This is Me, Debbi, David

Bonus: Nine Stories

by Alec Clayton

iiP Mud Flat Press

Cover art by Gabi Clayton.

First edition
Copyright © 2018 by Alec Clayton

ISBN:

Printed in the USA

DISCLAIMER

This is a work of fiction. The characters are the product of the author's imagination. Resemblance to any person living or dead is utterly coincidental.

Acknowledgements

Nani Poonani is a performer with Tush! Burlesque in my home town of Olympia, Washington. Hattie Hotpants is the hostess for Tush! I interviewed the two of them for an article in the Weekly Volcano, and after writing that article I pestered Nani with a deluge of emails with further questions about burlesque for a book I was working on at the time. I eventually abandoned that book, but much of what I learned from them—some of it taken word-for-word—found its way into this book. So thank you, Nani and Hattie, great performers and wonderful human beings.

Actors Heather Christopher, Pug Bujeaud, and Christian Carvajal, and playwright Steve Schalchlin were tremendously helpful in talking to me about the audition process (despite more than fifteen years as a theater critic, I have never sat in on an audition, so I had to call on them to find out what it is like).

Carvajal also helped me with invaluable critiques of the short story "Lyla Goes to the Mall."

Laurie Porter Obrien edited a couple of the short stories. Good job, Laurie. Thank you. Jack Butler offered helpful comments on the first drafts of "Hot on the Tracks" and "Ruination." And thanks to Jane Sammon for an enjoyable chat about the Catholic Worker houses in New York.

Special thanks to first readers Angie Banks and John Knold and to my wife, Gabi, who does an outstanding job of editing my books.

Also by Alec Clayton

Fiction
Until the Dawn
Imprudent Zeal
The Wives of Marty Winters
Reunion at the Wetside
The Backside of Nowhere (Freedom Trilogy Book 1)
Return to Freedom (Freedom Trilogy Book 2)
Visual Liberties (Freedom Trilogy Book 3)
Tupelo

Non-fiction
As If Art Matters

www.alecclayton.com
www.mudflatpress.com

This is me, Debbi

I'm a loudmouthed, fun-loving, rabble-rousing, perverse woman. That's just the kind of gal I am. I'm wild as wild can be, except for one thing, I don't curse. Or hardly ever. Strange, I know, for a twenty-first century party gal, but at some point growing up I just got fed up with hearing the f-word every day from everybody every other sentence. F-this, F-that, what the F is that all about, you effing F-wad? I figured there had to be a better way to talk. I was an English major, after all.

Want to know what kind of wild woman I am? I got arrested once for yanking off my top and running down Bourbon Street with my beauties bouncing in the rain. And it wasn't even Mardi Gras. It was just me letting it all hang out in a fit of exuberance. It was when the Saints won the Super Bowl. I was watching it with about a gazillion other people jammed into Lipstix, a bar on Bourbon Street. I didn't even like football, but I joined in for the excitement of the crowd. Plus David loved the game. Everybody was screaming and sloshing drinks on each other, and I jumped up and yanked my top off and ran out in the street, oblivious to the crowds and winter weather. I got from the corner at Bienville all the way to St. Phillip before the cops stopped me and hauled me off to jail. They made me wear something like a hospital gown, and they tossed me in with the drunks and told me to sleep it off. That wasn't the wildest thing I ever did, but it was doggone close to it.

David came to get me out of the slammer the next morning.

I think he was embarrassed. He's something of a prude, kind of old fashioned, which is kind of cute. Kind of sweet. But oh how I loved that man. Leaving him for Bryce was just about the dumbest thing I ever did.

1

This is me, David

I've always been something of a nebbish little mama's boy. Can't help it. Never took a chance on anything in my entire life. Not until the day Debbi walked into the bookstore. Well, actually it was the third time she came to the store. She spent a lot of time perusing the shelves, mostly the fiction sections and self-help, and she glanced up at me a lot. She wanted me to ask her out. Dropped hints all over the place, but I didn't catch the hints. Hopper was there the second time she came in, and after she left with her purchases he said, "Man, that woman wants to jump you."

"What do you mean?"

"I mean she's got the hots for you. It was written all over her."

Apparently I couldn't read the message. I've always been that way. I never notice when they're hinting, if they are, and even if I do notice, I never let myself believe it.

The next time she came in she asked, "Are you ever going to ask me out or not?" Well, I couldn't exactly ignore that now, could I? So we dated, and dating became an almost every day affair. We spent almost every moment together for a glorious month, and then she moved in with me—with me and Lucy and Randy and Hopper in our Ninth Ward menagerie. It was not too awfully long after Katrina. Well, actually, a few years, but the Ninth Ward was still a mess. The few rentals that were available were dirt cheap, and the four of us—five after Debbi moved in, took advantage of the cheap rent. But then not too long after she moved in, she left. It was after she ran off that I took what was the most foolhardy or courageous leap I ever took in my life.

Me, Debbi

Leaving New Orleans headed for Dallas with Bryce Fisher, we followed behind a car with a bumper sticker saying "Show me the birth certificate." They were all over Louisiana. It seemed like every third or fourth car on the road. That or "Tanned, Rested, Ready," Governor Bobby Jendal's campaign slogan. I don't think anybody knew what the slogan meant. The tan part I got. Jendal was a brown-skinned man from India. Was he seriously trying to pass himself off as a white man with a really good tan?

It was Halloween, cool and rainy, windshield wipers battling mist from cars and trucks in front of us. Monstrous trucks. It was scary. Horrifying. I'd never seen anything like it. Can you believe I had never been out of New Orleans? Thirty-two years old, and I'd never seen big trucks kicking up spray on the interstate highway. You think of people in places like Clarkton, Missouri and Hot Coffee, Mississippi leading such sheltered lives, not people who grew up in an apartment on Bourbon Street above a strip club called Lipstix.

And now I was leaving the only life I'd ever known and probably the only man who had ever truly loved me. (There had been dozens, scores, countless men who have lusted after me, but none who loved me.) I was leaving to live with another man, one I didn't really know all that well, for what well might be the rest of my life. You gotta know I was dazed, my head was spinning. I couldn't believe it was me, Deborah Allison Mason, an almost white Southern belle born and raised in the French Quarter. Sure, I'd led a pretty freewheeling life up to then, but never anything like this. Hopper warned me against going off with Bryce. He said he just had a feeling about him. I don't think David even knew I was dating Bryce. David and I had not discussed the nature of our relationship. I assumed it was not

3

exclusive, but I suspected David had different ideas. He said he loved me more than life itself, and once said he could not imagine living without me.

Sometimes things happen too fast even for me. I had not been with David all that long when I met Bryce and went out with him a time or two, and then he surprised me by asking me to live with him. I was even more surprised when I heard myself say yes. It was a done deal before my head stopped spinning. We had packed up all my worldly goods in a truck driven by a couple of college students for hire. We emptied my closets and chest of clothes, Bryce choosing what to keep and what to get rid of. "This one's precious. Keep it for sure. That one too," my favorite cardigan, "let's take it. That blouse is ridiculous. Toss it." And he did exactly that, tossed it onto a discard pile.

"Kitchen next," I said when everything in my bedroom had been sorted.

"I got a kitchen," he said. "Anything you need for cooking or eating, I got it. And a helluva lot better than this bargain basement junk. I got a cook, too. No need for you to cook unless you really want to. Do you like to cook?"

"Not really."

"Me neither. So neither of us ever needs to set foot in the kitchen. Tell the truth, I don't even know what's in there. Don't care. When it's time to eat, dinner arrives on the table, and when I'm through eating the empty plates go away. That's what money does, honey. Get used to it."

I thought maybe getting used to that could be fun.

The only other things I cared about keeping were my books. I had hardback (fake leather) collections of classics handed down from a grandfather I never knew. There were the complete works of Shakespeare, matched sets of novels by Hemingway, Faulkner and Steinbeck, plus tons of paperbacks I had bought over the years at used book sales. They were well-worn but precious to me. I couldn't stand the thought of leaving them behind.

When everything was packed, I asked Bryce what we should do with the stuff we weren't taking. "Just leave it," he said. "Let the landlord deal with it." We ended up leaving behind more than we took.

Before taking off with Bryce, I had to kick David to the curb. Sweet baby-faced David Parker, the boyfriend I had been living with for the past year. Being a first-class chicken, I broke it off by email. I couldn't face him in person. Chances are he had not even read my email yet, since he didn't own a cell phone and was not big on using his computer. Sometimes he would go for weeks without checking his messages. "What if there's a warning of a tsunami or a hurricane?" I challenged him, and he was like, "Hey, I watch the evening news. Besides, you'd tell me. Nothing happens without you telling me all about it."

Yeah, nothing except me dating another man, I thought but didn't dare say.

As soon as I packed my stuff and left the house I knew I was making a huge mistake, but I would not listen to that inner voice that kept telling me to turn around and go back. That's the way I am. No matter how surely I know that I'm wrong, once I make up my mind it stays made up. But oh my god, we had had such fun together, me and David. We were simpatico. We thought alike. We liked the same books and movies, we both loved theater, and we had similar dreams, the difference being that I chased my dreams and he ran away from his.

There was not a practical bone in either of our bodies. And that was just the problem. If we stayed together we would end up as eighty-year-old bohemians living off scraps, with nothing to look back upon but a few good times and lofty ideals.

Bryce Fisher, on the other hand, was a man a girl could only dream about. He was a man of substance, a take-charge, get-things-done kind of guy who, furthermore, was heir to a rather substantial fortune—or so he claimed, and I believed him—and you can't scoff at something like that. Mucho moola is not something to be cavalierly turned down, right?

David was a gentleman, so polite his actions were a parody of courtliness. He pulled out chairs for me, helped me on with my coat, held doors open not just for me but for everyone, tipped generously even though he had little money and—literally, literally, no joke— went out of his way to find little old ladies to help across the street. Until I found out where he came from, I pictured him as the pampered

5

only child of antebellum plantation owners right out of a nineteenth century Mississippi Delta plantation, transported over time to twenty-first century New Orleans.

Bryce could not have been more different. Six feet tall, with short, almost black hair and movie star good looks, he comfortably wore tailored clothes and expensive jewelry. This much he held in common with David: he was gentlemanly in the Southern manner. If I pictured David as the favored child of a plantation family, I could not imagine Bryce having family at all, certainly no father or mother or any other authority figure to look up to. Of course he did have parents, and I was on my way to meet them, which was just about the scariest thing I had ever done.

I imagined him hatched like a Roman god from the mating of a stallion and an eagle. Once we took one of those tourist cruises on a paddle wheeler around the city and standing by the rails I pictured him as a river boat gambler. We did that too, gambling on The Creole Queen. He lost a few hundred dollars and laughed it off like it was nothing.

We outran the rain, and Bryce turned off the wipers when they started going squee, squee, squee. Cruising into the afternoon sun at seventy miles-per in his brand-new Mercedes, snuggled close by Bryce's side in a short skirt and a heavy tunic sweater over a cotton top, "Ramblin' Man" blasting from his MP3, I felt vaguely and lazily erotic. I wiggled my ass against the hot leather seat, and the movement hiked my skirt up even higher. I caught Bryce's eyes glancing down and then back up to catch my eyes and beam at me with a smile that rivaled the sun. Oh boy, I had a good idea what he was thinking, and it meshed well with what I was feeling. But you know, we were in a car barreling down the highway, so whatever we might be feeling had to be put on hold. Or so I thought.

"Is the heat OK?" he asked, shouting over the music.

"It's perfect. You?"

"With you by my side I could be toasty warm in a blizzard."

Aw, that melted my heart. Bryce didn't often say romantic things, but when he did it was golden. I'm doing the right thing, I told myself. I'll be happy with Bryce. He loves me, and he'll be true. Not that he had ever come right out and said he loved me, but he had made it abundantly clear. He said he was a one-woman man, and I could tell right away that he meant it. Plus, well, look at him, the way he dresses, that three-hundred-dollar watch on his wrist and the ring from the best fraternity at Tulane, the Mercedes with those plush seats and the top-of-the-line sound system, the way he speaks—so articulate and calm, well-reasoned and confident, that soft Texas drawl, nothing like the way we talk in Nawlins. Nothing like the hesitant way David stumbles over his own tongue. Yeah, yeah, yeah, Bryce was solid, dependable. He was a good four or five years younger than I, as was David (I seem to have a thing for younger guys). But young as he was, he was already well established as a leading businessman and, I gathered from things he said, a leader in his community—Dallas, Texas, not some little Podunk hollow but a city where being a community leader meant something.

He spent as much time in New Orleans as he did in Dallas. He never explicitly told me why. I liked to think it was because of me. He often stayed three or four days at a stretch at the Bourbon Orleans Hotel. All I knew was it had something to do with his business and that he managed or bought merchandise or something for his father, who owned a bunch of businesses in Dallas. He got snippy whenever I asked him about his work. "I don't want to talk business. It's boring."

I gazed at Bryce's face, the strong jaw with the five o'clock shadow, but what I saw in my mind's eye was David's face. Ha! Where did that come from? David was nowhere near as handsome. You could almost say he was funny looking, but in a nice sort of way, medium in every way, medium height and weight, soft features, big Picasso eyes behind round, black-rim glasses. All his sweet little nervous quirks. He wore his hair long and swept back on top with a buzz cut in back and sides, and he habitually ran his fingers through his hair, sweeping the long top part to one side and then the other, sometimes practically tying it in a topknot with his fingers. Oh, I missed him already. He was so sweet, so kind, and so funny. He had ideals, worthy ideals that a person could be proud of, and he treated me like . . . not like a queen or a princess exactly, not like a dream lover, but like an equal, a comrade, someone worthy of respect. But there was no possible way I could see a realistic future with him. David the dreamer. Bryce, on the other hand, yeah, I could see a future with him. Damn if the seats in his Mercedes weren't dreamy comfortable.

With his left hand on the wheel, he reached his right hand up my skirt like he had every right to do that, and he did, too. Hadn't I given him that right over the past few months? And wasn't I feeling horny already? But there was something about the commanding way he did it that made me stiffen—the old fight or flight reflex, I guess.

But my tenseness was momentary. Bryce slipped one of his long fingers inside my panties, and then another, and he set my veevee to laughing, and yet he kept talking to me as if he were not even doing what he was so clearly doing. Get this, he was talking about his mother and father while doing what he was doing with his fingers. I could barely pay attention to what he was saying.

"You're going to love my parents," he said, while setting my nerves a tingle from toes to scalp.

"Oh, I'm . . . I'm sure I will like them. I can hardly wait to meet them." I could feel myself start to pant heavily between words. What words I could manage to get out coming in short bursts of air.

So, he goes on with like, "You'll have to be careful what you say to them. Probably best to just smile and follow my lead. They'll want to know what you do. Just tell them you're going to college."

"Well, I am. I mean I was. I . . . oh my, keep doing that. I plan to go back."

"Yes, I know. But they don't need to know about the other things."

I jerked away and slapped at his hand. "What other things?"

He laughed, and his hand went right back where it had been. It sounded as if he was ashamed of me, or like he was afraid his parents would think I was not worthy. We'll see about that. I can't abide snooty people. I wanted to tell him just where they could stick it if they couldn't accept who I was. But I stuffed it. I couldn't very well stay all petulant while his fingers played me like a fiddle down there.

Now I'll tell you something. I hated myself right then for being so easy. Was this what I had to look forward to? A lifetime of him being able to put me down and me letting him get away with it because he was such a bold lover?

I refused to dwell on that.

8

Me, David

A year ago at about this time I was standing on the side of the on-ramp to I-59 in New Orleans with my thumb out, begging for a ride, my worldly possessions stuffed into a backpack sitting in the damp grass beside my feet. What did I have in that backpack? Two shirts, a pair of jeans, a raggedy old sweater, toothbrush and shaving kit, and three paperback books: *On the Road, The Electric Kool-Aid Acid Test*, and *On the Technique of Acting*.

It was a couple of months after Debbi had taken my heart and tossed it in the bayou, a little more than two weeks before Christmas, temperatures in the fifties in New Orleans, a light drizzle dampening the road. I stood by the ramp trying to talk myself into sticking my thumb out. My immediate destination, assuming I didn't tuck my tail between my legs and turn around and head back home, was Slidell across Lake Ponchartrain, and then on up north and east through Mississippi. I was excited, hopeful, still broken hearted and full of self-doubt, yet determined, and shivering like a scared little yappy dog inside the army surplus jacket Lucy had given me, which she said had been given to her by a previous house mate in a different house. The lining had been ripped and some buttons missing, but Lucy repaired it. Lucy was the practical one in our little menagerie, the one who reminded us when we had appointments and insisted we set the alarm when we needed to get up early. She was also the one who gave me the back pack.

I had wasted pretty much my whole life up until then, mostly because I was too damn scared to do exactly what I was now setting out to do. To take a chance. Go for the big prize. Four years at Tulane majoring in English Lit had prepared me for exactly zero decent jobs and acting in six college plays (one decent role in *Twelve Angry Men* and throwaway roles in the other five) had not given me the confidence to try out for anything in any of the local theaters, even though I continued to think of myself as an actor—just not actively engaged in the profession at the moment, the moment being the past eight years. I never joined Actors' Equity. I never went to an audition. Since college I had worked something like twenty crappy jobs.

I figured after we got married I'd get a good job somewhere doing god knows what—maybe teaching in some college, maybe even in New Orleans if I was lucky enough—and we'd have a couple of kids. We had talked about it as something that would probably happen two or three years down the road.

And then she met Mister Hotshot Bryce Fisher and sent me that email. I shouldn't have even checked my messages that day. But I looked. I read her message. And then, before I hardly knew what had happened, I found myself huddled in Lucy's old army surplus coat standing with my thumb held high on that highway out of town as speeding cars passed me by. Me, just about the most risk-averse guy ever to come out of the Big Easy, hitchhiking to New York with dreams of becoming a Broadway star. I would never have done it if Debbi had not thrown me over for that trust-fund cowboy. How could she? And how could I compete with him? He was like a young Richard Gere. Gorgeous and tall and self-assured. But he was not our kind of person, not at all. In fact, he was the kind of person we loved to vilify. So why couldn't she see that? Bryce Fisher rode into her life like a rodeo rider on a handsome steed and she was a goner.

There was nothing for me in New Orleans after Debbi left. Striking out for a new life in New York City was a little extreme, but the hurt I felt when Debbi left was like nothing I'd ever felt before. It was as if I had been picked up by the talons of some great vulture and carried out over the swampland down below New Orleans and then dropped in the sharp grasses and knee-high water where there were no roads and no landmarks in any direction. What had I ever done? Got a degree in English Lit, and that was 'bout as useless as tits on a boar hog.

And something happened to me in that swamp of my mind, the bog of my soul. I switched in my heart from being a lifelong risk-averse twerp to a newborn man who craved adventure. My friends told me it was crazy to hitchhike. "Nobody hitchhikes anymore. It's not 1970," Randy said.

"You can be an actor right here in New Orleans," Lucy said. "There's plenty of opportunities here. Go to New York and you'll be eaten alive."

Randy said, "At least catch a bus. I know you don't have much money, but you can at least afford a Greyhound ticket. But for God's sake, don't hitchhike. That's like Woody Guthrie kind of stuff. Like for hobos. Nobody picks up hitchhikers 'cept for rapists and robbers."

I gave out a bit of a rueful laugh. "Nobody would want to rape me, and it's clear as the stains on my coat that I'm not worth robbing." Whatever good sense I might have still had told me they were right, but I had to do it anyway. I don't know why. I didn't know then, and I still don't.

And now I'm telling tales of my life in a cabaret blocks from Washington Square. Me, the guy who was too shy to ask Debbi Mason out (she asked me the first time). Now I'm simply talking about my oh-so boring life and people are laughing with me. Not at me, with me, laughing like the nuts they are. It's a fluke that I ended up here. In college I majored in English Lit because I thought it was a practical alternative to what I really wanted to major in, which was acting. I acted in school plays throughout high school and college, never a major role. I was usually the butler or an unnamed waiter—characters as non-descript as a clerk in a bookstore, which as I've already said was what I was in real life before I came to New York. Coincidentally, Debbi had also been an English major at Tulane, but not at the same time I was there.

I was so shy growing up that I was in college before I ever worked up the nerve to ask a girl out on a date. Beverly. The first girl I dated and the first one I slept with. Howzabout that, sports fans? Beverly was a Poly-sci major, as quiet and shut-down as I was. We exchanged tentative smiles in English class for almost the entire semester before I asked her if she'd like to go see *Brokeback Mountain* with me—a great movie, but a poor choice for our first date, because she assumed I was gay. People do. She asked if I wanted her to be my beard, and then she had to explain what that meant. Nevertheless, we dated throughout our junior year and halfway through our senior year, until she met Sam Cranston.

That was Beverly. Next came Debbi.

But whoops, I'm getting ahead of myself. Before Beverly and before I fell in love with Debbi, there was Diane Fairchild, and thanks to Diane, I fell in love with theater. I was in the tenth grade, I decided to audition for a school play. It was *My Fair Lady*. I tried out for a part to get close to Diane. Everybody knew Diane would get the part of Eliza because she got the lead role in every school play. She always had, since *Snow White and the Seven Dwarfs* in the second grade. Because she was gorgeous. I didn't get cast, but they asked me to stay on as a stage hand, which I did, and eventually I did get cast in a couple of plays. I even got to kiss Diane Fairchild in *Sleeping Beauty*—the first girl I ever kissed who wasn't a cousin. That sealed the deal for me. I made up my mind then and there that I was going to be an actor.

Fast forward to 2007. And then came Debbi. It was summertime. She was wearing short denim shorts that were molded to her perfectly round derriere like Spandex. The sight set my heart to pounding. She bought a book with a title something like *How to Make Men Want to Date You* and another with a title something like *Dating Tips for Single Women*. Nonchalantly plopping those titles down on the counter, she might as well have had "I'm Available" printed across her chest. Instead, she was wearing a t-shirt with the Jane Austin quote, "What is right to be done cannot be done too soon."

And I'll tell you something crazy about that. She had no intention and no desire of ever reading those books. She bought them so she could plop them down on the counter in front of me. The next day she brought them back and asked for a refund, telling me some cockamamie story about buying them for her cousin and then finding out her cousin already had them.

She came back again the day after that and the day after the day after, hinting blatantly, which we joked about later, and finally it was she who asked me out.

The thing that most attracted me to Debbi was her complexity. There were many versions of her. The self she liked to present to the world was wild, fun loving and devil-may-care. She didn't give a hoot what anybody thought of her. But I could plainly see that was a façade behind which hid a soft and sensitive woman, the kind of woman who would feed stray dogs and take care of the hurt and the crippled, who would never say an unkind word about anyone but would stand up against bullying and injustice with the fierceness of a mother lioness. Could it be I was projecting something onto her?

There was something else about Debbi and about me that maybe made us perfect for one another but maybe could have been an omen that was not so good, and that was our shared penchant for describing everything as analogous to movies we had seen or books we had read, an indication perhaps that neither of us was in touch with the real world. We even chided each other about it. She would say something like "That's just like the such-and-such scene in *Hello Dolly* or I would say something like "You look like a Tahitian girl in a Gauguin painting," and we'd each call the other a dreamer and an idiot.

She moved in with me after only three dates, and we were boyfriend and girlfriend for a long time. She said she loved me, and I sure as shootin' loved her. Or maybe, now looking back on it, maybe, just maybe we were just kids playing at being in love, even though were well into our adult years. But what is love, anyway? Does anybody know?

As I said, or at least I think I said this, I figured eventually we'd get married, not that I ever thought of asking her; it was just something I assumed would happen someday. And then she talked me into going with her to a bar where she used to hang out. Come to find out—well, she told me—it was actually in the same building she had lived in when she was growing up. It was a strip club. "You gotta learn to loosen up a little," she said when I balked at going in. "Are you afraid your boss or some friend is going to see you. Not going to happen. Nobody but tourists come here."

Let me tell you about the bar. It was called Lipstix, one of many such joints on Bourbon Street. There was a display window facing the sidewalk that was like the ones in department stores but only about four-by-four-by-four feet and without any glass on the side facing the sidewalk. A swing on golden ropes hung from hooks in the ceiling and the walls were covered with red silk with valentine hearts, and every night the strippers that worked the club swung on that swing in the briefest of costumes, swinging out over the sidewalk where pedestrians who gathered to watch could almost touch them. A sign on the building said "Girls! Girls! Girls! Fully Naked," which was a lie. They never got fully naked.

Debbi introduced me to the bartender and a couple of the girls who danced on stage. There was one named Stormy, a gigantic Black woman, and another called Babs, and some others I can't recall very well. She knew them all. I felt out of place in Lipstix, but they treated me like we were old friends, and eventually I learned to relax and enjoy the somewhat debauched atmosphere. I ended up spending a lot of evenings there, but that's not something I want to talk about right now.

Debbi was tattooed from shoulders to fingertips and down to her ankles with intricate art. I asked her about the one on her shoulder, the initials DGM. "That's my mama," she said. "Deborah Gabrielle Mason. My middle name is Grace, so it's my initials too. Mama died when I was seventeen. She caught a cold, and it went into pneumonia, and she died fast. I went to live with her sister, my Aunt Jamie 'cause my daddy was already long gone. But I could tell Aunt Jamie didn't want me, and I never felt at home with her, so soon as I turned eighteen I went off on my own. I lived on the street for a while. Did what I had to do to get by."

Suddenly brightening, she said, "Want to see my other tattoos? Turn on the overhead." We were in bed, undressed. It was our first night together, and we had undressed under the sheet. I had not yet seen her dance at Lipstix and had not seen her fully naked. I turned on the little bedside lamp.

"No, the overhead," she said.

Snakes, flowering trellises and coils of rope encircled her arms. A large butterfly spread its wings shoulder-to-shoulder on her chest. Cherubs and flowers danced on her stomach. Poetry spelled out in old English script covered her legs. On one thigh was a poem by a poet whose name I could never remember (Jack Butler, I looked it up later) that I always thought of as a description of Debbi herself:

> Because the floor and air were cold, she waited
> until the covers warmed her to undress,

then slipped naked in a rustling lightlessness
except for a blue shimmer that palpitated

like an especially hesitant firefly
over her glimmering skin: a stroked cat's ear,
touched in a properly crackling atmosphere,
will so illumine its gesture. But why

insist on classification of the spark?
What does having a name for it change?
Thinking of it is still wild and sweet and strange —
She sat there flashing softly in the dark.

Isn't that beautiful? It could easily be a description of what I saw while drinking in Debbi's loveliness that first night.

On the other thigh she sported a portrait of Edgar Allen Poe.

Her parting note to me when she ran off with that guy came in the form of an email. Did I tell you that already? Yeah. She wrote: "I truly thought I loved you, but I came to realize I never did. I don't love Bryce either. Maybe the truth is I don't know how to love. But I know Bryce can give me the security I need, and I know you never can. Please remember me with kindness."

I thought she must have been drunk or stoned when she wrote that. She wrote some other stuff too. Wished me a happy Halloween, happy Thanksgiving and merry Christmas, letting me know in no uncertain terms not to expect to see her ever again. The essence of what she wrote was she didn't love me, and she was leaving me for a man who could provide for her, throwing away what we had for a shot—or so she thought—at a secure, upper middleclass life in the suburbs, something I knew, despite her pretensions to rebellion, she had always wanted. She was going to Dallas with Bryce to be the wife, I guessed, or concubine or whatever, of a wealthy Texan in a white cowboy hat. She signed her message with nothing more than her initials, DGM.

"White cowboy hat" is just my attempt at metaphor. I don't think he ever wore one for real.

An email. Can you believe it? How impersonally can you say something so personal?

I pictured her and Bryce as Victoria Principal's Pamela and Patrick Duffy's Bobby in "Dallas"—the original series, not the new one. But standing on that road that morning I pushed their images out of my mind by imagining myself on a Broadway stage, oddly, not as some matinee idol but as Ethel Merman singing "Everything's Coming Up Roses." All right, David Parker, I scolded myself, you're not Ethel Merman.

Before Debbi moved in I had been living with Hopper, a twenty-something guy who worked the offshore oil rigs, and his friends Randy and Lucy, in a rundown apartment off a rundown courtyard in the Ninth Ward. It was a small apartment decorated in a style Hopper called Cajun Baroque. Fake gold or brass figurines of mermaids (I think they were painted plaster) swam over the archway separating the living and dining areas. There was an ancient oak table they had picked up at a yard sale that might have been but probably wasn't a valuable antique. Around it sat four mismatched chairs. There were faded red velveteen curtains with practically invisible floral patterns that put me in mind of stage curtains in nineteenth century music halls. There were posters from exhibitions at the Museum of Art: a Degas ballerina, nudes by Francois Boucher, a city scene by Stuart Davis, and a perfectly terrible all-blue French Quarter scene in pastel by some street artist that sold his stuff in Jackson Square. I sat in the overstuffed easy chair smoking one Marlboro after another and staring out at our pitiful little court yard. I was so despondent after Debbi left that all I could do was sit in that old chair and smoke cigarettes and sometimes weed and drink beer and feel sorry for myself. I didn't even go to work. Hopper said, "They're gonna fire your sorry ass."

I said, "So what? Who cares?"

When I told them I was going to hitchhike to New York, Randy said, "You're going to freeze your ass off up there."

Lucy said, "You don't even own a heavy coat."

Hopper just shrugged and took a hit off the joint we were passing around and said, "Whatever, man."

That was after they gave up trying to talk me out of it. It was mostly Hopper who, more adamantly than the others, argued against my leaving—until it reached the whatever stage with him. They asked me what I was going to do when I got to New York. I didn't have answers to any of their questions. All I knew was I couldn't go on sleeping on the queen-size mattress on the floor Debbi and I had shared, I couldn't walk the streets of the French Quarter she and I had strolled together. And I knew that the apartment I had once thought was bohemian perfection was suddenly the most drab and depressing place in the city.

I knew I would never again see Debbi, and yet I held tight to the insane fantasy that someday we would meet up, quite by accident. I would achieve my dream of becoming a star on Broadway, and she would attend the opening of my show—not even knowing I was the star because I had changed my name to something more star-like, Britt or Sky or Byrd. It would be an hour before sunrise on the morning after the opening and cast party and after reviews came out and we read them over-and-over out loud. Critics would have written that our play, whatever it was, was the most exciting new work in town and they would call me a sparkling newcomer. I would be in an all-night café like the one in that Hooper painting, and she would come in, stop dead still and shout "Oh my god! Oh my god! Oh my god!" and rush to me and hug me hard and tell me through a cascade of tears how greatly she regretted leaving me and how she had given up hope of seeing me ever again but had searched the country over nevertheless, praying that sooner or later she would find me.

It had to happen before a year was out. Otherwise I would have to slink back to New Orleans. That was the bargain I struck with myself.

Me, Debbi

We had done a joint before hitting the road, and I was as loopy as a dodo bird. Bryce still had his hand down there, and I had slumped down in the seat like a happy rag doll, lackadaisically enjoying what he was doing with his hand while half-heartedly listening to what he was saying. It was as if his mouth and his hand were not in the same car, not even in the same world; neither were my mind and my body. Ours was practically the only car on the highway. The sun was high overhead in a blue sky with scattered pillows of cloud, their shadows riding the landscape as if attached by monofilament lines, smoothly gliding over hills and valleys like in a Disney animation.

We were heading north under a brittle winter sun while driving seventy miles per hour on Highway 61, and Bryce Fisher was chattering inanely about his father, whom he called Pops and whom he apparently thought was Jesus Christ in a suit, and his mother, Moms, whom he talk about like she was Aunt Bea from Mayberry, all while doing tantalizing things with his fingers. I couldn't figure out if I loved it or hated it.

After a while he said, "Do me."

"Do you what?"

"You know."

"Are you kidding? Here in front of God and everybody?"

He said, "God don't care, and I don't care what other people think."

So he squirmed a bit to reposition himself and demanded, "Do it now." Authoritatively. No nonsense. His demanding tone was both thrilling and scary, and what he wanted me to do seemed like quite the sexual adventure, not that I hadn't done it before, but never while barreling down the highway.

A mile or so down the road, one of those crazy jacked-up pickups pulled up alongside us in the right lane. Its cab hovered above us like an Imperial Walker. The driver, a big man with a scruffy beard, looked down at me from his height and smiled a smarmy smile. How could I tell, you might ask. Well, I guess I must have sensed his presence and lifted my head long enough to see his leering face. He could clearly see what we were up to and was relishing the sight. I wanted to crush him like a bug underfoot. That thought brought to mind the crackling sound a cockroach makes when you step on it, and I shuddered. Bryce said, "What's the matter, babe, and what'cha stopping for?"

"That guy's looking at me like he wants to eat me." I had sat up but had not scooted back over to my side of the seat. That would have put me too close to the creep.

"Well screw him. I'll teach him a thing or two." He reached into a side pocket on his door and pulled out a pistol. I didn't know the dang thing was there. I've always been scared of guns, can't stand to be anywhere near them. He said, "Roll your window down and duck."

"What? No, I . . ."

"Just do it," he growled. I was afraid to do it and afraid not to. But I did. I rolled the window down and put my head between my knees, and Bryce shot the damn pistol. Bam! Like a rimshot on a snare drum. The bullet zipped right past my ear. The sound . . . oh my god, my ears were ringing. The bullet hit the truck's backseat window. I glimpsed the driver ducking and turning the wheel. He swerved to the right and slowed down.

"God damn! Were you trying to kill him?" I was shaking like a freezing puppy.

"If I'd of been trying to kill him he'd be dead. I was just trying to get his attention." He laughed at that and said, "Hey, don't sweat it. No harm done."

"No harm done? You shot out his window."

We were coming into Baton Rouge. In the rear-view mirror I could see that the truck driver had slowed to a stop on the side of the road.

Traffic bunched up as we pulled into town. Bryce pulled onto an exit ramp without putting his blinker on. "Let's stop for some lunch," he said. I was still so shaken I couldn't say anything. And my ears were still ringing.

We stopped off at Harrington's, a nice looking little café downtown, not far off the freeway. After looking over the menu, I said I'd like the blackened fish po boy. He said, "If you like blackened fish, then you should have the blackened fish topped with crawfish etouffee."

"Oh, you've been here before?"

"It's my favorite."

When the waitress came, he ordered for us. "We'll start with the grilled shrimp Caesar with sides of fried okra and the blackened fish topped with crawfish etouffee."

"Right away, Mister Fisher. Excellent choices."

In a way it irritated me that he was so presumptuous as to order for me without getting my approval, but then he often did, and I was getting used to it. Besides, those dishes did sound delicious, and his authoritative demeanor was impressive.

While waiting for the appetizer I swirled the water in my glass. "You're being awfully quiet," he said.

"I'm just thinking."

He was like, "You still shook up about the gun?"

"No, it's not that."

"Then what?"

I didn't want to tell him what I was thinking because I hadn't yet puzzled it out. But then I did. I said, "It kind of bothered me when you said I shouldn't tell your parents about my art. I'm proud of what I do and . . ."

"I know you are, and I'm proud of you too. You're wonderful. But Moms and Pops are kind of old fashioned. In some ways they're pretty sophisticated, but in other ways not at all, you know. Anything more cutting edge than *The Sound of Music* is decadent to them. And they think of actors, performers, even painters . . . well, they see them as kind of low-class professions."

"Then what are they going to think of me?"

20

"Oh, they'll like you all right. Just don't come on too strong. And whatever you do, don't talk about politics. Jesus, they were big supporters of George Bush. Both of them. Gave a shitload of money to their campaigns. They believed that birther crap about Obama. And, you know, they're against abortions and birth control and gun restrictions. The usual. But they're good people, and they'll come around. We just want them to get used to you before telling them anything. I just . . . I mean, well . . . the folks are kind of old fashioned, but they're good people. I think you'll like them."

"All right, Babe. I get the picture."

What happens to grownups when they go back home to visit their parents? Or is it just men? They become sniveling little boys again, desperate for their parents' approval. Women don't do that. Confronted by their mothers, they let the bitch out.

I said, "OK, yeah, I'll be good."

My mouth was dry. I took a big swig of water. I asked, "What do they think about teachers?"

"They love teachers. Moms was a teacher. She was principal of a private elementary school before she retired."

What a relief. I had taken a few education classes, and with a few more I could qualify for a teaching certificate. It was a compromise, a backup plan, and I thought an honorable and sensible one. They say follow your bliss. Ha! If I had been confident enough to follow my bliss I would have majored in dance and maybe kept up with studying English Lit because I had . . . well, some vague yearnings along those lines as well. But dance was my greatest love. I had watched all the greats on film: Twala Tharp, Martha Graham, Josephine Baker. To be like one of them, that was my dream. Before Bryce whisked me away I was working my way through college, but it got to be a bit much and I dropped out for a while with the intention of starting back the next year. According to my latest revised plan, it was going to take me three more years to get my degree. Realistically, I knew it might never happen. At least I had thought it was unlikely up until I started dating Bryce. But now, now . . . if we got married or even if we lived together with or without getting married, I wouldn't have to work anymore. I could find a good college near Dallas, and I could go to school full time and finish in two more years. Of course

I'd probably have to give up dancing. My art. What would Moms and Pops think about me being a dancer? In their minds I'd probably be no better than a whore at worst or one of those silly trained monkeys that dance to the tune of a music box. I could imagine them picturing me that way, silly little colored girl dancing for her supper, cute, but not really a grown-up woman.

"Moms would admire you for working your way through school on your own." He said they admired grit and determination.

The waitress brought our lunch. The plates were huge and piled high. "Gosh, I'll never be able to eat all that," I said.

He laughed. "It's a Texas-size meal."

"Hey, we're not in Texas yet." I laughed along with him but then expressed a real concern. Is it true what they say about everything being bigger in Texas? Are they all a bunch of blowhards that have to be bigger than anything and anyone else?

He said, "We may not be in Texas yet, but we're getting closer, and the closer we get the bigger things get." I had visions of going into a restaurant on the Louisiana-Texas border and getting hamburgers as big around as basketballs, burgers in Dallas the size of satellite dishes. Getting back to the subject of Moms and Pops, he said—after quickly shoveling three huge bites of fish in his mouth—"You're going to love them. Moms especially. She's so sweet. Quiet and polite. Oh god, please don't curse around her. She'll be flabbergasted. She's never said the words *shit* or *fuck* in her life. I think she would pass out or have a heart attack if you dropped an s- or f-bomb. I don't believe she has ever said a harsh word to anybody. She always looks for the best in everybody. She's just a sweetheart. Even people she doesn't like, she calls honey and blesses their little hearts. Pops, on the other hand . . . he's a glad-hander and a backslapper and a hugger of girls. He treats all females like . . . well, you can imagine. Let's just say he's certainly no feminist. I have no doubt that he had affairs when he was younger. I'm sure he did. That's just the way men of his generation were. Successful men. Oh, and he can be loud and overbearing, but underneath it all he can be as sweet as Moms."

I wondered just how much Bryce was like his father.

He said Pops owned a number of businesses in Grapevine. Whether he owned the buildings and leased them to the businesses or actually owned the businesses outright wasn't clear. What was clear was that the Fishers were rolling in dough.

I had a feeling Moms and Pops were going to be scary people.

I had thought I was famished when we entered the café, but when the meal was served, I found I could barely choke half of it down.

Me, David

Y ou could hardly see the rain coming down. It was a drifting ghost of a mist, but wet enough. After half an hour standing on the side of the road, my shirt was soaked through. My chinos were like wet bandages clinging to my legs. At least the coat Lucy gave me was somewhat water resistant. I had long since put my glasses in my pocket. I could not see well without them, but I couldn't see with wet lenses either. Every car that passed me—and there were a lot that did—tossed up a fine spray of water. I stood as far back from the edge of the road as I could. A few of them still got me with their spray. My worldly possessions, meaning two pairs of jeans, three shirts, two underpants, an extra pair of shoes, and my books, were stuffed in my backpack. And my wallet. I had a grand total of ten cents in my pocket. I had not thought I would need cash; everybody takes debit and credit cards, or so I naively thought, having never before tried to use plastic in Purvis, Mississippi or Rocky Mount, North Carolina. It dawned on me that places like those—places I might end up passing through or, worse yet, stuck in, might still exist in a kind of throwback 1920s way.

The gray sky darkened. Slowly. As if the unseen sun whose light seeped from behind the cover of a solid sky of gray had a dimmer switch. There came a sudden clap of thunder. I don't know why they call it a clap. It was more like the crash of a building falling in on itself followed by the deep rumble of timpani drums rolling in from the coastal swamps to the south. It sounded like a Mongol hoard riding in on elephants, like the clangorous coupling of freight train cars, like . . . this is where my writing teacher at Tulane would tell me not to pile on the similes. But you get the picture. The sudden darkness made me think of the Biblical story of when day turned to night at the crucifixion of Christ. Could it be that God or the goddess or the unknowable ruler of the universe was telling me to go home and forget the madness of hitching to New York? Or the madness of thinking that I who had yet to even join the actors' union, who was afraid to audition at second rate theaters in New Orleans, could carry my Southern accent and mediocre looks to New York and become an actor on Broadway?

A deluge of raindrops bounded off the pavement, getting stronger by the moment. I grabbed up my backpack and ran for the nearest cover, a bus stop about a hundred yards behind me. It was a backwards bus stop to my way of thinking, with the open front facing away from the street. Crazy, I thought. But everything in and around New Orleans was crazy. A fast-moving truck drove through standing water and threw a tsunami against the back/front of the bus shelter, and suddenly I realized that facing the open side away from the street was not so dumb after all, pretty smart engineering for a city that averages sixty-four inches of rain a year.

Slidell. That's what the lighted sign on the front of the bus said. Slidell would be the first town on my route, if I ever got out of New Orleans. The bus pulled to a stop with the shrill hiss of what I took to be pneumatic brakes. Shivering and soaked, I watched an old woman hobble off. She was wizened, skinny, with dry, cracked, colorless skin. She moved slowly down the three steps pushing a wire basket on wheels in front of her. The basket tipped over when the wheels touched ground, and clothing and food in cans and boxes and a black umbrella fell out. I scrambled to help her pick everything up.

"Thank you, sonny," she said, her voice raspy and quiet. I could barely hear her. "Could you help me get my stuff home? It's right down there, no more'n a block. I don't think I can get it up the steps by myself."

The driver shot me a questioning look. I waved him off. I would have hopped on that bus in a New York minute if I could have, but ten cents would not have gotten me anywhere.

"You gonna hep me or not?" the old lady asked.

"Sure. I can help you. But let's wait a bit. It's raining cats and dogs."

"You ain't made out'a sugar, sweet stuff," she said. "and you ain't a gonna melt."

Luckily the rain slackened almost as quickly as it had materialized. The cloud cover turned to vapor, and a blazing morning sun broke through. I pushed her little makeshift cart down the sidewalk to a house on the next corner. It was a six-step walkup to her front door. "Carry my cart up and set it by the door, then come back down here and hep me up them steps."

I wondered how she managed if there was nobody to help her up the steps. Maybe she didn't. Maybe she sat on the bottom step until someone happened along. I bumped her little cart up to the door, turned to look back at her, wondering if I would end up so feeble when I grew old. "You jest gonna stan there a starin' at me? Come gi' me your arm."

"I'm coming."

I didn't see the patch of wet moss growing on the top step. My foot shot out from under me, and I tumbled down the stairs, landing hard on my hip. I bumped into her, and she would have fallen if she had not grabbled my head for support.

"Tarnation, sonny. You all right?"

"Yeah, I think so."

She used my head as a steadying post and then helped me to my feet. Her hand on my arm felt like a bundle of sticks. I helped by grabbing the bannister. A sharp pain shot up my leg. I tried to ignore it. We hobbled up the stairs holding on to each other. It was debatable who was helping who.

She insisted that I have a glass of lemonade for my troubles.

"I reckon not," I said. I need to get on the road. I got a long way to go."

"Where you heading?"

I told her I was going to New York.

"Well New York can damn well wait long enough for you to have a glass of lemonade," she said. "How's your leg? Can you walk on it?"

"It's going to be all right," I said. "Just bruised, I think."

"Well go slow." She pulled off her coat and scarf and draped them over a chairback. "It's colder'n a witch's tit in here. You reckon you can get a fire started in that there fireplace while I get us something to drink?"

26

She hobbled into the kitchen while I hobbled to the fireplace.

My first sip of her lemonade was tart with an after taste of alcohol.

"Vodka," she said. "Just a tech. It'll warm you right up."

After the second glass and after I told her why I was going to New York, after everything in my mind poured out with the force of water over a damn, I told her how I had always been afraid to chase my dreams, afraid I was never good enough, and that now by god I was going to do it. After I told her about Debbi and how she had left me and how now I was determined to do something right for myself for once, she said, "That's the spirit, sonny. But the right thing for you is to chase after that gal first and then chase after your dream."

Something told me she was probably right. The pain in my thigh and hip was building up. She could see it in the way I winced when I moved, even though I tried to hide it. "When did you eat last?" she asked.

I told her I had breakfast before hitting the road.

"When would that be?"

"I guess about eight o'clock."

"It's nigh on four o'clock in the afternoon, Sonny. "You been standing out on the highway all this time?"

"I'm afraid so."

"Well tarnation. We need to feed you and rest you up for your trip. I got supper already cooked, enough for both of us and Cox's army too. It's in the fridge. All you gotta do is toss it in the microwave."

What a great dinner is was. Fried chicken and mashed potatoes and okra. After we ate, she made me take off my pants so she could rub some kind of ointment on my bruises. "Don't be shy, Sonny. I'm eighty years old. Ain't nothing under your britches I ain't seen before."

I don't know what kind of ointment it was, but it sure was soothing. She informed me it was "too dang late to hit the road. You get a good night's sleep and leave out in the morning. Head back into town and find that gal of yours."

She was right about one thing. It was too dang late to hit the road. Getting a good night's sleep and starting over in the morning might be a good idea. But I felt like a failure already. I had spent the entire day on the road and hadn't even gotten out of town. I had a horrifying vision of every day repeating itself: all day with my thumb out on the freeway ramp and them meeting . . . I just realized she never told me her name . . . and going home with her for dinner and a good night's sleep.

She said, "Let's us have another one of them lemonades before bed."

"Okay, sure."

"I'm a tell you something you just might want to take to heart. My first lover—the first of many, I'll have you know, was a get-down party man. His name was Jasper, and I loved me some Jasper. But I let him go. I figured out he was never going to amount to a hill of beans. I knew I was going to miss him something fierce, but I needed me a man I could depend on to take care of me and bring home a good paycheck every week. So I broke it off with Jasper, though it broke my heart, and pretty soon I hooked up with ol' dependable George, and we got married and right off I pushed out six screaming young'uns. We're Catholic. Now ol' George, he was a good man, but he couldn't hold down a decent job to save his life. When it come to ditching a lover I thought couldn't be dependable for one that could, man oh man did I ever mess that one up. And Jasper? He's a big-shot executive with some company in Shreveport now, and last I heard he's got three children and half a dozen grandchildren."

I got the impression she intended for Jasper and George to be her David and Bryce, but I couldn't figure out which was supposed to be which.

After I walked down those six slippery steps the next morning and turned to wave goodbye, she said, "Which way you going, sonny, New York or New Orleans?"

I said, "I'm going home. I'm going to find that gal."

"That's good. You won't regret it."

But I suspected she knew I was just saying that to make her feel good.

Me, Debbi

W e practically tripped over the kid sitting on the sidewalk out in front of the restaurant. He was wearing a torn sweater and a pair of brown corduroy pants worn to near invisibility at the knees. He looked like he had been sleeping on the street and probably hadn't eaten in days. He was about eight years old, a ragamuffin right out of a Dickens novel. "Are you all right, son?" Bryce asked, dropping to one knee next to the kid.

"I'm hungry," the kid sniffled.

"Where's your folks? What are you doing out here all by yourself?"

"Down yonder," the kid said. "Just a piece thataway."

It took Bryce a few minutes and a good deal of patience to wheedle out of the kid the information that his mama was gone—he didn't know where or when or how it came to be—and that his papa had lost his job and was begging on the street corner. Somewhere. The kid had wandered off and now didn't know where his papa was.

The kid was like, "I went back to where he was, but he wadn't there."

"He's probably looking for you," Bryce said. "Let's go see if we can find him."

Man, I liked this side of Bryce. It was a Bryce I'd never seen before, this solicitous, gentle side. Even his voice took on a soft tone unlike the Bryce I knew. We searched the neighborhood, stopping to ask everyone we saw on the streets if they had seen a man looking for a lost boy. A few had. The father had been asking everyone he saw as well. "Where did you see him?" Bryce asked, and they answered, "Right here not fifteen minutes ago. He was heading thataway." The next one we asked went, "Half a block down there, across from the movie house."

Pretty soon we found him, and he came rushing to us shouting, "Billy, Billy, oh Billy. There you are!" He held out his arms and Billy jumped into them and the father said, "I was worried sick. I didn't know where you were. Don't you ever run off like that again." And turning his eyes to Bryce, he said, "Thank you, Mister."

Bryce said, "The boy said he was hungry. Do you not have money for food?"

"No sir, we don't. I'm just down on my luck, Mister. I'm not a bum. I swear I'm not. I don't mind working, but times is tough. You risk your life, you serve your country, and you come back home and it's like they never known you."

After some more talk, Bryce said, "Come on. I'm going to buy you lunch," and we all went back to Harrington's, and Bryce and I watched them eat while the father told their story. He was an Iraq War vet. So was his wife. They had been sweethearts in high school and college and got married their senior year at LSU. In a patriotic rush, they agreed to drop out of college and join the army after 9-11. Billy was just a toddler at the time. Both parents were sent to Iraq, but they did not serve together. He worked in the motor pool. She was a medical tech. She saw enough horror to last her a lifetime. Billy stayed with his grandmother in Baton Rouge. Each of his parents came home dealing with post-traumatic stress, and the mother also with an opioid addiction. After failed attempts at rehab and after neither of them could find or hold down a good job, she took off to parts unknown, leaving the father to take care of Billy by himself. "If it wadn't for the drugs she never would have left. This boy was her heart."

From Harrington's, we walked a few blocks to Bank America, where Bryce got cash from a machine, I don't know how much, and he gave it to the papa. If I didn't love him at first—and I must confess I didn't love him at first; he was just a meal ticket to me, that's all, and gorgeous arm candy and a bundle of excitement to feed my craving for adventure—but doing things like feeding that poor man and his son made me love him. I knew that for a long time after, when he acted like he owned the world and the world owed him allegiance, when he did insanely scary things like what he did when he shot out the window in the truck driver's truck, when he stayed gone days on end without me knowing where he was, when things like that made me regret my decision to go with him, I would remember the homeless father and his son. But even then, I suspected such acts of charity on his part were not acts of love so much as easy gestures that cost him nothing but bought him the adoration he seemed to not be able to live without. God, I'm such a cynic. You see, that's the thing. You can be a paragon of charity out of the goodness of your heart, or you can be kind so people will admire you; in the latter case the motive cancels out the deed as far as I'm concerned.

Me, David

I don't remember how I ended up on the old, little used highway instead of hitching on the on-ramp to I-59, but I clearly recall the short-hop across the lake and through Slidell in a car full of teenagers celebrating Christmas early with beer and marijuana. Windows rolled up, the car reeked of it; I would have gotten a contact high even if I hadn't taken a toke of the joint they passed around, which of course I did, not being the kind of ingrate who turns down an offered gift. And then there was the farmer in a beat-up old Ford pickup. He was going somewhere in Mississippi. I don't remember where it was he said he was headed. He turned onto a dirt road near the little town of Picayune and let me out, saying, "This rat cheer's far as I'm going, Bub."

I trudged to where the freeway intersected with old Highway 11, a two-lane road. It was getting on to around two o'clock in the afternoon according to the cheap wristwatch that seldom kept accurate time. A Timex. It takes a licking and keeps on ticking. Pretty accurately too, so long as I remember to wind it. I had won it in one of those fair-type game things where there's a toy bulldozer in a case with lots of prizes that you try to pick up by manipulating handles. It took me less than a minute to snatch the watch. Leaving New Orleans, it took me five hours to go about fifty miles.

An African-American family picked me up. The hands and face of the father behind the wheel of their late model Pontiac were the color of coco butter. There was a streak of white skin across the back of his neck. He was dressed in the height of casual wear, a black-and-white striped pullover shirt, collarless, and a navy-blue denim jacket that I suspected cost more than a month's salary at my last job. With his gray-streaked hair, goatee and high cheekbones, he put me in mind of Frederick Douglas, and set me off on wild speculations. He

32

was an impassioned orator famous in certain circles but unknown to me, or a fiery evangelical preacher, also famous in certain circles but unknown to me—those circles being merry-go-rounds I would love to ride but in which I would surely feel out of place. I saw what looked to be a college class ring on his right hand and a wedding band on his left. Crowded next to him on the front seat were his wife, who said her name was Ginny, and riding shotgun was her father, who was bundled in a heavy coat that he kept trying to wrap more tightly around his skeletal figure. Ginny wore pants that matched her husband's and a colorful floral-print blouse. She was thin, with skin slightly darker than her husband's. I took her to be a college professor or a business woman, maybe a marketing director for some big firm in New Orleans. The old man kept honking up great gobs of phlegm and spitting out the window. The back window on the passenger side was streaked with it. I sat on something on the back seat between two rambunctious kids, my backpack on the floorboard under my feet and my knees raised high to my chest. The thing I had sat on and extracted from underneath my butt was a plastic pistol. "Oops. Sorry about that," the kid to my right said. He took the toy gun from me and tossed it in the back.

The girl said, "That's not even ours. We're too old for toy guns. One of our little cousins left it."

The kids were carbon copies of their parents, the boy about twelve years old and the girl a year or two younger. They started in playing some kind of hand-slapping game, which necessitated them repeatedly reaching across me, and they were talking excitedly about cousins they were going to see in Hattiesburg, including the one, the girl said disdainfully, who left the stupid gun in their car. They talked over each other, one answering the other before the other finished what they were saying—a rat-a-tat-tat of happy prattle. The adults did the same. Sound inside the Pontiac was a buzz like the lobby of a theater before the show starts, where nobody can hear anything because everybody is talking at once.

They were from Chicago, spending their Christmas vacation visiting their many relatives in the South.

"Where are you going?" the father asked.

"New York City."

"Really? My goodness, that's a long way to hitchhike."

The wife asked, "Are you going there for a job or just visiting or . . ."

"A job. I'm an actor, and I got a part in a play off-Broadway." That popped into my head and out of my mouth in an instant. I'm bad about making up outlandish stories when people I don't know ask me about myself. I don't know why I do that. Lack of self-confidence, I guess. In this case it might have been that I would have been embarrassed to confess I was going to New York questing a harebrained dream with no plans and no prospects.

"That's wonderful," the wife said.

The husband said, "I pray you get all the way up there without getting robbed or killed. You're taking a big chance, young man."

"Yes sir, I guess so."

"You be lucky we came along," the old man said. "Nobody picks up hitchhikers no more. Tain't safe. I read about a hitchhiker got picked up by a man what slit his throat and robbed him of a measly twenty bucks. Twenty dollars! Killed that sucka for twenty dollars. Or was it the hitchhiker that robbed the driver? I can't recall. It don't matter none. The point is you never know what kinda monster you liable to run into. Tain't like when I was a kid. Everybody hitched back then. Crazy hippies all over the place. Even girls. White folks. Hardly ever blacks. You didn't see black folks hitchhiking. Black folks walked. We knew if other black folks saw us they'd pick us up. Didn't have to stick no thumb out. But it's not like that nowadays. Mark my word. You be lucky to get out of Miss'ippi alive."

"Aw don't you go scaring him, Pop," the wife said. To me she said, "Are you really going to be in a play in New York?"

"Yes ma'am. It's not a big role—one of the jurors in *Twelve Angry Men*. But it's a start. I'm going to be Juror Number Two." It was the role I had played in high school. Juror Number two was described in the script as a meek man with no opinions of his own who is easily swayed by others. That was me, all right. Or it had been in high school. By the time I decided to make the move to New York, I think I had overcome some of that. At least I hoped that the big move would be the beginning of a new more confident me.

I lied about myself because I didn't want these people I didn't even know to think I was some dumb kid with unrealistic dreams. I gathered that they were wise—the mother and father, anyway, I wasn't so sure about grandpa—and I wanted to impress them. I didn't even give them my real name. I told them my name was Brad Paisley.

The father said, "That's a pretty big role. I mean there aren't any minor roles in that play."

"You've seen it?"

"Yes, I have. My drama department did it when I was in college. Of course I wasn't in it. There are no roles for black men in that one."

"There could have been," I argued. "The script didn't specifically call for white actors."

"But it was set in the fifties. Black men didn't sit on juries back then. If they had, there would have really been some angry men."

And then he said, "I did play Othello once."

"He was great," Ginny said.

I said, "Wow! That's pretty impressive. So you're an actor too?"

"In college. I'm an insurance adjustor now."

The old man said, "He didn't have the guts to chase after his dream. Just as well, I wouldn't a wanted my daughter married to some two-bit actor nohow."

I was glad, at least, that the play I had picked to lie about was one I actually knew. If I had said *Othello,* I would have really played the fool. I didn't even know Othello was black.

The mother said, "We're the Blacks."

"All the Blacks? I mean there are lots of black people down here."

That was humor. My feeble attempt at it, which I immediately regretted. Bad habit of mine, spurting out things without thinking. The driver barely chuckled, and his wife responded as if I had asked a serious question, explaining, "Black is our family name: Ronnie Black and Ginny Black, grandfather Dakota Black and our kids Minnie and Pauley Black; and we're every one of us awfully glad to have you join us on our little journey."

"Thank you, ma'am."

The father said, "I hope you're prepared to get a job after the play is done. It might be years before you get another part. The competition up there is fierce."

I imagined he was probably right.

Ginny said, "Don't be so pessimistic, Ronnie. Leave the boy with some hope." And then she said, "My sister Leeanne is an actor too. Just community theater, you know." They were on their way to visit Leeanne in Hattiesburg.

"I'm going to see my sister, too. In Laurel. Then on to the Big Apple."

"That's nice," the mother said. "Family's important."

The boy had a CD player on his lap, and he turned it on to listen to rap or hip-hop (I can't tell the difference). The father shouted, "Earphones! The rest of us don't want to listen to that noise."

The girl said, "I do."

"Don't you sass your father, young lady," the mother said. So the kids plugged in a set of earphones and shared the earbuds, one for his ear and one for hers, which necessitated them sitting cheek-to-cheek. I thought that was sweet.

Grandpa said, "How old are you, son?"

"Turning thirty in a couple of months."

"Then how come you ain't married? You oughta be making babies by now."

"Now Papa," the mother said.

I said, "I wish I was married and making babies. I almost was. I was engaged to get married. We had set the date and sent out invitations and everything," I lied, the compulsion to make up stories about myself, about Brad Paisley, was growing into a monster. That's the thing about lying, once I start I can't stop. I said, "She left me for another man. Out of the blue." I got a hiccough in my voice like I was about to cry. It was only partially an act.

"Well you can't just give up," the mother said. "You ought to turn around right now and go back where you came from, and you fight for that girl. Ronnie, you pull over and let him out."

"No, no, I can't go back. She's not even there. She left town with her new boyfriend. I don't know where they are."

The father said, "If she left you that easily, then you don't need to be with her anyway. Go on to New York. Follow your bliss."

"Aw pshaw," the mother said. "Don't you listen to Ronnie. He doesn't have a romantic bone in his body. You go on back, and you fight for your girl. You find her, wherever she is, and tell her how you feel about her. Get down on your knees and beg if you have to."

We talked about Debbi for the next fifty or sixty miles. I told them I couldn't work up the nerve to ask her out for the first date, so she asked me out. We went to the Gumbo Shop for an early dinner, and then we wandered the quarter on foot, people watching. I told the Blacks how smart Debbie was and how she loved all the touristy things most natives scorned. I told them she had grown up poor right there in the French Quarter with a single mother who worked as a caregiver for Hospice (not true). I told them how my friends—let's face it, I had no friends, just acquaintances—thought she was beneath me, not because she grew up poor but because of how she made her living.

"How's that?" Ronnie asked.

"She's a bartender in a . . . well, one of those strip clubs on Bourbon Street. She's not a stripper, but she does have to wear a revealing outfit, tight shorts and a little halter top, and the men are always trying to slip tips into the top or the shorts the way they do with the dancers. She slaps their hands away and says, 'You behave yourself,' always with a wink or a smile 'cause she can't be mean to the customers. She hates it, but you have to do what you can to make a living. She's clever at fending off the letches without making them mad."

I almost broke down right there in a car full of strangers and cried over Debbi, over a story about her that was only partially true, over the memory of our time together.

Coming into Hattiesburg I said, "Ya'll can just let me out where I can get to 59, and I can hitch on up to Laurel from there."

"No sirree, we gonna take you through town past all the local traffic."

"Well that's mighty nice, but you don't have to."

He drove right through the middle of town. "We gonna stop at the Choctaw and get some ribs and barbeque beef sandwiches. Best barbeque in the South. Our treat."

"Oh no. You . . ."

"You gotta eat, son."

I couldn't talk them out of it. I waited in the car with the mother and the kids and grandpa while the father went in. Now I hate to even bring this up, but I feel like I should. Mississippi was another world, a nightmarish world to me. Even though I lived right across the river and had visited the Gulf Coast towns of Gulfport and Biloxi a few times, I knew next to nothing about the state other than its history of racial injustice. I had heard horror stories about how Jim Crow was rampant in Mississippi and the Ku Klux Klan was still alive and well. The coastal area was another country in and of itself, with its white sand beaches and night clubs and casinos, but the steamy land north of there was scary and mysterious. I was afraid to be seen in the car with a Black family, so I scrunched down in the seat and pretended to be asleep until the father came back with the food. Was I being racist? Or just cowardice? I shudder to think what Debbi would have thought. Or the Blacks for that matter, if they knew. And perhaps they did.

The smell of smoke and the borderline burnt odor of barbeque sauce was overwhelming and tantalizing. Handing me two large brown paper bags when he got back in the car, the father said, "Here you go, son. Hold onto these for us, would you?"

Even after we pulled out of the parking lot and drove through the streets of Hattiesburg, I kept my head down.

The mother said, "Ronnie, wouldn't it be nice to bring this young man to Leanne's? Let him meet the family?"

"Why yes, that's a good idea. Whatcha say, young man?"

"No sir. I couldn't. I mean thanks, it's awful nice of you, but I need to get on up to Laurel and . . ."

"Don't you fret it, son. Tell you what. We'll have dinner with Leanne and Aunt Betty and them, and then I'll take you to Laurel and drive you right to your sister's front door. You can't argue with that, now, can you?"

No, I couldn't. It was a choice between hitchhiking at night with my stomach growling from hunger or eating some delicious-smelling barbeque and getting a ride thirty more miles up the road. That was no choice at all, but I made a feeble attempt at pretending to argue that I shouldn't take advantage of their hospitality.

We drove down Hardy Street, which I gathered was the main drag through town, past small strip malls and houses that had been converted into shops of all kinds. We turned onto a side street and made a couple of turns in an area of small frame houses with many cars and bikes and kids' toys in yards, and we pulled up to a small house painted pink with white trim, with bicycles and a basketball hoop in the front yard, and two more cars in the driveway. The kids jumped out almost before we got stopped, and three more kids burst out of the front door of the house, and they were all high-fiving and slapping each other on the back, and the boys were wrestling on the ground, and three dogs came running from around the side of the house and joined in the melee, barking up a storm and jumping on the wrestling boys.

There was a Christmas tree in the front window and those icicle lights I abhor strung across the front of the house. Three adults, two old and gray and the third, a good looking woman in, I guessed, her early forties, met us at the door, and there were shouts of greeting and hugs all around, and then the mother—meaning Ginny, Ronnie's wife—said, "Leanne, this here is Brad Paisley. He's an actor. Brad these other two are Uncle Roy and Aunt Betty."

"An actor. My heavens. What have you been in? Oh, I think I know. You were in that show about the two girls that drove off a cliff. You were that good looking young fella they picked up."

"No ma'am. That wasn't me. That was another actor. His name is Brad, too. I'm uh . . . I'm a stage actor, not in the movies."

"He's going to be in a play on Broadway." Ginny said that, beaming like I was her own creation.

"Well it's an honor to have you in our house," Leanne said. Her manner was so demure she was like a shy little girl. She said, "I'm an actress myself. Not professional like you, but I've been in a bunch of plays at the Little Theatre." It seemed like it hurt her to say it, but she had to get it out before she chickened out altogether. "I was Calpurnia the maid in *To Kill a Mockingbird* and I got to play Celie's little sister Nettie in *The Color Purple*, the musical."

39

"That was when she was much younger," Ginny said. "You should have seen her. She was precious."

"That was six years ago," Leanne huffed. "It was such an honor just to get to be in those plays."

I told her I had seen *The Color Purple*—the movie, not the play. "I bet you were a great Nettie."

I noticed a calico cat eyeing me from her perch on top of a shelf as if I were game and she was a huntress. "That's Preacher," Aunt Betty said. "She's a little wary of strangers, but she'll warm to you in no time."

I couldn't keep up with the conversation that pinged like balls in a pinball machine while the food was set on the table and ice tea was poured into tall glasses.

I felt more than saw a hand reaching for my hand and realized the family was holding hands around the table. Leanne was to my right and Aunt Betty to my left. They clasped my hands, and I followed suit when all heads bowed. Ronnie said, "Leanne, would you kindly say grace?" and Leanne said, "We thank you, Lord, for this sumptuous meal and for a fine and loving family, and please look after Uncle Josh and Brother Duke. And thank you, Lord, for bringing us this nice young man, Brad."

Everyone squeezed hands before letting go. Platters piled high with food were noisily passed around. I probably made an ass of myself chomping on that barbeque so voraciously while trying to take part in the scattershot conversation as best I could. Aunt Betty brought out a black bottom pie for dessert. "Ooh I dearly love your black bottom pie," Dora said.

"I'm afraid this'un ain't mine. It's store bought. I simply don't have the energy to bake no more. These old bones are getting weary."

Grandpa said, "Leanne, honeybunch, ain't you got some a that good sippin' whiskey in the cabinet?"

"Why sure, Pop."

She brought out a bottle of Jack Daniels Black Label and Cokes to mix it with, and all the adults except Aunt Betty had an after-dinner drink while they went on and on about food and fishing (Uncle Roy caught a six-pound bass in Lake Serene last week) and the Southern Mississippi football team. Names of different friends and relatives, and I guess enemies too from the tales that were told, were rapidly fired like shots from one of those T-shirt guns at ball games. My head was spinning from it all.

I missed family, or the idea of family. Never really had much of a family. One younger brother and no other siblings. My folks were good people, but we never talked a lot or did family things together. They both worked, and when they came home the TV went on and stayed on until bedtime. Dinner was more often than not take-out or reheated Sunday dinners eaten in front of the TV with plates on laps. Those reheated Sunday dinners were more often or not a big pot roast with peas and potatoes or a lasagna or some kind of casserole Mom fixed and we warmed up in the microwave three or four times during the week. Or else we'd do take-out, Church's fried chicken or Pizza Hut. Eating on the couch followed by three hours of TV every night was what passed for family time. I never experienced the kind of raucous love and togetherness I saw with the Black family.

Somebody said, "Here, have another slice of this delicious black bottom pie, and someone else said, "Let me freshen up your drink." Aunt Betty said they brought a DVD of the last family reunion, the one at Paul B. Johnson State Park, and Ronnie said, "You gotta watch this, Brad."

"But I really need to get on up to Laurel." At the rate I was traveling, I figured it would take me more than two weeks to get to New York, and Laurel, half an hour up the road, was an insignificant mile marker on the way. I'd likely run out of money and food long before New York, and I'd never meet my goal of landing an acting job before next Christmas. But on the other hand, I was being royally fed and feted so far. Chalk up one on the plus side.

Ronnie said, "Don't you worry, son. I'll get you there in plenty of time."

So we settled in to watch the home movie, me and Ginny and Leanne and one of the kids all crowded together on the couch. About the time the DVD started playing, as if it were a starter's pistol, Preacher the cat leapt from her perch and ran down the hall and back like a shot out of hell, her little paws on the laminate floor sounding like a herd of mustangs stampeding across a wooden bridge. She jumped across my lap and onto the back of the couch, where she settled down right next to my shoulder. Everybody hooted at the cat's antics. "Don't pay her no nevermind," Uncle Roy said. "She spazzes out like that just about this time every night. It only lasts a minute or two, and then she calms down." She had already settled down, her little head nestled against me, and she was softly purring.

"Would you just look at that," Leeanne said. "Preacher took right to you." And then, while we were watching the film of some of the kids wading in the shallow water near a spillway, Preacher came down from her perch and crawled onto my lap and circled a few times trying to settle into a comfortable position—sticking her butt in my face in the process. Aunt Betty said, "It looks like you've been adopted. You're part of the family now."

The Blacks insisted it was getting late and that I should spend the night there, and I was too tired to argue. Bedding down on their couch with Preacher was nicer than fitfully sleeping in a car while rolling along the highway. Ronnie took me to Laurel the next day. Ginny and Leanne both hugged me and wished me well, and the kids wished me a merry Christmas and gave me hand-made Christmas cards, for which I thanked them profusely.

Thirty miles just to drop me off at my sister's house and right back home for him, all because he was a nice man and he felt bad about delaying my trip. So that was nice. I got a place to stay for the night and a free meal—breakfast the next day, too, sausage and biscuits slathered with maple syrup, and a ride right to my sister's front door, which was kind of weird because I had made up the part about having a sister in Laurel.

Me, Debbi

Not far out of Baton Rouge I started drifting off to sleep but was shocked awake when Bryce suddenly braked and swerved. "Goddamn idiot!" he shouted. Somebody had cut in too close in front of us. I was surprised he didn't go for the gun again, and he probably would have if the guy that cut us off hadn't taken the exit for Opelousas. Thank the goddess Bryce didn't take off after him through the streets of Opelousas. All he did was cuss a blue streak for the next mile or so while my heart beat like a conga drum. "I got a good mind to turn around and chase that bastard down," he said.

"Oh please don't."

"Ah, he ain't worth it. The loser in Opelousas. Screw him."

What a relief that was. And what a weird name for a town. Wasn't an opelousas some kind of horse? I had to ask Bryce. He said it was a kind of catfish. Naming a town after a fish? Or a horse for that matter? Geeze. Come to think of it, Natchitoches, the next town name I saw on a road sign, was a weird freaking name too, and so was Coushatta. Where did they come up with these names? Buncha crazy Cajuns, I figured. My mama's family. Except I don't think they were Cajuns. Indians maybe, Choctaw. Or maybe just plain old white trash rednecks.

Sometime later, when I was bored out of my gourd waiting for Bryce to come home, I Googled those names and found out Opelousas was an Indian name meaning the color red ochre. Whoopie! Or was that Natchitoches? I can't remember. I know one of them was the spice capital or the world. Double whoopee. Coushatta was an Indian tribe. That's America for you. We kill the Indians and take their land and name our podunk towns after them.

It was about three-thirty in the afternoon when the dude cut us off and Bryce cussed him. He calmed down quickly—he had that ability to changes moods lightning quick—and we took the next exit to gas up in Red Ochre; i.e., Opelousas. While Bryce was gassing up, I went to the restroom. Oh my god. It was around behind the little convenience store. I had to get the key from inside from a guy wearing overalls and sporting a beard that looked like a haystack. There was wet toilet paper stuck to the seat, and the smell of mold and piss was overwhelming. I jerked handfuls of paper from the dispenser to wipe the seat clean before sitting down. Ha! I must have practically emptied the dispenser, and even with all that paper for protection, I still wasn't willing to touch flesh to the toilet seat. I squatted, hovering with my rear end a few inches above the seat looking at posters and photos of local points of interest pasted to the grimy walls. Like that stinking crapper was the Louisiana tourist bureau. Pictures of Southern plantation homes with broad porches, and everything shaded by massive oak trees; photos of a serene lake with homes nestled amongst trees on the shore, cypress trees in the water; a photo ripped from a magazine of what I took to be downtown Natchitoches; and a sign declaring the town the bed and breakfast capital of Louisiana. Another whoopee. Scribbled across everything were the usual mélange of restroom graffiti: *call so-and-so for a good time, Billy S sucks, from my cold dead hands*, crude drawings of naked bodies and body parts, and a poem, "Here I sit all broken hearted," followed by something that had been crossed out with an indelible marker.

I got out of there as quickly as I could and joined Bryce inside the store where, in addition to the usual convenience-store goodies, they sold fishing tackle and hunting and fishing licenses, and worms and crickets. We bought Cokes, and cheese and peanut butter Nabs. He said we'd need snacks because it would be after suppertime before we got to Dallas. "I texted Martina while you were in the bathroom. She'll have supper ready for us."

I was like, "That's cool, but who's Martina?"

"She's my maid."

"Is she Black?"

"No she's not. She's Mexican, if you really must know. And before you say any more, she's not a servant. She's a domestic employee and well paid. And she's an American citizen."

I guess I offended him. Here's the thing: I didn't mention this before, but I'm part Black myself. So I'm kind of touchy about the whole maid-servant thing. My mama was half Black. That makes me a quarter Black, a quadroon in the old way of saying it. Mama says I could pass as white if I wanted to, but why would I.

Mama was a voodoo woman, and she played it to the hilt. She wore a bandana on her head and wore long flowing flower-print skirts with long splits up the thigh and plunging necklines. She was one sexy mama, and she knew it, and she loved it. It was all an act, a persona put on for the tourists. Folks say I'm sassy and brassy. If so, I get that from Mama. Mama told fortunes in the quarter. I could just see Bryce busting a gasket if he knew that, or if I told him my daddy was a dirt poor ol' dumbass Creole fisherman from Thibodaux with no more than a sixth-grade education. I had not told Bryce anything about my family, and he hadn't asked. I guess we'd be trash in his estimation if he knew anything about what I came from, but I don't think he gave a hoot.

But when he told me he had a maid whom I correctly assumed must live in and cater to his every whim, he read in my tone of voice that I was implying his help was chattel, a step up from a house slave. And I guess I was. Who could blame me? The way wealthy whites treated Blacks, and more and more these days foreign-born domestics, was degrading, and I was quick to assume the worst.

He got his dander up. He said, "Martina is a respected and well-paid employee. She's my housekeeper, cook, you name it." What he didn't say was that Martina's mother who worked for his parents was an undocumented person. But maybe that was another thing about which he gave not a hoot.

I said, "Well all right. Climb down off your high horse. I get it."

He said Martina was well paid. Ha! I wanted to ask just what that meant in dollars and cents, but I didn't. I let it slide. I gave myself a little talking to. Calm down, Debbi. Get to know what's what before you get your panties in a bunch.

We had only gone a bit more than a hundred miles and had well over three hundred more to go, and already Bryce had shot at a man and fed a homeless man and his son. I couldn't imagine what else could happen. But it was smooth sailing from there on. Drive-wise. Talking-wise not so much. Engaging him in conversation was becoming a challenge. Nightfall arrived before Tyler. All I could see of that town in the beam of our headlights was a scrim of tall pine trees against what seemed to be softly glowing lavender fleece in the blue-black night sky. When I commented on it, Bryce said it was the reflection of city lights off low-lying clouds. Traffic was light. Bryce cruised at about seventy-five. I was relaxed but no longer sleepy. Lane markings and occasional signs meeting us and receding behind were hypnotic, but I kind of wished it was lighter out so I could see more. I'd never been in Texas. Heck, I'd never been much of anywhere. A travel virgin, that's what I was. One trip to Gulfport when I was about ten years old and a week at dance camp at LSU when I was fourteen. That was it. Dance camp was where I lost my virginity. Bobby Billings raped me. Bobby was seventeen. That three-year age gap was humongous. All us junior high girls idolized him. I never told anyone because I thought it was my fault. I wanted him to sweep me up in his arms, to hold me tight, to kiss me; but I did not want him to do what he did, and I did not know how to say no. Bobby, of course, prob'ly thought it was consensual. What a thing to think about at this late date. Bobby is probably a successful businessman now with a wife and three perfect kids. He's probably in the Chamber of Commerce somewhere and a deacon in his church. Pfft!

Soon we skirted Dallas, and I felt more at home. Back in a city at last, but I was tired and my nerves were on edge. Heavy, stop-and-go traffic. Steel and concrete and glass. Traffic came to a dead stop, and then we inched along a few feet at a time with Bryce cursing like he thought everybody else on the road should pull off and make room for him. As if they didn't have places to be also. Dang construction. Down to one lane in a half-mile stretch. We were both getting hungry, and Bryce was increasingly irritable. He was cursing other drivers and cursing the construction crews and complaining that their lights were blinding him.

"There's nothing we can do," I said. "We might as well just relax."

"Just shut your trap," he snarled at me.

I said, "Don't you talk to me like that."

"No? What you gonna do about it?"

For once I couldn't come up with a snappy comeback. What could I do about it? Get out and walk? Hitchhike into town? Or back the other way all the way to New Orleans? That's what I was tempted to do.

Me, David

"Turn right here. It's the last house on the right. The white one."

Ronnie let me off and I hefted my backpack and crawled out of the Pontiac. "Thank you so much," I said. "For everything, the dinner and the movies and bringing me all the way to Laurel. I'll never forget you and your family."

I meant that, too. They would come to epitomize for me the ideal family such as I might someday have. But with whom?

I trudged up to the door of the house. A woman about my mother's age opened the door as Ronnie drove off. She was wearing a robe and fuzzy slippers. I said, "Hi. I'm Brad, George's friend from New Orleans. He's expecting me."

She shot me a quizzical look that morphed immediately into a look of disgust, like she thought I stank to high heavens. "George? There's nobody here named George. You got the wrong house, young fella."

"Are you sure? Isn't this . . . the uh . . . what's the address here?" I was sure I was acting confused as convincingly as could be.

She said, "It's 2020 Fir Street."

"Oh gosh. Fir Street. Silly me, I was looking for 2020 Pine. I knew it was some kind of tree." Quick thinking.

She said, "Pine is down that way about six blocks."

I apologized for disturbing her and thanked her for setting me off in the right direction. I don't know why I had told the Blacks I had a sister in Laurel anyway. Just another bit of the made-up biography that was puddling out of me one drip at a time. I liked my avatar Brad Paisley better than I liked me. Brad had a sister in Laurel who lived in a neat but modest home with her three children, my cousins, and a husband who had been a star running back for the Ole Miss Rebels before his career ended with a torn cartilage. Brad's mother wrote mystery novels under a pseudonym and acted with the Laurel Little Theatre (I assumed there was a Laurel Little Theatre). See how easily I constructed my own version of Brad's family? My real mother was dull. She had migraines and hated doing housework. Our meals when I was growing up, the only child of Gladys and Roy Parker, were same old same old. You heard about it already. TV dinners, frozen pizza, leftovers. For a special treat we sometimes had red beans and rice with cornbread. I grew up in a two-bedroom house right near the river bend about halfway between the French Quarter and the Ninth Ward, walking distance from where I later lived with Lucy and Randy and Hopper and Debbi. Mama hung around the house all day and Papa came home bone tired. They both chain-smoked, and the house reeked of cigarettes. We never went anywhere, never did anything. No wonder I was creating a more adventurous life for Brad Paisley.

I hiked past stately old antebellum houses, imagining histories of the families who lived in them, past the art museum, which was housed in another antebellum home with an expansive lawn, and through parts of a small downtown and finally to I-59 headed north and east. After a couple of short rides, I got picked up by a woman in an old Thunderbird from back in the days when Thunderbirds were sports cars. This one was a classic, a real beauty, painted a light pea green. She was a large woman, not what I'd call fat, but monumental. Lots of flesh, like one of those big babe sculptures by Gaston Lachaise, but without the tiny feet. She had kicked off her boots, black cowboy boots with a printed red rose on each. They were lain on the floorboard by my feet. She was dressed like the hookers on Bourbon Street, flaming fuchsia hair, a jean jacket with cut-off sleeves over a light-colored blouse, a dark bra showing through, black leather skirt hiked up almost to her crotch, where a silver whiskey flask was propped between meaty thighs. Looking down at the floorboard, I could see her toenails were painted crimson. As it turned out, she was in fact a hooker on Bourbon Street. She told me so. She said, "If you're gonna ride with me, you might as well know who it is you're riding with. Does that shock you?"

I said, "I live in the French Quarter. Not much of anything shocks me."

A hearty laugh at that. She said, "All right, sweetie pie. I think we're going to get along just fine."

She slipped a CD in the player and thankfully adjusted the volume to a level that didn't hurt my ears. I recognized Buckwheat Zydeco playing "Waiting' For My Ya Ya." Great song. This was going to be a fun ride.

She told me she was a heroin addict but easing off with a methadone regimen. "I'm heading to Atlanta to visit my boyfriend. He's in jail for armed robbery. How 'bout that? You freaked out yet?" She exploded with laughter that blended with the fiddle and accordion sounds from her CD.

I told her that no, I wasn't freaked out yet (but I kind of was). "Like I said, French Quarter." It takes a lot to shock Brad Paisley.

She said, "He didn't rob the damn Seven-Eleven, but the stupid old biddy that worked in the store identified him. So I don't know, maybe he did do it after all. Maybe he lied to me about it. But you know, Buddy—that's his name—he looks 'bout like just about anybody. I mean there's nothing special about the way he looks. He could be mistaken for anybody. Like whoever did rob the stupid store. Light me a cigarette, would you? In the glove compartment." She gestured with a free hand. Long cherry red fingernails.

I opened the glove compartment. It was stuffed as glove compartments always are. Bunches of papers, a hairbrush, pack of Wrigley's gum, a pack of Marlboros and a disposable lighter, and lying on top of everything, a small black pistol.

I gasped, then tried to look unfazed. "Is that thing loaded?"

"Of course it is. Wouldn't do no good if it weren't. A girl needs protection. Just reach me a cigarette, and don't fret over the gun."

I pulled out the pack, lit two of them, one for her and one for me, slipped one between her waiting lips. Puffy lips painted red as the rose on her boots, red as her nails. She rolled her window down a bit to let the smoke out, and I did the same. The cool air felt good. We were passing by clusters of buildings: a farm equipment store with tractors out front, used car lots; Jake Malone's Discount Sports, One Stop Shopping for the Hunter and Fishers; a Wendy's, a Taco Bell and McDonalds ahead on the right.

She said, "Hey, don't let the gun freak you out."

"Yeah, OK. Nah, it doesn't freak me out." I took a deep drag on my cigarette and choked on it.

"Not a smoker, huh?"

"Actually, yeah I do smoke. That just went down the wrong way."

"Are you a drinking man?"

"On occasion," I said.

"Well this is as good occasion as any. So, kiddo, drink up." She handed me the flask from between her thighs, and I took a drink.

"Not bad. What is it?" handing it back to her.

"Just some cheap whiskey. Nothing special."

"Well it hits the spot."

"Good. Have another." She handed it back, and I took another swig. Loved the fire of it going down.

The noonday sun was warming the car. She was passing cars in quick succession. Speedometer needle hovering around seventy-five. That little T-Bird was a sweet ride.

"You hungry? I could go for a burger. My treat."

I said, "Sure, thanks." I looked at the cheap watch on my wrist. It said three-fifteen, obviously not the correct time. That would have been when it stopped the day before. I was always forgetting to wind it.

She pulled off at a Birmingham exit and found a truck stop restaurant. "I don't know about you, but I'm starving," she said.

The place was jam-packed. We managed to find an empty booth and squeezed in. I couldn't help but noticing the leering looks the truckers shot her way, the sneak peeks from men in the restaurant with their families, and the withering looks of disapproval from those men's wives. She seemed to take it all in stride, or simply not notice. It was interesting to me to see how prostitutes navigated the daytime world when they were not prostituting. This one seemed self-assured and jolly. We ordered burgers and fries and beer. She pulled a cell phone out of her bag and started texting somebody. I sipped on my beer and looked around. A clock on the wall said it was 3:20 in the afternoon. Maybe my trusty Timex was right after all.

She put her phone away. I said, "I never told you my name, did I? It's Brad. What's yours?"

"Molly."

"Well it's nice to meet you, Molly."

I thought maybe I should use Brad as a stage name when I got to New York.

I napped a bit between Birmingham and Atlanta. It was dark when I opened my eyes.

"Nice nap?"

"Yeah."

"We're just about there."

She took an exit marked Douglasville and soon pulled into a motel parking lot. "This is my destination. As far as I'm going tonight. It don't cost no more for two than one, so you might as well stay the night."

I thanked her and offered to chip in on the cost of the room. "Forget it," she said. "Like I said, it don't cost me no more for you to stay. Besides, I can see you ain't no Bill Gates."

There was only one bed in the room. It was a queen size with four large, fluffy pillows and an equally fluffy quilt, a TV from before flat-screens, and some insipid art on the walls. She said, "I don't mind sharing the bed, but keep your hands and your you-know-what to yourself."

"Sure. I'll behave myself."

"You better. Ha! I've seen how you look at me."

She was flattering herself. I had not looked at her with anything more than idle curiosity. Okay, maybe there had been a bit of a lustful glance at her thighs when she was driving.

Molly took a shower and spent a long time in the bathroom. When she opened the door, the whole room was steamy. The mirror was fogged. She came out wrapped in a towel, vigorously drying her hair with a second towel. She grabbed something from the bag she had carried in and sat down on the edge of the bed and said, "You ever see anybody shoot up?"

"No, I haven't."

"Well get ready. You're about to."

She shot the inside of her thigh with a hypodermic needle, and then she stood up and pulled the towel loose and started vigorously toweling her body from shoulders to feet, acting like standing buck naked in front of a hitchhiker she'd just picked up was a common everyday thing. I think I had told you that Debbi was something of an exhibitionist, so naked Molly wasn't totally shocking, but it caught me off guard. My early comparison with a LaChaise sculpture didn't hold up because she had heavy calves and ankles. She looked more like a Rubins nude. Creamy skin glowing pinkish. She stepped into thong panties and pulled a T-shirt over her head. The shirt pictured a band I had not heard of. "Are you going to shower," she asked.

"Uh huh."

She turned on the TV, and I went into the bathroom and showered, and came out in my underwear and a T-shirt, figuring I might as well follow her lead when it came to night dress. We watched television for an hour or so, in bed, propped up on those big pillows and covered with a sheet and bedspread. (We'd kicked the quilt off because the room was warm.) We didn't talk very much other than a few comments about the show. It was a movie on HBO, some action adventure flick with Denzel Washington and Jodie Foster. And we finished off the whiskey as the movie ended, and she said, "I'm 'bout ready to turn it off and go to sleep. How 'bout you?"

"Yeah, I'm ready."

And then she said, "Tell you what, you're kinda cute. Maybe I'll give you a freebee if you want."

I opened my eyes to blinding white light. Molly must have woken at the same time. We looked at each other and then looked at the window. Snow dusted the grass and bushes and piled on the windowsill. We broke into laughter. "A white Christmas," I said.

"It'll be melted in less than an hour. We don't get real snow down here."

"I know. I wonder what time it is."

She checked the clock on her cell. "Almost eleven o'clock. I guess we'd better get up and get going."

The continental breakfast was free. After downing coffee and eggs and muffins, she said she would take me out to I-85 north of the city. "It's the best place to catch a ride."

But it didn't seem like she was heading to a freeway. As best I could tell—and frankly I hadn't paid much attention when we went to the motel the night before, nor had I paid attention to where we were going after leaving—we must have been a bit west of Atlanta, probably southwest, and where I was hoping to hitchhike from was northeast of the city. She took a bunch of turns, searching for something, I knew not what. She was silent. She drove with an intent look on her face until we turned a corner where she saw something that caused her to spark up with a eureka expression and announce, "That's it. That's the jail house where they got my Buddy."

She slowly drove around a big, fortress-like building, brick and glass and white concrete or plaster on what looked like the front or showy side and dead white with tiny windows on the other side. Parking half a block away, she reached across me to open the glove compartment and reach for the pistol. I caught my breath. Felt chilled throughout my body. I watched her as she casually and slowly loaded the chamber with bullets. She said, "I'm going to break his ass out of jail. Scoot your butt over behind the wheel when I get out, and when you see us coming pull up and be prepared to gun it when we jump in. You're going to be our getaway driver."

"Jesus, Molly! You can't expect me to . . ."

"If you ain't gonna do it, then you can just get out and start walking, and I don't care if you walk all the way to New York City."

"But I . . ."

"Hey, was last night for nothing? Now you gonna do what I ask or get gone."

It was as if she had suddenly become a totally different and more vicious person, a lap dog suddenly turned into a wolf. I didn't know what else to do. I stammered, "I'm sorry, but I . . . I can't drive," another lie. What I meant was I couldn't be a part of a jail break. I lifted my backpack out and started walking, my body held stiff as an iron pipe, expecting any moment for her to let fire with the little gun. I had never felt such fear. I took a step, another, and another. She didn't fire the gun. I turned my head to look back, and I saw her walking into the jail house with head held high.

I didn't know where to go. If I was a Boy Scout I could have navigated by the position of the sun or by what side of a tree moss grew on, or something like that. But I was never a Boy Scout. It was mid-day and the sun was almost directly overhead. A cold wind had come up, and I was shivering. I didn't know if it was from the cold or from fear. The smattering of snow had already melted. Half a block away there was a bus stop enclosed on three sides with glass. I walked to the bus stop and sat on the bench and watched the jail house for an hour by the Timex on my wrist. I smoked the last of my Marlboros and crumbled the pack and stashed it in my backpack with the intention of dumping it in the next trash can I came across. I never saw her come out. Of course not. They probably had metal detectors and would have found her gun and detained her. I could imagine how it went down. After taking the gun away from her they would have checked her driver's license and run a computer check and found she was wanted back in N.O. for drug possession or something. Heck, maybe even for armed robbery. Probably she and Buddy were robbers all along. Now they'd both be guests of the Douglas County Jail.

I didn't board the bus, but I stood on the step and asked the driver how to get to I-85. He said, "Not this bus. Catch the 21."

Me, Debbi

The view from Bryce's window was like something out of the movies. We were sky high over the city with a wall of windows, and through those windows I saw the city laid out against the blue-black night sky like a million diamonds arranged in patterns of overlapping rectangles, tower after tower after tower of lighted windows. I thought New Orleans was big, but you could have put two of New Orleans inside of Dallas.

We had zipped up from the parking garage in a supersonic elevator that opened not to a hallway the way elevators were supposed to, but directly into Bryce's living and dining rooms, one gigantic open area sparsely furnished with sleek modern furniture, a large fireplace that was crackling hot, fired up earlier, I presumed, by Martina, whom I had so far only heard about but not seen. There was a glass-top dining table that sat eight or more. The view was breathtaking, and the room was toasty, and yet there was something oddly cold about Bryce's penthouse. It took me a while to figure it out, but it was this: there were no pictures on the walls, no photographs or paintings, and no books or magazines anywhere to be seen, no robes or jackets draped over a chairback and no newspaper open on the coffee table. The place was as sterile as an operating room.

My legs ached, and my lower back. Too long in the car, especially that last part, inching through the construction zone. I stretched and bent to get the kinks out, and then I started slowly dancing in front of the window to the music in my head. Bryce kicked back on the couch and crossed his ankles on the coffee table, watching me dance. I could picture myself as I must have looked to him, moving in flowing motions against the backdrop of the city skyline, so much more sublime than dancing at Lipstix.

A small, black-haired beauty stepped through an open door into the dining area. I stopped still. At first, I thought she was a child, probably no more than five feet tall and thin, but with a shapely figure—a teenager perhaps, but no, when I got a closer look at her face it was clear that she was at least as old as I. I was surprised at myself for being struck with how small she was and how young she appeared, because I was hardly an inch or two taller and probably looked just as child-like. Of course I knew who she had to be, even if I had for a moment thought I'd gone down the rabbit hole with a Latina Alice. She said, "Welcome home, Mister Bryce" with less of an accent than my mother's. I recognized the use of *Mister* followed by a first name as an expression of deference once commonly used by domestic help in the South when addressing their employer's older children. Do they still do that? Yeah, I think so.

Bryce said, "Thank you, Martina. This is Debbi."

"It's nice to meet you, Martina. And just Debbi, please, not Miss Debbi. That sounds like the name of a porcelain doll."

"Thank you, Miss Debbi, it is my pleasure to meet you."

So much for not addressing me as Miss. But I didn't correct her. Turning to Bryce she said, "Dinner is ready, but I need to warm it up and toast the bread. I can have it on the table by the time you clean up."

"Thank you, Martina," he said, and throwing me for a loop, he kissed her, a rather chaste and casual kiss, but right smack on the mouth. From my point of view, it seemed there was no response from her. Her lips were an empty receptacle. But she didn't resist or protest, and I got the impression greeting with a kiss was a commonplace occurrence she neither welcomed nor objected to. She turned and walked into the kitchen to be about her duties—duties the nature of which I was beginning to question in my mind if not out loud.

I followed Bryce down a short hallway past an open door to a gymnasium fitted out with a leather-covered exercise bench, weights stacked neatly on racks, a stationary bike, punching bags both speed and heavy. Everything was shiny and neat, with white hand towels laid out as by an attendant (Martina, or did he have other domestics? I envisioned a butler and a chauffeur and a fitness trainer). He slipped on a pair of leather gloves and punched the speed bag a few times to show me (to show off, I thought). And then he said, "I only use a small part of this room. You could have half of it for a dance studio. That wall over there? I could put mirrors along there and install a bar. I've seen dance studios in the movies. How would that be?"

"Expensive," was the only response I could think of.

"No biggie."

I was flabbergasted. "You'd do that for me?"

"Sure. Why not?"

The next door was closed. "Martina's room," he said. And the next. "Company bathroom. We have a private bath, as does Martina." An archway across the hallway from the bathroom opened into an entertainment room. "This is pretty much where I live when I'm home," he said. There was a large-screen television against the wall and a huge sectional sofa. Magazines were spread on the coffee table. *Sports Illustrated*, *Financial Times*, *Playboy*. It was warmer and more inviting than the living room. In a small alcove at one end of his entertainment room was a glass-fronted cabinet with pistols and rifles that were not so much stored there as on display as in a museum, and there were museum quality ancient guns including an old blunderbuss and a musket from the seventeen hundreds and what Bryce called a tommy gun that had once belonged to a famous gangster called Machinegun Kelly. I learned all that later when Bryce gave me a history of his collection and let me nervously hold each of the guns. "Don't worry," he said. "They can't hurt you. They're not loaded. Hell, they don't even make bullets for many of them anymore."

I hazarded to ask if he had any guns he keeps for actual shooting. "Just that pistol I keep in the car for protection. I did some hunting when I was younger, but I used Pops' guns. Never had a hunting rifle of my own. And to tell the truth, I found hunting boring as all get-out. I haven't done it in ages and don't intend to ever start back."

"Thank god," I said.

Finally, we ventured into his bedroom, now our bedroom. There was a king-size bed and a large, triple-mirrored dressing table. He slid open the doors to a closet wherein his clothes were neatly hung on one end, with dress shoes and Tony Llama cowboy boots in a rack on the floor. Suits and pants and shirts and jackets were arranged by color and style. I wondered if he or Martina did that. With a theatrical flourish, he slid the door in the opposite direction to reveal the other half of the closet. It was empty. "This is yours," he announced, sounding like a proud groom escorting his bride into their new home. "Put your suitcase in there. Martina will put everything away for you in the morning. Tomorrow we'll shop for enough clothing to fill it with the best of everything. My welcome-home present for you."

"Oh my gosh," I said. "This is too much. It's . . . it's overwhelming," my usual sassy-brash self reduced to oh gosh, oh golly gee.

As in the living room, there were large, sliding glass doors against the outside wall that opened onto a small balcony. "The great thing about the view is we can see out but nobody can see us."

You mean they can't see through?"

"No. But that's a good idea. I might look into it. I mean 'cause we're so freaking high. A helicopter maybe. We can walk around bare-ass naked if we want to. Here and in the living room too."

"What about Martina? Do you walk around naked in her presence?"

"Oh, she doesn't mind."

OK, so the son of a bitch must be sleeping with her. Or he thinks so little of her that he subjects her to seeing him strut his nakedness in front of her. But wait. Maybe nudity and the casual kissing I had observed was non-sexual. Pure affection in the instance of the kissing and a healthy attitude about the naked body. I of all people should not be offended by nudity in others. I despised body shaming and had long held the belief that if nudity were commonplace it would not be erotic—advocated for non-threatening and non-eroticized nakedness in principle, but when it came to my boyfriend and his lovely maid, I wasn't so sure. I was butting heads with my own hypocrisy and jealousy.

I had my doubts about Martina's immigration status, despite Bryce's assurances. I wondered if she was here on a temporary work visa and was afraid of being fired or caught by the immigration people, and so she had to put up with his . . . whatever you want to call it. Crapola! It dawned on me that I might be, in a different sort of way, an immigrant beholden to Bryce, just like Martina. Me, an immigrant from the French Quarter and she from Mexico City or some South American city, both of us imprisoned in this gilded cage by our need for security from want.

Soon I would come to understand that at least metaphorically she and I were each immigrants, but literally not. She was born in a hospital in Dallas.

Me, David

I had only the vaguest idea where I was or how to get anywhere from there, so I depended on the people who picked me up to direct me. "Stay on 20 West," one driver told me. Another said, "85 will get you there quicker. Or 78. It might be slower but you're more likely to get rides." A series of short rides somehow got me through the Atlanta metropolitan area—sort of. There were so many crisscrossing roads and railroads and overpasses and underpasses that I felt like I was in some sort of bizarre dream about getting lost in the city. Somehow I ended up maybe an hour, maybe two, after escaping on a street in a grimy industrial area of what I guessed to be Atlanta but maybe it wasn't but still prob'ly part of Douglas County. Might as well have been Hong Kong. Heavy traffic. Warehouses, closed-down or barely operating businesses, trucks and buses, a nearby rail track.

It had started raining, a steady downpour that turned gutters into rivers in a matter of minutes. I held out my thumb to the continual stream of vehicles, the drivers of which never even glanced in my direction, water plastering my hair down on my head and into my eyes. I was just about to give it up and head for the nearest shelter, thinking nobody would pick me up with me dripping like a sieve. And then they passed me and slammed on their brakes. It was Molly and Buddy, the whore in her classic Thunderbird and the boyfriend she had broken out of jail. How had she gotten him out? Had she shot a guard? Were they murderers now in addition to being a whore and a drug dealer and a robber? And by what impossible stroke of fate had they wound up in the same god forsaken part of the city?

Buddy the boyfriend—I presumed it must be him—hopped out of the T-bird and started running my way splashing, through puddles, intent on murder.

I snatched up my backpack and slung it over my shoulders and took off running as fast as I could, across the street, darting between cars and trucks, behind a service station, across the railroad tracks, between parked boxcars, into and out of a warehouse of some sort where the workers halted their work to stare at me, slipping once and sliding on the pavement like a base runner into home plate. I picked myself up and pushed forward, glancing back over my shoulder to see I was losing him, thinking heavens-to-Betsy, of all the bleak and crappy industrial neighborhoods in the world where a fellow could get lost, how did we both end up in this one, and why was he chasing me and how in the world had she gotten him out of jail and which one of them had that goddamn gun?

I guess there are some question that can never be answered.

I was faster. I was breathing in heavy gasps, and there was a sharp pain in my side, knots in my calves, shins burning. But when I looked back again he was almost out of sight, leaning against a brick wall.

I lost them. Or they gave up.

A couple more rides got me out of the city, and I eventually ended up on a smaller highway in mountains in either Georgia or Virginia or maybe even Tennessee, unsure if I was even going in the right direction. By then it was nearing mid-day, and I was beginning to feel emptiness in my stomach. I never eat much at a single meal, but I eat often when I can—I'm a grazer. I hear that's healthy, but that's not why I do it. It's just the way I'm built.

The rain had come and gone and come again. The road I was on now was slick with water that glistened like polished silver. Rainbows of oil on water in places. The sun had come out. Blue skies behind me and heavy gray clouds ahead. I love the smell that lingers after a burst of rain, and the quality of light. The sunny side of trees were fiery orange and white against a backdrop of blackened evergreens on the shady side. Tree trunks as black as coal. The whole world glowed like embers in a campfire. It was so enchanting that I could have stood there all day, which was exactly what it was beginning to look like I was going to do.

There were hours and hours of standing on the side of the road with very little passing traffic. And what road it was, I could hardly guess. What little traffic there was whipped by as if I were a ghost. I watched the cars that passed me by vanish around curves and then reappear minutes later as they rounded other curves far ahead and across a cavern. The road was doubling back on itself like a tangled rope. The sun rose higher overhead and appeared smaller, a bleached white disc that was soon covered with a translucent veil of cloud. The wind was gusting and cold. I crammed my hands in my pockets and pulled out only my right hand to stick out my thumb when a car came by. I started walking slowly forward. Half the day had gotten away from me, when someone finally stopped on the shoulder up ahead and waited for me to get in. He was a large man in an old Ford sedan. I tossed my backpack in the back seat and got in the front.

"Hey there."

"Hey yourself. Thanks for stopping."

"Glad to, fella. It's my Christian duty." With that, he reached over, patted my thigh, squeezed my leg, and then put his meaty hand back on the wheel.

I had never seen such a man before. Obese? Yes, but obesity of a repellent nature. No neck whatsoever. His chin oozed into the space between sloped shoulders. He wore a lumberjack shirt with gaping spaces between buttons where curly black hair crawled out. His eyes darted snakelike, and the unfiltered cigarette that dangled from his flaccid lips was wetted at the mouth end. He smiled at me and put the car in gear and took off. It was a straight shift, and he seemed to get a kick out of running through the gears from first to second to third. My guess was he was pretending to be drag racing. I imagined he was going vroom vroom inside his head. The heat in the car was cranked up, and so was the volume on the country music blaring from his dashboard radio. At first the heat felt great, until I got over the shivering from the outside cold and wet, but soon it became oppressive. The man drove with both hands on the wheel. A gaudy high school or college class ring dug into his fat index finger. There were letters tattooed on his fingers, the first letter partially concealed by his ring. It spelled out something that ended with the letters *uck*. I guess it could have been *luck,* but you can guess what I immediately thought. At any rate, it was a cheesy ring. This hippopotamus of a driver was a bloated river creature dredged up from the muddy deep with the smile of a salesman plastered on his face. What looked like a three-or four-day growth of salt-and-pepper beard dirtied his jowly cheeks. His belly spilled over a belt that was not buckled, the top button on his pants open. I gathered he needed breathing room.

"Where you going?" he asked.

"New York."

I knew what he was going to ask next.

"What for?"

I didn't think the acting story would lead to any interesting conversations with this guy. "Oh, uh, going for a new job. I got a girlfriend up there I'm gonna stay with."

"I'll pray for a safe trip and a life filled with love."

"Uh, thanks." I wasn't comfortable with that, but I didn't know why. I asked about his tattoo.

"It says Buck. Not what you think."

"Oh, uh, I wasn't . . . Who is Buck?"

"Buck is my husband."

That was a surprise. I must admit I harbored some preconceived notions of what gay guys were like, and he certainly didn't fit the image.

He lit another cigarette and slapped my thigh again in a glad-handing manner, and squeezed it again, this time leaving his hand there longer that was comfortable. I was starting to sweat. He said, "God loves you, brother. Have you accepted Jesus as Lord?"

"Yes I have," I said, in hopes that if he thought I was already saved he'd hold off on the preaching. "I was baptized in the Catholic church."

"Catholic!" He shouted. His cigarette shot out of his mouth and landed on his lap, and he brushed it off onto the floorboard. "Catholics are heathens. They worship false gods and saints. They are ruled by the Pope in Italy who is under the control of Russian Communists."

He slammed on his brakes. The car skidding to a stop at an angle across one traffic lane. He got out of the car in the road and said, "Get out. Come around here."

I gripped the edge of my seat ready to hold on for dear life if he tried to pull be out of the car.

"Get out, you heathen." He bounded around to my side of the car and jerked the door open. I thought he was going to yank me out. What could I do? The guy must had had at least two-hundred pounds on me. He pried my hand from the edge. But he didn't yank at me. He was surprisingly gentle. He coaxed me out of the car. "Come on, come on. I ain't a gonna hurt you."

I got out, afraid not to, and, I must admit, somewhat out of curiosity. He told me to stand in front of him and bow my head. This was all happening in the middle of a road where he had come to a stop blocking one or only two lanes. I did as I was told, and instinctively I took off my glasses and put them in my pocket. He hovered over me like some kind of giant blob of meat and muscle and put one hand on top of my head and raised his other hand to the heavens and prayed, "Dear Lord Jesus, creator of all mankind, please bless this young sinner and guide him back to the straight and narrow path before it is too late and he is cast into the fiery lakes of hell." And he went on and on, babbling exhortations to God and his son, Jesus, and finally he ordered me to get down on my knees and ask for forgiveness. Again I did what he commanded of me, and he said, "Out loud. I want to hear you say it," so I said, "Forgive me, Lord Jesus."

Back in the car and back on the road, he preached about the end times coming and talked about trials and tribulations and war and the coming of the anti-Christ, and I did not say another word.

Up and down and around what I was afraid was going to be an endless succession of curves, we finally leveled out into a stretch of farmland, broad fields on either side of the road and smatterings of rundown barns and farmhouses. I watched him roll down his window and toss his cigarette out and immediately light another. I looked away from him, watching now the shadows of clouds as they rode the fields, afraid to look him in the eye, afraid that if I did meet his eye he could see right through me and know I wasn't truly saved. Watching him smoke made me want a cigarette too, but my pack was empty and the carton in my backpack was too hard to get to and I didn't want to ask for one of his. I pulled my glasses out of my pocket and cleaned them with the tail of my shirt before putting them back on. The sun was getting low in the west. Shadows were long. He slowed down and turned onto a dirt road.

"This is it," he said. "This is as far as I go. Right up yonder is where me and Buck live. You can come on up if you want, have a bite of supper with us, even spend the night. It's getting dark, and this old road ain't no safe place to be after dark."

Me, Debbi

Practically sleepwalking, I groped my way into the kitchen. It was mid-morning, ten-thirty or eleven I guess. That was like the crack of dawn to me. Crusty gunk glued the corners of my eyes shut, my hair a mess, no makeup, wondering where in the world Bryce was. The door to the gym was closed and a hellacious noise came from behind it. I dared to open the door a crack and peek in. There were workmen in there installing a mirror. By god, he had done it. He had brought in a work crew to create my dance studio. I was overwhelmed by knowing he would do something like that just for me. I almost broke into a happy dance, singing "He loves me, he loves me," but my desperation for strong coffee and a face wash and a couple of pain pills prevented any such action.

Bryce and I had sat up late the night before, drinking a bourbon concoction of his devising in front of the fireplace, talking about our childhoods. His childhood, as he told it, seemed idyllic. Hunting and fishing with his father and a big bother named Harrison, trips to Disneyland, flying in his father's Cessna to Destin, Florida, where they rented a cabin on the beach and fished for tarpon in the Gulf of Mexico two years in a private military academy, which he hated, and college at LSU, where he was active in the Young Republicans. I wondered if our political differences were going to turn out to be an insurmountable strain on our relationship.

I told him as little as possible about my growing up. Not much to brag about. Mama was a voodoo woman, Madame Ernestine, a beauty of Jamaican and English ancestry, or so she claimed. Mixed race for sure, with high cheekbones and a delicate jaw and blue-black hair. She told fortunes and worked healing magic, was often asked to cast evil spells but said "I only do good magic." During my lifetime she scraped by with a succession of menial jobs, mostly house cleaning for wealthy people in the Garden District where she often pilfered decorative doodads. Oh how she loved her trinkets, the tackier the better. She caught pneumonia and died when I was in high school. With no living relatives (I never knew my old man), I was cast out to survive on my own. I did what street kids do to get by. Nothing to talk about. At seventeen I started stripping at Lipstix. Lied about my age. They're not exactly sticklers for checking IDs in the French Quarter. Been there off and on ever since. It paid the rent and put me through two years at Tulane. You better believe I developed a tough hide in those years. I lived a double or even triple life, learning to get along with my fellow students whose growing up might as well have been in a different world, and still hanging out some of the street kids I had grown to love, and then the strippers and musicians and the drunks at Lipstix. And I didn't take lip from anybody. If anyone dared to disparage strippers or sex workers or queers or street kids, I let them have it with both barrels, calling them spoiled and privileged trust-fund hippies and daring them to walk in the shoes of those they criticized before shooting off their mouths. Yeah, I know, "walk a mile in their shoes" is a cliché unworthy of an English major, but I enlivened it with a fusillade of creative cursing. That was before I decided to give up cursing.

So that was my life before I met David, the first man who ever loved me for my heart and my mind and not just for my tits and ass, and before I met Bryce. Lipstix was where I met Bryce. He tried to pick me up right off the bat. He congratulated me on the elegance of my moves. *Elegance* was the word he used. He said I reminded him of Josephine Baker, which was right smack on target because the routine I was doing the night he came in the first time was patterned on one of her dances. I was bowled over by him even knowing who Josephine Baker was. Of all the men who hit on me in Lipstix, and you'd better believe they were legion, Bryce was the first one to talk about admiring the art of burlesque—the beauty of it, not the sexiness of it. Oh yes, I fell for him right then and there. And yet, here I am living in his beyond-imagination penthouse apartment where he has hired workers to build me a dance studio and where we will someday soon travel together the few miles out in the country to meet his parents. And he has instructed me to not let them know I'm a dancer.

That somehow negates a huge hunk of the good stuff. Whatever happened to his admiration of my art? How can he be both proud of my art and ashamed of it?

I wandered into the dining room and was headed to the kitchen door when Martina opened it and greeted me with, "Good morning, Miss Debbi," her perkiness like xylophones playing in my head, and I wasn't ready for music—a funeral dirge, maybe, but her voice was more like calypso. "What would you like for breakfast?" she chirruped. "Eggs and grits, maybe? Sausage and biscuits with gravy? You will love my buttermilk gravy."

" Nuh . . . uh, no, nothing please. I never eat breakfast. Just some coffee if you don't mind. Do you know where Bryce is?"

"Oh, he's gone to work, Miss. How do you want your coffee?"

"Black. Black and strong."

"Chicory?"

"Oh lord no, I can't stand coffee with chicory."

"I thought all you folks from New Orleans drank your coffee with chicory. And lots of heavy cream."

"That's for tourists. Where'd you say Bryce was?"

"He's at work, Miss."

"He said he was going to take me shopping today."

Martina responded with a little bit of a shrug and a one-sided smile. Her chirpiness so early in the morning irritated me, but I tried to not let it show.

"What time is it anyway?" I asked her. She said it was ten-thirty.

"When did those workmen start?"

"About an hour ago."

She served the coffee in a delicate little cup. It was just the way I liked it, scalding hot and so strong a spoon could almost stand up in it, but the white demitasse with the single silver band around it simply didn't get it. I needed a mug, the bigger the better. She stepped back into the kitchen, leaving me to sip my coffee alone. I drained the demitasse in about five quick slurps. Through the open kitchen door, I spied Martina sitting alone on a stool at a counter drinking a cup of coffee of her own. In an honest-to-god coffee mug. What's with this separation of employers and employees, I wondered, what's with the diffidence? I stood up and stepped halfway through the kitchen door, stopped and leaned against the door frame in what I realized was a rather slatternly pose. So I straightened up quickly and said, "Could you bring the newspaper in here and let's have our coffee together?"

"Yes, Miss."

"And please, don't call me Miss."

"Yes, Miss. I mean . . ."

"Debbi. Call me Debbi." Hadn't I told her that already? "And bring me some more coffee, and put it in a real mug like yours. "

I asked her just what kind of work Bryce did. She said, "Well, Miss . . ."

"Debbi."

"Debbi. I'm sorry. He works for his father. I don't rightly know just what he does. Something in finance or real estate. Mister Fisher also owns some stores, a lot of them. He owns Grapevine Hardware and Discount Sports Center, and some other things. Mister Bryce and Mister Fisher are very important men."

She poured another cup of coffee for me and refilled hers. Her hands were unsteady. She grasped her cup with both hands to drink. I tried to draw her out in conversation. It was torturous. I asked her about herself, her family. She said she was an only child. Her mother, Gabriella, worked for Mr. and Mrs. Fisher, Bryce's parents. She was born in the cottage that sat on the senior Fishers' property—servants quarters, I thought—and lived there until she was grown. Four years younger than Bryce, she had been his playmate starting when she was three and he was eight or nine. By the time she was as old as Bryce had been when they first started playing together, he started telling her she was a child and he had no interest in playing with her. Her mother told her, "Mr. Bryce is becoming a young man now, it is time you start addressing him properly as Mr. Bryce."

She said, "I cried about that. It was like my playmate had been taken away and replaced by someone I didn't know." Almost tearing up at the memory, she cleared her throat and said, "Mama still lives in the cottage and still works for them. You will meet them tonight."

"Tonight?"

"Yes, tonight. You will be having dinner with them."

It was disturbing that Bryce's maid knew what I was going to be doing before I knew it.

We heard the barely perceivable swoosh of the elevator door sliding open and looked up to see Bryce coming home. "There you are," he said, stepping quickly past us, pausing long enough to give each of a perfunctory kiss (I didn't think I would ever get used to seeing him kiss her) and on into the kitchen, striding quickly to the coffee pot to pour himself a cup, using a large mug he snatched from the overhead cabinet. That was when I caught on that the delicate little tea cups were only for company. Or maybe they were for ladies, not for big strapping men like Bryce or for the help. Martina quickly stood up and carried her coffee to the sink, rinsed it and put it in the dishwasher. It was like she was not allowed to take a break and had been caught goofing off. "Is there anything you need, Mr. Bryce?" she asked.

"No, I'm fine. Thank you, Martina."

She excused herself and left the kitchen. Bryce turned to me. "You're not dressed. The day's half gone. Get yourself dressed. I told you I'm taking you shopping."

"Now?"

"Yeah. Come on. Chop, chop."

The remainder of that day and evening is a blur in my mind. It left me confused, a fairy tale princess one moment and a pampered but unloved child the next, swooning with romance and conflicted by outrage. We went first to the biggest shopping mall I had ever seen. First stop, Macy's. We went to the women's department, and Bryce said, "Have at it. Pick out whatever you like."

"Really? Anything?"

"Sure. But if I don't like it I'll let you know. Believe it or not, I have excellent taste in women's fashion."

"I believe it."

He was right on both counts: didn't hesitate to say "That's stupid" or "Are you kidding me?" and did have good taste, if a bit more conservative than mine. The first thing I picked off the rack was a sleeveless navy-blue ruffle dress, the ruffles descending at a slant from left shoulder to the right at waist height. I spotted the price tag: on sale for $47, marked down from $79.50. Not bad. Then a simple black dress with three-quarter-length sleeves and a plunging v-neckline priced at $89.50 but on sale for $56.90. He approved of both, and I approved his thrift in giving the go-ahead to sale items. I had expected him to be extravagant and to hell with the cost in a show-offy way, but he wasn't. He was more businesslike. I needed clothes, and it was his job to see to it I got the very best at the best price.

Bryce started picking dresses, jeans, tops. He piled them on my outstretched arms and told me to try them on. "Ooh la la," he said when I stepped out of the changing room in the black number with the plunging neckline. I had never known a man to have so much fun watching a woman shop. I thought men hated shopping, but shopping with Bryce was turning out to be a playful delight.

"Shoes," he said. "Gotta have shoes."

"Oh no. I don't need any shoes," I demurred.

"Don't be silly. A woman can never have too many shoes."

That was what I hoped he'd say. So then I was like, "Well, I guess I could use a pair of boots." I ended up buying knee-length cowgirl boots, $199.00, and some red and white Converse sneakers and heels. . After the shoe shopping, we went to lunch. Burgers and fries. Coffee for him and a chocolate milkshake for me. And then he said, "Ear rings. I love big dangly ear rings on women." So we went to a jewelry store and bought five pair of ear rings and a diamond necklace.

"Now for the best part. Underwear. Victoria's Secret."

"Oh gosh no. I don't need underwear."

"Oh yes you do. I've seen those old lady cotton panties you wear."

"But I like them. They're comfortable."

Needless to say, we made a stop in Victoria's Secret. And for dessert, dance togs and ballet slippers. "You got a brand-new studio. You can't dance in just any old thing. You can't dance naked."

"Oh, I don't know. I bet you'd like that."

"I would. But you wouldn't get in much rehearsing."

You just don't say no to Bryce Fisher. I saw the tab. It was $212 and some odd cents. That was just at Victoria's Secret. I didn't see the charges at Macy's or at the jewelry store, but I had looked at the price tags and mentally added it up as best I could remember. Bryce ended up spending more than a thousand dollars on me.

Me, David

Escaped from the grasp of the evangelical ogre, I found myself once again standing on a narrow strip of earth on the side of the road. And it was snowing again and getting uncomfortably late. My toes should not have been numb from cold and wet, but they were. Somehow moisture was getting into my shoes. What little sunlight filtered through the veil of cloud spread out along the western horizon. The snow wasn't sticking to the road, but it was beginning to pile up on the strip of dirt and dead grass on the side where I stood. I plodded onward, heading north and then east and then west and northeast as the road curved and switched back upon itself like a corridor in a midway house of horrors. I started thinking about the Donner party.

What was I doing there, I wondered. Had I passed up another meal and place to sleep for the night because I had been afraid of an obese Christian evangelical who, gay or not, would surely not have tried anything with me since he was inviting me into the home where his husband was making dinner. So no, it wasn't that. I'm no homophobe, and I think fat people deserve the same respect as thin people, but there was something grossly repellent about that guy's obesity and the slovenly way his fat, wet lips clamped around the cigarettes he chain-smoked. Plus, I had known from too many previous experiences that rabid Christians can be impossible to escape. Asking to pray for you, asking again and again if you're sure you've been saved, preaching their version of the gospel, they can be more threatening than a madman with a gun. So rather than accept an offered meal despite my hunger, and a safe if somewhat rustic place to spend the night (as I imagined since I had not seen their house), I chose to wander a road to I knew not where. So far, I thought, though I had gotten hardly anywhere, I had been extremely lucky to be offered a bed and meals with almost every ride. The old lady in New Orleans, that oh-so-nice African-American family, the prostitute. I still had change in my pocket and had not needed to pull out my credit card once. Up to that point, the only drawback to my adventure was that it was taking forever to get anywhere. And now, because I felt repulsed by a man who was probably harmless, I was stranded in the darkening cold in the middle of a mountain range where I would surely be attacked by a wild animal if I didn't simply freeze to death on the side of the road.

There were places where the band of earth between the pavement and steep hillsides, chasms and gullies, was no more than three or four feet wide, depending on the curve of the road. I was afraid if it got any colder the wet snow underfoot would become treacherously slick. I pictured cars sliding sideways toward me, and me with no place to run. My steps left clear impressions on the soft ground. I imagined my footsteps freezing solid, hardening until spring, and I imagined little boys and girls a thousand years in the future looking at the petrified footsteps in a glass case in a museum and reading a plaque that said, "Petrified shoe print of David Parker who froze to death on the Appalachian Trail" guessing that where I was might be in the Appalachians. (I later figured out that I must have been somewhere in the Great Smokies near the border or Tennessee and the Carolinas.) Geography and I are not on the best of terms.

I should have bought some decent shoes for the trip. Maybe combat boots to go with the army surplus coat. I was cold, but not yet in danger of frostbite or anything so drastic. Only my feet felt icy, and my cheeks and lips. When the sun peeked out from behind the low-lying clouds, it was the cold white of a china plate, not the burning yellow sun I was accustomed to seeing. Come to think of it, that might have been an early rising moon I was seeing. I didn't know. I don't think I was thinking clearly at that point. I was feeling weak from hunger and cold, and perhaps even from lingering fear. I was seriously beginning to doubt that hitchhiking to New York was a good idea. I estimated I was about halfway there. Maybe I should just turn around, cross to the other side of the road and try to hitch my way back to New Orleans. Soon it would be fully dark, and the temperature would surely drop precipitously. I had no idea whatsoever what I was going to do about an evening meal or a place to spend the night. The idea of trudging through the night on that almost deserted mountain road was depressing. Who would pick up a lone hitchhiker in the dark? A murderer? A rapist? Another creep like the one I had just escaped? To try and force such frightening thoughts from my head, I called to mind visions of Debbi. Oh God, how I missed her! I pictured her in my mind. At thirty-two, only three years older than I, she was beginning to get a few gray streaks in her wheat colored hair. Otherwise, she could pass for twenty-something. She was small to medium in height and build. When we stood side-by-side she could rest her cheek against my chest, and I could rest my chin on the top of her head.

I remembered her waking up in the morning, kicking off the covers and standing up naked as the day she was born, rushing to grab a flannel robe on cold mornings or casually walking on bare feet to the bathroom when the house was warm enough, her body the color of sand on a beach. She knew that seeing her naked body thrilled me, and knowing that gave her a jolt of pride. She was something of an exhibitionist. Nudity excited her. She once talked me into going to a clothing-optional beach and she felt much more comfortable there than I did. If she sauntered out of our bedroom sans clothing and bumped into one of our housemates, she would casually say, "Oh, are you headed to the bathroom? I'll be just a minute." The housemate would likely say "No problem, I can wait." That's the way we were. It was an unusual living arrangement. Lucy, Randy, Hopper, David and Debbi. I guess it was an unusual household in which values from the sixties and seventies still held sway. Nobody wanted to be considered up-tight or prudish. If any one of us thought nakedness was anything other than natural, we didn't dare say so. Lucy and I once accidentally opened a door and stepped out into the hall at the same time, and she was unclothed. Reflexively she covered herself but then immediately moved her hands. The covering was due to modesty; the uncovering was shame at being modest. I think that was common to most of us, except for Debbi and Hopper. Debbi was more natural about the body than any of the rest of us, and more philosophical about it. "Nakedness doesn't have to be sexy. If we all went naked whenever we wanted to, nobody would get all excited about it," she preached, and everybody said they agreed. She used the term *naked*, not *nude*.

She had an interesting take on that, which made a lot of sense to me. She said, "Nudity is for artists' models and pin-ups. They show off their nude bodies, and are meant to be seen and admired, even lusted after. But to be naked is to be oneself with nothing to hide, neither body nor soul. Nakedness is never prurient."

She got that from a book called *Ways of Seeing* by John Berger. I kind of got what she meant, but this is an arena where physical and intellectual arousal go their separate ways, with the former being beyond my control if not beyond everybody's. I mean, I could say very emphatically, yes I agree with that on principle, but evidence of a philosophical principle doesn't make my heart rate shoot sky high. Emotion tramples the snot out of intellect.

But there was so very much more to Debbi than a gorgeous, well-muscled body. She had a brilliant mind. She had been an honor student. She wanted to be a writer and, in fact, had written some excellent short stories. She made costumes for the theater department and had toyed with the idea of going into costume design as a profession, but when I last spoke to her about it—she did tend to veer off into different directions—she was set on becoming a ballet dancer. We had talked about going to New York together, she to study ballet, and me to try and make it as an actor. At the time, I thought of it as a pipe dream, not something either of us would ever do.

I loved her passion when she talked about dance. She idolized Martha Graham and Isodora Duncan and Josephine Baker. I had heard of all of them but was not familiar with their dancing, so Debbi found videos of them and showed them to me, and she learned their routines and showed them to me and to Randy and Hopper and Lucy in the small stage of the living room of our apartment.

This is when I have to tell you what Debbi did for a living. She was a burlesque dancer at Lipstix. For a woman who loved dancing and was comfortable with nudity—I mean nakedness, using her definition—burlesque was a natural. And speaking of natural, my natural reaction when she told me was to shout, "You're a stripper!" an exclamation and a question. I was horrified at first, and intrigued, and that was when she let loose with a tirade about strip tease and burlesque the likes of which I had never heard.

"Burlesque has a historic tradition of beauty, sophistication, humor and class." She was in lecture mode. "It comes from the parody plays of the Victorian era, done with humor and often based on political or social issues of the time. The audience is expected to hoot and holler. Remember what I said about the difference between nakedness and nudity? It's like that. In a strip club, you're a canvas, in burlesque, you have to be a cartoon. Despite the girls on the swing and the salacious posters, Lipstix is not your typical strip club. It's burlesque of the highest order, the real McCoy. For the performers, it can be a very empowering undertaking. Burlesque tells a story. Each performance has a theme that is carried out by each of the performers, and it involves elaborate costumes and choreography. And many of us, myself included, design and make our own costumes and plan out our own choreography, and practice. And since we perform almost every night, practice has to be in moments when we should be sleeping. Most importantly, perhaps, burlesque is funny. It's good sexy fun—more like Vaudeville than stripping, and in some ways like musical theater." She took a deep breath and then plunged into her tirade again. "We spend around six to eight weeks preparing for each show. There aren't any men stuffing dollar bills in our G-strings. It's all about emphasizing body positivity and healthy admiration for the human form instead of just nudity for the sake of titillation. It's about reveling in the beauty and grace and yeah, the raunch and the humor, but also the teasing aspect of stripping."

I seemed to me the phrase *the tease of stripping* sort of contradicted everything else she was saying, but I let it go.

She said, "Each burlesque act represents a huge chunk of my heart; so much time and thought, sweat and blood goes into it. Every stitch of the costume is mine, the song choice is mine, the concept is mine. I'm responsible for making all of it work for all those people, not just the ones who came looking for what I'm already serving up. And taking off clothes smoothly is not enough, and it's not enough to keep time with the music. The thing that defines a great burlesque act is how the performer fills the space. You have to throw your persona, intentions, and ideas so far that you slap the cheap seats in the face. It's terrifying! But that's what's great about it. It forces you to grow. It's a magical thing when it happens, but it can be super elusive when you're juggling tricky hooks, technical difficulties, and nerves. Burlesque is definitely the deep end of the peeling pool."

Talk about waxing poetic. I think that was when I really fell in love with her mind.

I walked, I walked. My feet grew heavy. I finally stopped moving and stood immobile facing in the direction I hoped traffic would come from. The road was deserted. Dark. Standing alone on the lonely road, I thought about the first time Debbi and I went out together. We went to the O'Henry, a coffee shop a few steps down from the bookstore. While we were drinking our coffee, a latte for her and Americano for me, she told me she was an English major at Tulane. "No way," I said. "I was an English major too."

"Really?"

"Yeah, really."

"Did you have Professor Kline for Introduction to Shakespeare?"

"Oh lord, yes. The way he droned on and on with that whiney nasal voice almost killed Shakespeare for me."

"Speaking of Shakespeare, did you see *Shakespeare in Love?*"

"I loved it. What a brilliant writer Stoppard is."

"And how weird."

"And I loved Gwyneth Paltrow."

And our conversation flew from books to movies to favorite bands.

Another time we spent an hour or more in Louis Armstrong Park, the most gorgeous park in America as far as I was concerned, although I must admit I would have loved it even more if it was a little less pristine—a little wildness wouldn't have hurt. We sat in the grass by that sensuously curved stream and talked about our youth, about all the times we had done things we never should have done. There was a lot more of that on her part. And as it always did, our talk came back to movies we had seen and books we had read. We discovered that we had both watched *Cabaret* many times. I told her I still had it on VHS tape, and she said, "Oh my. Let's watch it tonight." And we did.

Once she told me she had a hankering for raw oysters. I had never eaten them. "Oh my God, you've got to. There's nothing like it."

"But they're so slimy. It would be like swallowing snot."

We laughed like crazy at that and she told me I was chicken. It was Debbi and not I who was always the adventurous one . . . well, at least until I embarked on this hitchhiking journey.

She challenged me to eat oysters. "Right now. Do it. I double-dog dare you. Just slurp one right down."

I couldn't bring myself to do it.

We walked hand-in-hand through the art deco arch and found a funky little café not far away on Rampart, where I ate fried shrimp and watched her eat raw oysters dipped in a hot sauce. I can't even remember the things we said that made us laugh insanely.

Cold and lonely and a little bit afraid in the spooky dark, I remembered our first kiss, our first and only fight, the first time we made love, and sadly, I remembered the last time too.

My revelry was interrupted by Ned Flanders in a Mini Cooper. Ned Flanders, the nebbish character from the cartoon series *The Simpsons*. It had been so long since a car had passed me by, I thought I would never get a ride. For a long moment I stared at the little car that had pulled off the road in the only place it could, about fifty yards ahead of me. And then I shook myself back to reality and jogged ahead, tossed my backpack in what passed for a luggage compartment and then took my first look at the driver as I hopped in the front seat next to him. It was the sweater that made him look like *The Simpsons* character. That and the buttoned-to-the-neck shirt poking out from the crew collar, and the mustache and the glasses. I immediately thought accountant or librarian—stereotypes, I know. He was actually a nice-looking chap, smaller than me with delicate hands at ten and two on the steering wheel, just like they teach it. (Who drives with both hands on the wheel? Probably Ned Flanders.)

"My goodness," he said. "How in the world did you wind up on a road like this in the dark of night? Did your car break down?"

"No, I don't have car. I was hitching north on . . . I guess it was I-40, and I got a ride with someone who detoured onto this road.

He said it was quicker. And I've been kind of been stuck out here ever since. No traffic and nobody wants to stop."

"Oh my goodness gracious. You've got yourself in quite a pickle. I'm Ned Smith. I'm afraid I'm not going far. I live just up the road a piece."

"Your name is really Ned?"

"Yes. Does that seem odd? I mean, Ned is a common enough name." After a brief pause and with a silly grin, he said, "Oh, I get it. I've been told that before, that I look like that cartoon character. I've never watched it, so I don't know. So where are you going, anyway?"

"I'm going to New York."

"My, my, my. That's quite a trip. Why in the world are you going to New York?"

For a change, I did not feel the need to make up a story. I spilled the beans about how Debbi had left me for another man and about how I had dreamed all my life about being a star on Broadway and had finally decided to take the big chance. The heater in the little Mini warmed me up nicely and quickly, and I was beginning to feel lethargic in a dreamy way. Ned said he admired my courage. "I could never take such a chance," he said. "I dream of doing romantic things, but I never do anything. I'm a clerk in a department store. I drive twenty miles in and twenty miles back and take my lunch in a tin lunch bucket decorated with a scene from *Lost in Space*. How dull is that."

I said, "I never before had the nerve to try anything either, but sometimes you just have to."

We didn't talk about much else that I can remember. I closed my eyes, thinking it would be just for a moment, and I fell asleep. I dreamed that I had AIDS but a friend cured me of it by hooking me up to some weird contraption that hung me upside-down from the ceiling, and the friend pricked my toe with a needled and the virus dripped out onto the floor and I was cured. And then my dream changed to something I remember as being lovely, although I can't remember what it was.

When I woke, I felt Ned's hand in my lap. I woke slowly, and when he felt me move a little he pulled his hand away and back to the steering wheel. "Sorry," he said. No explanation, no excuse, just "Sorry." With both hands gripping the steering wheel and his eyes unblinkingly on the road ahead, he looked so terribly sad, that rather than being mad at him for touching me inappropriately while I slept I was overcome with sadness for him, for how terribly lonely and uneventful his life must be. Imagining what life must be like for him living in some isolated house somewhere in these mountains, an apparently gay man who probably felt as if he were the only gay man in the world, I didn't know what to think or what to say, so I didn't say anything. What bothered me a little, but not much, was not him putting his hands on me uninvited while I had dozed off but that he was not the first but the second of two gay men in a row to pick me up. And it wasn't just them. Gays seemed to be attracted to me. It had happened enough to make me worry about myself. Was I some kind of gay magnet? Granted, the last guy wasn't after me sexually, he just wanted to bring me to Jesus. But oh my god, he was so repulsive. And now this one putting his hand on me, that should have been the final straw. But this guy was so nice, so polite, interesting, and interested in me, not just in where he'd had his hand but interested in what I thought, where I'd been and where I was going. That was clear from what little we'd talked about. But I couldn't shake the nagging worry, because they weren't the first or only. There had been others back home over the years. I recreated in my mind the men, the situations. It wasn't like it happened all the time, I told myself. But still, it was enough to be worrisome. Did they sense something in me that I couldn't even recognize in myself? Or maybe it was because I was not boisterous or threatening in any way. In other words, safe.

"Why so quiet?" he asked, and then, "I really am sorry about what I did. I had no right."

"It's all right. I'm just . . . just remembering stuff."

"Stuff you want to talk about?"

"No, no. Nothing important."

He pushed a button on his dashboard and music started. "That sounds like Judy Garland," I said.

"It is. Judy and Liza together. It's from a live concert in London."

"That's great. I love them."

The headlights of his little Mini Cooper spotlighted empty pavement. Somehow, we got to talking about movies. (Weird, I had just been remembering how Debbi and I loved to talk about movies. Maybe it wasn't queers that were attracted to me, maybe it was movie lovers.) He said his favorite movie of all times was one with a lot of singing and dancing called *All That Jazz*.

"I've heard of that one. Always wanted to see it but never did."

He said, "I have it on DVD. It's fabulous. If you came home with me, we could watch it together."

"If I . . ."

"Why not? It's getting late. You can't hitchhike in the snow at night. Come home with me. I'll fix you a good supper and we can watch movies. You can spend the night, and I'll take you to a good spot for hitching in the morning."

So here we go again, I thought. This offering of meals and a place to stay and a ride back to the highway was getting to be a habit. I felt extremely lucky. But I had to get one thing clear. "You're not going to try and get me in bed, are you?"

"Not if you don't want me to."

And that was that, so straight forward and natural. I wondered why everyone couldn't be like that.

Ned prepared a marvelous meal. Lasagna and a tossed salad with walnuts and cranberries and biscuits. Nuts and berries in a salad was something I'd heard of but never tried. It was delicious. He heated up a peach cobbler in the microwave for dessert and topped it with vanilla cream. The all-natural kind with vanilla beans. And then we watched *All That Jazz* on a thirty-something-inch TV, sitting together on a love seat, the only seating option with a good angle on the television. He mixed us Manhattans, which he said were to bring me luck in New York. I drank three of them. All that time seated so close together in his dimly lighted living room and he never made a move toward me. I felt safe and comfortable and grateful.

"Isn't this great?" he asked.

I felt he meant not only the movie but the drinks and the coziness, but I responded only about the movie. I said, "Yes, it is. It's beautifully done. The dancing is amazing."

"That's Bob Fosse. The whole thing is his life story thinly disguised as fiction."

The dancers made me think about Debbi. Where was she now? What was she doing? Would her new life with the Texas millionaire end her dreams of being a dancer? That would be such a shame.

I drifted into fantasy, imagining I was a successful actor on Broadway, and on my way to rehearsal one day I would pass a billboard on a theater with a photo of dancers, and there she was front center, the lead dancer, like Katie, Gideon's girlfriend in the movie. I imagined meeting her backstage with a bouquet and a bottle of wine, a hug and a kiss and tears of joy.

Ned paused the movie and shuffled off to the kitchen to refill our drinks. Setting our drinks on the coffee table in front of us, he said, "Are you not enjoying the movie?"

"Yes, I am."

"But you seem so far away. Just like in the car earlier. I can tell something is bothering you."

"It's nothing, really."

"Don't give me that," he said. "Something's eating at you."

I was surprised such a nebbish little man could speak so authoritatively. I said, "It's the dancers. My girlfriend was a dancer. I miss her terribly."

He kept the video paused while I told him all about Debbi, my love for her, how much I missed her. I told him about how throughout my life I had time after time let opportunities slip away. I told him I felt like I didn't deserve her because I had not fought for her when I had the chance. He tried to tell me I should go back home and fight for her now. "It's never too late."

"Yes it is. It's plenty too late."

When I convinced him that winning Debbi back was impossible, he said, "Then set your mind on what is possible. Think about the glorious career you're going to have as an actor. Pursue that goal with everything you've got in you."

Suddenly he pushed himself clumsily to his feet, clutched his chest with one hand and then kind of kneeled or fell onto the coffee table, knocking over our drinks.

"My heart," he gasped. "I'm having a heart attack."

I stood up and helped him back to a seating position on the love seat, asking, "What do I do?"

"My key chain. On that shelf there. There's a little metal container on it that holds nitroglycerine tablets. Get me one." He was sweating and gasping for breath. I got the container on the keychain. It had a screw top. The tiniest pills ever shook out, and he put one in his mouth. He said, "Hold my hand. Please." I thought he was going to die. I think he knew he was about to die. He wanted someone to hold his hand while he was dying. And then he passed out. CPR! I remembered I had been shown CPR once but I wasn't sure I remembered how to do it. Yet I had to try as best I knew how. Blowing air in his mouth while holding his nose closed and then pressing his chest. I did what I could. I was sweating now more than he was. I don't know how long I pounded on his chest and blew into his mouth. I thought he was a goner for sure. And then he came to, opened his eyes, blinked a few times and started breathing shallowly. He even smiled at me, a crooked little smile. Some more time passed before he could speak.

"I need you to get me an aspirin from the medicine cabinet in the bathroom, and I need you to take me to the hospital in Spartenburg. I can direct you, but I don't think I can drive."

Me, Debbi

Moms and Pops lived in a secluded house, or should I say a country estate or compound—I don't know what to call it—near the town of Grapevine. Approaching the house from the main road was like driving through a long tunnel. It was not quite dark when we got there. Low-lying oak branches draped with lolling tongues of Spanish moss canopied the long driveway. Old-timey gas lamps spaced every twenty feet or so created halos in the fog that had descended on us. In places, the moss came close to sweeping our windshield. It was like driving through a carwash with those strips of felt flapping against the windshield. It brought to mind visions of "Twelve Oaks" in *Gone With the Wind*. Oh my gosh, I watched that movie when I was a little girl and simply devoured it. I must have watched it a least six times. But guess what. The last time I saw it, it was as if I were a different person watching a different movie. I hated it. I hated Rhett Butler, and I really, really hated Scarlet O'Hara, and I was sickened by the glorification of the Southern way of life.

So, slap me upside the head and call me an idiot for even bringing up the analogy, because—get this—the twelve oaks of the estate in the movie didn't line the drive like at the Fisher home, but surrounded the house, and the Fisher house itself was nothing like the one in the movie. It was more like the home of some cattle baron in a wild west movie, a sprawling ranch house with treated but unpainted wood and forest green trim on doorways and shutters. Had there been snow on the ground at Bryce's childhood home (I'm tempted to say ancestral home) it would have looked like a Christmas card. So my response was more emotional than accurate. Whatever. The view made me feel as if I were entering an unreal place, not unreal as in surrealistic or otherworldly but as in fake, phony, a stage set. It didn't make me want to venture in.

Behind the main house and connected by a covered walkway softly lighted by the same gas lamps was the cottage Martina had grown up in. I tried to picture her gamboling in the grass, but no picture would come. What little light shone from the windows of the big house was soft, warm and yellow. On the outside, a couple of lights on either side of the front door illuminated a broad porch that stretched around to infinity where the light petered out. Wicker chairs sat on the porch. There was a circular drive in front. I imagined it had been where coach drivers a century earlier pulled up to be greeted by a butler who helped their passengers down and carried their luggage into the great house. The butler would be a Black man in a tuxedo, or perhaps an Apache with long black hair tied back with a colorful cloth.

No coachman led us in. The double front doors were not locked. Bryce opened the door, and at the flick of a switch as we entered, a huge chandelier lit up the large front room. There were two couches and many chairs cushioned with red velvet, a grand piano and a fireplace against one wall. Soft, deep maroon carpets with an Indian or Arabian pattern in shades of blue covered the floors. On the walls were portraits of men and women, mostly men in sedate poses painted with burnt sienna skin tones. I took them to be ancestors. A trophy deer hung on the wall and—too freakin' clichéd to be believable—there was a white bearskin rug complete with snarling head on the floor in front of a roaring fireplace. I couldn't believe it. I was in the Cartwright's home in *Bonanza*.

No sign yet of Moms and Pops.

I was scared of them before I even met them.

In the kitchen, which was surprisingly small for such an ostentatious country mansion, stood Gabriella, Martina's mother, cooking our dinner like Aunt Jemima herself, only Latina instead of Black. She looked to be in her sixties, a good looking woman, like her daughter, no more than five feet tall if that, but with plenty of meat on her bones. She obviously doted on Bryce, yet it was immediately clear that in her there was none of the obsequious attitude I had observed in Martina. Interesting, I thought. You would have expected it to be just the opposite, with the old mother bowing and scraping and the daughter rebelliously having none of it. Gabriella proved to be feisty and sharp of tongue. I liked that.

"I been working for the Fishers since before this'un was born," she announced, dismissively tilting her head in Bryce's direction. "He thinks he's the boss around here now, but I changed his poopy diapers when he was little and tanned his hide when he got too big for his britches. He don't know how lucky he is I'm still willing to wait on him hand and foot."

Bryce laughed. "If anybody rules the roost around these parts, you're looking at her."

Gabriella said, "That's right, kiddo. And don't you forget it."

I wondered why Martina had not inherited any of Gabriella's spunk. Maybe she had, and maybe it had been beaten out of her. Growing up in a household ruled by an autocratic master, as I imagined Bryce's father to be, and with a mother who could shame the feathers right off a peacock, could cause a gal to be easily intimidated. I was projecting all kinds of stuff onto the Fisher family and their hired help, and I had to remind myself that none of it was based on anything real.

"Is that a real fish?" I asked, nodding in the direction of a large tarpon hanging on the wall in the living room where we had settled with drinks in hand while awaiting the senior Fishers' appearance. The fish was longer than Gabriella was tall, with silver scales and a haunting eye that made it look alive, a fishing lure dangling from its mouth. I felt like I should have been wearing jodhpurs or waders instead of the elegant red dress Bryce had bought for me. Surrounded by deer and bear and fish, I felt I was inside a sporting goods store.

Bryce was like "Of course it's real. Pops caught it off the coast of Florida."

"What about that fat one" It looked like a giant pancake with fins and a face. Creepy.

"That's a pompano. Pops caught it too. It was a world record for a short time. Twenty-five pounds. They usually run about four or five pounds. But then somebody caught one that was half a pound bigger, so he didn't hold the record for very long. Can you believe it? The guy who beat his record caught his pompano in the same spot in the Gulf."

I said, "I don't know if I feel comfortable eating in the midst of dead animals."

That was when his folks made their appearance.

"Moms, Pops, this is Debbi."

"Ron Fisher, but you can call me Pops," the old man said. His voice was deep and soft, nothing like what I expected, although I don't really know what I did expect. I could see exactly what Bryce would look like in twenty years: still handsome, even more so, in fact, white hair and unruly eyebrows, fine lines around his eyes like cracks in a dried-up river bottom and deeper crevices on his brow. He was smoking. When he lifted his hand to take a drag I noticed two things: first the cigarette he was smoking was a non-filtered brand, and second, he held it between fingers that were stained dirty yellow. I figured it was the mark of a lifetime of smoking, probably starting when he was about nine years old.

"It's nice to meet you, sir." I grasped the hand he extended, a dry, firm grasp.

He said, "And you too, young lady," and turned his head to cough, covering it in the prescribed way with his elbow. "Excuse me."

Bryce jumped in to introduce his mother. "Moms, this is Debbi."

That was when I noticed that Moms had been standing mouth dropped open as if in shock, as if she had seen the stuffed tarpon open its mouth and say hidy. "You're colored," she blurted out, and before I could respond she turned to Bryce and said, "She's colored," and quickly back to me to stammer, "Du-don't get me wrong. I don't dislike colored people. What is it you people call yourselves nowadays? Blacks? Or African-Americans or . . . or what's the new one? People of color? Some of my best friends are colored . . . uh, Black. Black lives matter. Yes, I know all about that, and it's . . . it's absolutely true, but then don't all lives matter, really? But like I said, some of my best friends . . . why, Ron, what's that woman's name in the garden club?" She couldn't remember her "best friend's" name. I chuckled and flashed her a warm smile. I wasn't offended. I thought it sweet that she was really trying, but oh so ineptly.

I said, "It's so nice to meet you, Mrs. Fisher."

More composed after that first outburst, she said, "Debbi, is it? I'm Charlotte. But please call me Moms. Everybody calls me Moms. Welcome to the family."

Welcome to the family? Had Bryce told them we were married? Had he even warned them he was bringing a woman home? A *colored* woman no less? Had he written them or called them without my knowledge? Suddenly I feared . . . well, I didn't know what I feared. Were they racist or just like so many old Southern aristocrats who casually use racist terms—even the n-word—out of habit and without any evil intent. That was something I had argued about with Stormy, the only dark-skinned Black woman at Lipstix and one of the few Black burlesque performers in N'Orleans. She was more forgiving than I was. She argued that white people who casually used the n-word without meaning it in a bad way are not racist. "It's not like they're Klan members. They don't even dislike us. It's just habit. That word's been in their vocabulary all their lives. They're just everyday racists."

My argument was that they may not hate us, but they think we're inherently less than them, and their lessening of us is racist in my book. And in my opinion, it was obvious that dear old Moms was racist to the bone. To heck with her honky stuff. If I had not been dependent on Bryce for transportation, I would have walked out right then and there and made my way back to Dallas, if not even all the way back to New Orleans.

And then she surprised me with a big, warm welcoming hug, and even a little peck on my cheek. And she rubbed my hair, I suspect to see if it felt like a Brillo pad.

She was just getting started. Before I had time to respond to anything, she came up with this: "Are ya'll married? How dare you, Bryce, getting married without telling your own parents. How could you? I hope at least it was a decent Christian wedding in a church, and I mean a real church, not some Catholic or Mormon or some kind of hippie-dippy church." She rattled all that off in a rush of words, and Bryce was barely able to sneak in, "No, mother, we're not married."

"What?"

"I said we're not married."

"Then I pray to God you're not sleeping together." Then she turned to Pops and said, "Are you not going to say anything?" and I wanted to ask Bryce the same thing.

Pops was slow to respond. His glance traveled from face to face as if trying to decide to whom he should address his remarks. I was still shocked at Moms' tirade and at the lack of reaction from the two big men. Pops didn't respond to his wife but quietly turned to me and said, "I'm afraid Charlotte doesn't react too well to surprises. She'll get over it." It was if he were excusing the ill manners of a precocious child.

I had expected Pops, the hunter and fisherman and bigtime business tycoon, to rule the household with an iron will, and I had expected Moms to be the subservient kind of old fashioned Southern belle who holds Saturday afternoon teas and raises money for Baptist missions to Africa—money to help Christianize natives she'd cross the street to avoid if she ran across them in Dallas.

Pops, it turned out, was some kind of milquetoast, and Moms was a tyrant. But as soon as I thought that, I told myself it couldn't be that simple. There's always more to people than you think.

But this much was clear, Moms thought Bryce and I were living in sin. Ha! If she even knew the half of it she'd have me pegged as a trollop, a whore, a loose woman. I guess she already did. Come to think of it, I kind of liked the term "loose woman." I could live with that.

We took our seats at the dining table and Gabriella brought in the dinner, deep fried bass (Pops said he caught them himself) with cornbread and hushpuppies and fried okra, sweet potatoes and English peas. Food I had been eating all my life. We chatted over dinner as if the imbroglio that had just transpired had never happened.

Pops said Moms was a stay-at-home housewife. "She keeps the home fires tended." (Funny, I thought Gabriella did that.) "Plus, she's involved in just about every community activity you can imagine. Busiest little woman in seven states." Now he was proudly painting her exactly as I had envisioned her, and reinforcing my earlier vision of them, he patted her on the head. I swear to God he did. He kept laying it on. "My darlin' Charlotte is on the board of the little theater, treasurer of the women's auxiliary of the Chamber of Commerce, plays bridge every Wednesday afternoon with a bunch of biddies, volunteers sometimes at the children's hospital in Dallas. Can you even imagine any one woman doing all that?"

Charlotte beamed and blushed.

"So what do you do, young lady?" Pops asked me.

I told him I was a student at Tulane, majoring in English, but said I had dropped out temporarily. "I plan to go back next year. Or maybe I'll transfer to SMU or Dallas Baptist."

"Can't decide between the Methodists and Baptists, huh? Heck, it don't matter none. They're both the same. Don't neither one of 'em believe in dancing or sex." Pops guffawed, and for the first time I knew what a guffaw was.

Moms said, "Oh Ronnie, you're such a card," and she tipped up her glass and took a big swallow. I hadn't noticed what they were drinking, but it looked to be some sort of alcoholic beverage. They hadn't offered me any. It was as if they considered me a child too young to drink.

I don't know why I said what I said about transferring to a Dallas-area college. I had blurted it out without thinking, which was not unusual for me. Old fire-from-the-hip Debbi. Unconsciously, I guess I was trying to let them know I intended to stay with their son. It was my way of saying you can't run me off with a shotgun. It had not exactly been established that I was sleeping with their son, who so far was not putting his two bits worth in, but it had certainly been implied. Not liking even one little bit the thought of keeping my relationship with their son ambiguous at best, I looked to Bryce for a clue, but he didn't even look my way. He was busy piling food on his plate. He picked up the bass—a slice from its tail to where the head was mercifully cut off—took a large bite and wiped his mouth with the back of his hand. "Damn, this bass is good. Ya'll better dig in before I eat it all." To me he said, "Watch out for the bones."

He wiped his mouth on his sleeve, and Moms told him to use a napkin.

"Nobody fries 'em up like Gabriella," Pops said. He also tipped up his glass and finished it off. In the direction of the kitchen he shouted, "More booze, Gabriella!"

I nibbled at my fish. I had to admit it was good. Crisp on the outside and chewy inside.

Moms said, "What's your last name again, dear?" She was squinting at me, probably nearsighted but too vain to wear glasses.

I said, "Mason."

"Oh yes, the New Orleans Masons." Pops piped in as if assuming everybody who was anybody knew who the New Orleans Masons were. "You must be Herbert's daughter. Or granddaughter, I guess it would be."

"No, I'm afraid I don't know Herbert Mason."

"Well surely you know who he is."

"No, I think not."

"Then who is your daddy, dear?" Moms asked.

"I'm afraid I don't know that either."

Bryce shot me a cancerous look.

Moms said, "Oh pshaw. Don't be silly. Everybody knows who their own daddy is."

What I wanted to say was "Not me. Mama had so many lovers she hadn't the slightest clue who the unwitting sperm donor was." That was the truth, but it was clear Bryce didn't want me telling the truth. Maybe he should have coached me more thoroughly ahead of time on what I could and could not say—more thoroughly, I mean, than saying I shouldn't talk about dancing. He should have given me a playbook. On the one hand, I felt like a worm; on the other, my righteous indignation was coming to a boiling point. I told myself to chill.

Moms didn't even respond to me when I said, "No ma'am, I honestly don't know," but she turned to Pops and said, "Did you hear what she said, Ronnie?" and turning back to me she said, "Are you all right, darling? I mean, you haven't had any, uh, mental . . . uh, problems, have you?"

Once again I was stunned by Moms' reaction. She was implying I must have been traumatized and rendered mentally incapacitated by a mother who slept around so much she didn't even know who the father of her child was. At least that was the impression I got. Slow boil, about to spill over. But I focused on my breathing and brought it to a simmer.

The rest of that evening is mercifully erased from my memory, just a few indecipherable smudges remaining. Bryce and I spoke very little on the ride home. Back in his penthouse, he poured himself a drink and carried it into his study. I went to bed and read Barbara

Kingsolver's *The Lacuna* until he came to bed, the words in the book barely registering on my consciousness.

I wanted to know why it was that his parents were drinking like lushes but never offered either of us anything other than iced tea. He said, "They think I have a drinking problem. I don't, but I did drink pretty heavily for a while, a few years back. It's easier to let them think I'm an alcoholic than to argue it. They feel like they're protecting me, and that makes them feel worthy. That's the whole thing with Moms. She thinks she's nothing but a reflection of Pops, that on her own she's a big fat zero."

My impression had been quite different. I read Moms as the matriarch that ruled the family. But Bryce said his mom's insecurity was the reason she got involved in so many community activities that she didn't really give a hoot about. And as for her thinking he had a drinking problem, he said, "Thinking she's protecting her poor son from falling off the wagon makes her feel worthwhile."

Bryce had the uncanny ability to fall asleep the moment he puts his body in a recline and shuts his eyes. Oh how I envied him that. Long after he fell asleep I lay still by his side going over and over the events of the night and letting my imagination run wild with scenarios about me blasting Moms and Pops with sarcasm, wit and venom, and wondering what I could possibly say to Bryce about how he reverts to childhood around them and lets them bully him. And I wondered how much I would be willing to endure. Most of all I hated pretending to be something I wasn't.

I got up out of bed and slid on silent slippers into the gymnasium/dance studio and sat on the leather exercise bench and looked at my image in the wall-to-wall mirror. With Tchaikovsky in my head, I stood up and began to dance. Slowly, smoothly, the music in my head lulling me into putting the day and night out of mind. It took a while, but eventually I began to feel drowsy and at ease. But I had developed a headache, so I went back into the bedroom and picked up my purse to dig out a bottle of Tylenol, feeling for it in the dark, not wanting to wake Bryce.

My fingers touched a folded piece of paper not much bigger than a postage stamp. I pulled it out and opened it and slipped into the bathroom where I could see what it was by the light over the mirror. It was a note written in a tight hand that said, "Run, girl, run." I quickly jabbed it back in my purse and clasped the purse shut.

Me, David

There was another guy standing on the entrance ramp with a backpack on the ground and holding a sign that said DC. He was wearing army fatigues and a brown coat. I wasn't sure about the protocol. Should I join him? Would two hitchhikers together be less likely to get a ride than a single man? Probably. I didn't want to intrude, but I didn't want to be standoffish either. I waved at him, and he waved back. I headed toward where he was standing. "I'll back off if you want me to," I said. "I just wanted to say hi."

"That's okay," he said, and added a howdy.

"Going to D.C.?"

"Uh huh. You?"

"New York."

We stood together for a while and chatted. He had been out of the army for about half a year, he said. He had been in Afghanistan and had not been able to find a decent job since he got out. He had an old girlfriend in D.C. "It's not like we're still a couple or anything. She's with some other guy now. A guy that has some kind of government job. They're gonna let me stay with them while I look for a job. What about you? What are you going to New York for?"

"Same thing. Looking for work. I have a friend in the city I can stay with."

"Well good luck to you. Hey, you wouldn't happen to have a cigarette on you, do you?"

I said I did, and I fished one out and handed it to him, and then another, saying, "One for the road."

I withdrew about a hundred feet or so and started to take my stand there, but then I realized that wouldn't be fair to him. In that position, I'd have first shot at all the cars that came by. Plus, even though I looked pretty raggedy myself, he looked even worse. I thought if I was a driver I probably wouldn't feel comfortable picking him up. There was a forested area off the side of the road, and so I wandered into the woods. I found a fallen tree trunk and sat down on it. I rested my elbows on my knees and my chin in my hands, and I thought about my situation. Was I ever going to get to New York? And where would I stay when I got there? I didn't have any friend to stay with like I had said, and I didn't have a heck of a lot of money. What hit me like a sudden whiff of ammonia was the truth, and the truth was I should have never undertaken this stupid adventure in the first place. A trip of more than a thousand miles, and here I was right about halfway there on road in a town I'd never even heard of sitting on a log with my head in my hands wondering what in the world I was getting myself into. I wanted to give up, but I couldn't even imagine what giving up would mean.

Me, Debbi

Looking back over the brief time since I left New Orleans with Bryce, I came to realize that the chivalry that so endeared me to him when we were dating in the Big Easy had flown out the window the moment we crossed the Texas state line. Sooner than that, even, as soon as I agreed to go with him. It was as if once we entered his territory, he owned me, no longer had to be nice, no longer needed to turn on the charm and capture my heart. But it snuck up on me. When I wasn't looking, he switched from being charming and loving to ignoring me or treating me like a kept woman. I never knew what to expect, and I never knew when he was going to be there and when he wasn't—both literally and metaphorically—as he was often gone for days at a time. I had thought I was capable of handling any situation with humor or brashness or my native wit, which I thought was pretty keen. But this was something new to me. It was getting to where I couldn't even recognize myself when I looked in the mirror.

Some of the best times were when we were together in the gym with Bryce lifting weights and doing calisthenics or punching the bag, and me dancing, music courtesy of the DVD player in the entertainment room that piped music to speakers all over the house. We connected in those moments as if by osmosis, both of us sweating, our bodies glistening, and I certainly noticed the bright muscularity of his body as I'm sure he noticed mine. The music, whether classical or jazz or the eighties and nineties rock of our youth, was like on a direct current from him to me. Dancing for me was a transformative religious rite, and exercise was the same for him. After our time in the gym, we often showered together and then drank cold drinks in the entertainment room, usually with robes thrown over out freshly scrubbed bodies.

Those were the good times. The bad times were when he was gruff and impatient with me. (Do this, do that, now; who do you think you are; did I ask you to talk; what makes you think you can think? And me shooting right back, do it yourself; God gave you legs, use them; I'm a person with thoughts and rights and feelings, not some arrogant windbag of a backed-up toilet like you. But fighting back wore me down and soon seemed not worth the effort.)

And when he was gone. When he was gone was sometimes the best because being free of him was such a relief, but equally the worst because of the loneliness and because of I missed the good Bryce who was quickly becoming little more than a memory, seemingly a fantasy I had dreamed up. He seldom told me where he was going or when he would be back, like I didn't matter. I could call him if I needed to. I had his cell number. But he was usually especially gruff when I called him. I cringed in advance whenever I called, expecting a verbal slap in the face. "How many times do I have to tell you not to call me when I'm at work." That was never a question, it was a demand, and it didn't take me long to learn not to call him unless it was an emergency.

When he was gone and I was stuck at home with nothing to do and nowhere to go and no way to get there if there was a there to go to, I had only Martina to keep me company; and Martina, still shy and diffident, was not good company. I asked her if she liked her job, and she said, "Yes, Mister Bryce is good to me. I have a place to live, and I don't have to buy anything."

I couldn't let that go. I was like, "What does that even mean?" and she went, "Well, Mister Bryce buys me whatever I need."

That took some explaining, and she seemed unable to explain the living and work arrangement she had with Bryce. As she stumbled through an attempt to make it clear, it gradually became clear she didn't get paid at all. She got room and board. He bought her clothes and gave her spending money when she needed it. If she needed to go somewhere, Anders from the second floor could take her. If he wasn't available, she could catch the bus. Bryce expected the same of me vis-à-vis Anders or the bus. There was a petty cash stash in a kitchen cabinet from which Martina and I both were welcomed to draw when needed. Not that he told me any of this. I had to drag it out of him. How he expected me to know these things if he didn't tell me was a great mystery. It was like one day I was grumbling about needing something from the grocery store—I don't even remember what it was—and not having money to buy it or any way to get to the store, and Martina said, "You get money from the petty cash. Didn't he tell you? And Anders will take you."

"What petty cash? Who's Anders?" I was like totally in the dark. So she filled me in and took me down to the second floor to meet Anders. Thanks a lot, Bryce, for abandoning me upstream without a paddle. Anders was a handyman who did various jobs for Bryce as needed and would gladly take us anywhere we wanted to go if and when he was available.

"Does Bryce pay you for this?" I asked him, and he said, "Not exactly, Miss. Not a salary or not by the hour or anything like that. But he gives me money now and again, and when my mama was sick and couldn't afford a doctor, he took care of it. He's a very generous gentleman. I am happy to help out."

I learned that Martina had never lived in any place that was not owned by a Fisher. She moved directly from Moms and Pops' cottage where she was born to Bryce's penthouse. Her only experience of not being a child of the Fisher family, as she thought of herself, was summer camp three years running when she was in the eight, ninth and tenth grades. She still got dreamy-eyed and spacy when she talked about it, about the games they played and swimming in the river and telling stories around a campfire at night, and about the yellow-haired boy she had a crush on who never spoke to her. "I never spoke to him either. I would not have known what to say."

I wanted so very much—oh, I was itching like crazy to ask her—about the kissing, about Bryce kissing her, which was something she didn't look like she enjoyed but something she was willing to let happen. But I didn't. Maybe I was afraid of what she might say. The way I justified my not asking was it was so meaningless and routine she probably never even thought about it. It had probably started with a twelve-year-old Bryce-Martina crush about the same time she was going to those summer camps, and over time the kissing became as common as saying "good morning" first thing in the morning and "bye" when walking out the door.

One day Bryce brought home a shopping bag from Charlene Ride, an exclusive women's shop. Tossing it to me, he said, "It's party time, my dear, and I brought home the most luscious party dress you've ever worn." It was luscious all right. It was metallic emerald green with a mid-thigh hemline and a plunging neckline. It was lovely, I had to admit, but why did he want me to wear something that revealing? "Is it your intention to put my body on display for all and sundry?" For a girl who stripped for a living and had once scampered down Bourbon Street topless, wearing a skimpy party dress was no big deal, but I didn't like the idea that for him I was just a pretty accessory like an expensive watch or a diamond ring.

"You're damn right that's my intention," he said. "Exactly. Now get into this, baby, and let's see how you look."

I couldn't figure out if I was flattered or incensed. But I did look good in it. Oh my oh my, I would have hit on me. I turned and turned in front of the full-length mirror, and what I saw looked delicious. Bryce whistled and shouted, "Martina, get in here and take a gander at this lovely gal of mine."

"You're beautiful," Martina said, when she came in to see what the fuss was about. To Bryce she said, "Are you eating out or should I prepare dinner?"

He said we were eating out, and to me he said, "Now do something with that face and let's get going. We have eight o'clock reservations."

The party was in a private banquet room in a swanky restaurant. I don't remember the name. It was one of those places where they have too much silverware. I watched other people to see what fork was for the salad and which for the entrée and what was with all those spoons. I was reminded of a tale David once told me. He swore it was true. He said a friend of his father knew some big-shot celebrity. I don't remember who it was. Oh wait a minute, yes I do. It was Andy Warhol. And so his father's friend invited another friend to eat with Andy and his entourage. The other friend was not exactly the worldliest guy in the world. When David's father's friend saw the other guy was confused by the lineup of implements on the table, he whispered to him, "Watch Andy and do what he does." But Andy, who was quite the joker, overheard, so he picked up a tea spoon and placed the spoon part inside the larger soup spoon and ate his soup using both spoons. Of course the guy copied him, and David said nobody dared laugh at them or correct them. In fact everyone else at the table followed suit.

It was a great story, but I never believed it, not for a moment.

Now back from Andy Warhol to Bryce Fisher and his friends. Everybody in the banquet room was friendly and boisterous. There was too much laughter and so much chatter flying around the table that I could hardly hear any of it. The talk blended into a cacophony of bubbly sounds.

My beauty was greatly appreciated, and that made Bryce happy as a clam, and I've got to admit it pleased me too. I can't even count how many people said I was lovely or my dress was beautiful.

"Where in the world did you get it?"

"I don't know. Bryce bought it for me."

"You're a lucky girl. I wish my Winston would shop for me."

The men mostly talked about football. It seemed the Cowboys were having a great season.

I honestly can't remember what the women talked about. Nothing of note it would seem.

On the way home, Bryce said, "You did good."

"Oh, thank you." I didn't know how to respond. Had I undergone some kind of test? It seemed so, and it seemed I passed. At home we finished off the night with more drinks. He was friendly, charming, jocular, sweet for the first time in quite some time. The next morning he left again without saying anything, and it was four days before he came home.

Me, David

I thought the evangelical gay ogre and the jailbreaking prostitute and her boyfriend were bad, but they were nothing compared to the next people to give me a ride. A ratty pickup truck with big Rebel flag across the back window braked to a stop in front of me, and a bald head and long beard poked out, and a mouth nestled between the beard and a red nose shouted, "Haul ass, dude. We ain't waiting forever."

The signs were not auspicious: a redneck looking dude poking his head out of a truck sporting a Confederate battle flag. Not my ideal ride, but I wasn't sure if there would be another offer so I was in no position to be picky. I hustled to get in the pickup, thinking I had to get out of the Deep South and the sooner the better. If I had to ride with some modern-day night riders, at least they were headed north. Charlotte and then Richmond were ahead, and then Marilyn and Delware, where I hoped to run into people who were not still fighting the Civil War.

It was one of those double-cab pickups with about six inches of leg room in the back, which was littered with crushed beer cans and empty cigarette packs and a cooler and brown paper bags containing who knows what. At least I was on a major freeway thanks to Ned, who had not died after all and had arranged for me to get a lift to the on-ramp to I-85. All night the night before, I had slept fitfully in a chair next to his hospital bed, and I stayed there while they wheeled him into the catheter lab and put in a stent. He thanked me profusely for taking care of him and then he called for a friend to take me out to the highway. I was going to miss Ned. He was a sweet man.

Things got ugly in a great big hurry. The guys in the pickup were drinking beer and talking nasty. They told me—loudly, boasted, in fact—that they had met in prison. The driver, who had a knife tattooed on his neck, said he had killed a man. "Yeah, I killed him. You'd a done the same," he growled. "I caught him messing with my old lady. Caught 'em in the act. Flagrante delicto. You know what that means?"

"Yes, uh huh. I do." I was surprised he did.

"Yep. Caught 'em doing the nasty. Right on her living room couch in broad daylight. She thought I was out of town, but the guy I was going fishing with, he come down with the flu, so we called off the fishing trip. The TV was going. Some dumb soap. They was getting it on so hot they didn't e'em hear me come in. I jerked him offen her and slung him halfway 'cross the room. And I sliced him up and gutted him like a deer. She watched me do it, crouched up against a wall and crying her eyes out."

The guy sounded gleeful, like he had enjoyed gutting the man and was getting a kick out of telling me all about it.

"After that I didn't wanna have nothing to do with her. They give me twenty years for gutting that sumbitch, but they let me out after six."

For what it's worth, the driver told me his name was Sean Campbell. The bearded one never told me his name, but Sean called him Randy. He said he was a kidnapper. He said he kidnapped the daughter of a wealthy real estate developer. Held her for ransom, which her father paid. Ten thousand dollars. But the cops were waiting in ambush when they met to swap the cash for the girl. "She was ten years old and cute as a button. She had yaller hair and a missing tooth right in front. I kindly wished I could keep her and raise her as my own daughter."

They were both stinking drunk, and they were both laughing like crazy men when they told their tales of crime. I thought, or at least I desperately hoped, that they were joking. Just trying to scare me. It really did seem that way to me.

They were quiet for a while, finished off their beers—Bud Lights—and tossed the empties on the floorboard. The kidnapper turned sideways in his seat and hung his face inches from mine and said, "Lemme see your watch."

I held up my arm for him to see, and he said, "Naw, don't just hold it up. Take it off. Lemme get a good close look at it."

Stupid, stupid me, I don't know why I said what I said. This making up stories had become some insane impulse that took over my brain from time to time. It was . . . well, I guess it was my way to convincing myself they were playing with me and my only hope of not getting butchered was to make light of it. I said, "I can't take it off. My mother gave it to me on her death bed, and I promised her I'd never take it off."

I didn't think the guy who said he was a killer really was a killer. He looked more like a tax preparer. Glasses. Hair bald on top and not much on the sides. Skinny. A mild case of acne. He said, "Aw, that's so sweet about the watch and your poor mama. Let him keep the watch, Randy."

But Randy said, "Uh-uh." And he pulled out a pistol. Does everybody keep a goddamn pistol in their glove compartment? I thought I was dead for sure, but he said, "I'll trade you this pistol for the watch."

That was when I knew I had been right all along. They were putting me on. I laughed and said, "All right. Here you go," and started to pull the watch off my arm when Sean the killer said, "Put the damn gun away, man. And you, don't give him your damn watch."

So Randy stashed the pistol back in the glove compartment, and laughing, he told me they were playing with me. "I ain't no killer and he ain't no kidnapper," Sean said. "We're just funning you."

"Oh, I knew that all along," I said. But I was still scared out of my wits.

"Give him a beer," the driver said, and the bearded one reached into a sack on the floorboard and pulled out a can of Budweiser. It was not exactly warm, but tepid and tasteless.

A few miles farther along they stopped at a convenience store and went in to get more beer. As soon as they went inside, I jumped out and ran as fast as I could and hid in the nearby woods until I was sure they were long gone. I was beginning to feel like I was spending as much time on this trip hiding as riding.

Me, Debbi

Martina wanted to be friends. Not right off the bat, but soon enough. She like me a lot and told me so. She also thought I was pretty, which she also told me, often enough that it was embarrassing. But there was an unmovable barrier between us. She was the help; I was the boss's girl. I was more than willing to bridge that gap, but for her it was impossible. Diffidence had been pounded in far too strongly. She couldn't even call me by my given name without prefacing it with "Miss." She practically bowed before me and always smiled. But I detected an underlying sadness, or perhaps fear. I didn't know what it was, but it was there unmistakably.

I was never quite sure what Anders did when he wasn't running errands for Martina or me. I guess he was a contract worker for the building manager. Martina referred to him as the superintendent. Whatever was needed, he did it, and he did it with a smile. "If you need to go anywhere or have someone pick you up something from the store, call Anders," Martina said. "He takes me to the grocery store and waits in the car while I shop."

"He doesn't go in with you?"

"No. He can be surly that way, if you must know, but he's as kind as can be."

Martina did not drive. Neither did I. My mother never owned a car, and living in the city, I never needed to, so I never learned.

Anders was a large man whose skin and hair were almost the same bleached tone of tan. His hairline blended into his forehead, looking from a distance like he combed his skin back on top of his head. His conversation consisted of one-and-two-word answers to direct questions. He was friendly, and he smiled a lot, but engaging him in an actual conversation was beyond my abilities. Come spring, we saw him working in the yard a lot. I would shout "Hi" from the balcony, and he'd look up, shading his eyes with his hands, and say, "Hello, ma'am." He was always so formal with me. I wouldn't say Martina was exactly the opposite, but she did eventually get to where she talked to me freely. I liked her, or at least thought she was pleasant enough, but the topics we were able to converse about were limited. Almost out of necessity, I buried my nose in books and spent hours in the studio practicing dance. I worked up my own choreography to ballets or modern dance performances based on favorite stories from my childhood. That was fun. Ballet *Winnie the Pooh* and *Alice in Wonderland* to made-up songs in my head.

I kept that note in my bag, the one slipped in there after that first dinner with Bryce's parents. It had been months. I finally dug it out and showed it to Martina. "Was that you?" I asked. "Did you write this?"

"Oh no, Miss Debbi. I wouldn't do anything like that."

"Well, it had to be you or your mother one or the other. Ya'll were the only ones that had a chance to slip something into my bag."

"Moms or Pops could have done it."

"Don't be silly, Why would they do something like that? They didn't even know me."

"Neither did I. What reason could I have had?"

That made sense, but who else could have done it? One of our housemates from back home? Could it have traveled all the way from New Orleans? That made no sense either. I would have noticed it long before. I decided my only option was to chalk it up as a mystery and forget about it, but that was not so easy to do.

I asked Martina about her family. "Are you an only child"

"Oh no. There's a bunch of us."

She was a middle child in a family of six, three boys and three girls. Two of her sisters were older and one younger. Her brothers all younger. Both the older sisters were maids for wealthy white families in Dallas. The oldest of her little brothers came home from the war in the Middle East minus a leg. The next younger was in college. The younger sister and the youngest of her brothers, still lived at home with their mother. I had no idea where they were the times we visited Moms and Pops. That younger sister was in high school, and her little brother went to Dallas County Community College. There was quite the age spread. "Renny (the youngest brother) gonna go places, that one," Martina said.

"What about your father?"

She said, "Who knows?" with a shrug. Said he had been out of the picture pretty much forever. "And good riddance. He was nasty. He drank whiskey all the time. Whiskey and cheap beer. If I never see Papa again, that's fine with me. He always put me down. Told people I was fat and stupid."

"How could he possibly think you were fat? You're a waif."

She went, "I don't know what a waif is, but I was a chubby girl back when Papa was at home. And he told me I would never amount to anything. He was right, too. Look at me. I barely finished high school. I could have gone to college. Mister Bryce offered to pay for it. But I blew it. I just . . . well, I guess I wasn't prepared for all the studying. I couldn't keep up. I thought all those white girls were so much smarter than me. Now I'm working as a maid for the boy I used to play with. I guess I'll be doing that until I'm old and useless. I'll never get married neither. Who would marry me? Just like Papa said, I'll never amount to nothing. At least Mama had the excuse of being an immigrant and being uneducated, and that was not her fault. She never had a chance to make more of herself. But me, I had every opportunity and didn't do anything."

I felt sorry for her, but I didn't know what to do with that and the conversation ended there.

It got to where Bryce was away from home more than ever. I seldom saw him anymore. He was usually already gone to work when I got up and was often late coming home. I confronted him once when he came home about five o'clock in the morning with liquor on his breath. "What are you doing, banging your secretary? Hanging out in strip clubs? Hey, I really don't give a flip. Bang away all you want to. Just let me know when you're not coming home. Please."

Boy, did he ever have an answer for that. He went, "If I didn't hang out at strip clubs, I never would have met you. So quit your complaining. It's my business what I do when I'm not here."

"I just want to know," I said, realizing as I said it that I sounded whiney.

"When I'm not here, I'm working, if you must know. If I didn't work so hard you wouldn't have all the good things you have."

"What? Like the dresses I never asked you to buy me? I never wear them anyway, because you never take me anywhere."

"Well maybe you oughta give 'em to the Salvation Army."

"Yeah, and maybe you oughta stay out of strip clubs and casinos," I shot back.

He said, "I do what I want to when I want to, and I don't have to tell you doodly squat. I sure as hell don't have to ask your permission. If you don't like it, you can leave. Go back to New Orleans. See if I care. You're not a prisoner here." But it felt like I was. Other times he would say something like, "So I had a few drinks with some of the boys after work. It's good business. It's important to let 'em know you can be one of the guys. But not all the time. You gotta let 'em know who's boss too. It's a delicate balance."

It sounded like he was giving me lessons in how to conduct business, but what he was doing was inadvertently telling me his secret for how to keep me in line, keep me dangling, indebted to him, while all the time he was out drinking with the boys and playing with the girls. Had I not worked in a strip club long enough to recognize the pattern? Not going out with the customers at Lipstix should have been rule number one. Oh my god how I missed David Parker. I should get Anders to take me to the Greyhound station, and I should buy a ticket home and beg David to take me back, and if he was no longer there I should search the whole country until I found him.

Springtime in Texas. Time for renewal, rebirth. Yeah, right. Want a ten-cent synopsis of the time since leaving New Orleans with Bryce? Thanksgiving and Christmas were barely endurable. Dinners with his parents, watching football games on television. Opening presents. His folks gave me a book. A lousy book. At least I guess it was lousy. I didn't read it. It was one by the guy who wrote *The Da Vinci Code*. The dinners were good, but there was no company, no activities. They didn't even have a Christmas tree.

I missed David. He and Lucy and Randy and Hopper probably played board games and smoked dope and danced while we watched football. They probably celebrated New Year's at Tipitinas with Dr.

John or Fats Domino. No wait, I think Dr. J and Fats were dead already. So many entertainers I loved have died recently. I can't keep up. The world had passed me by. Next thing I knew it was Superbowl Sunday, and Mardi Gras and—whoops, it's springtime already. The crew at Lipstix would be planning a wild equinox party. Understand, at that point I assumed David was still in New Orleans.

And bless my soul, I was in still Texas. I was there for a tiresome Thanksgiving and a boring Christmas and a New Year's Eve that was celebrated, so far as I was concerned, only on television. I watched the ball drop in Times Square and went to bed alone.

And then it was Easter when Bryce's family, including far-flung aunts and uncles and cousins and nieces and nephews, came in from all over the Southland for the only church service Bryce ever attended and for a huge family dinner. I looked to the coming Fisher family gathering with dread.

Me, David

So anyway, I made it to New York. Once I picked my butt up off that fallen log north of Spartanburg, it was easy. One sweet ride with a pleasant young man in a Chevy Corvette all the way to the airport in Newark, New Jersey, where I could catch a city bus right into the heart of Manhattan. That was where a pulled my debit card out from my wallet for the first time since before I left New Orleans to get enough cash from a machine in the airport to catch a bus to Grand Central. As it turned out, it had been an amazingly good trip after all, and I had not spent a single cent the whole way. That had to have been a good omen.

Now life was going to be glorious. I was going to capture hearts of Times Square. But first I had to stroll along Broadway in the snow and amidst all the Christmas decorations, and then I had to figure out where and how to live. But not yet. Not on my first day. I remembered an old joke about a good ol' boy from the South moving to Chicago (Chicago, New York, interchangeable in this joke). The old boy, a country bumpkin if there ever was one, had heard there was so much money in Chicago it was falling from the sky. Sure enough, no sooner had he arrived than he saw a fifty-dollar bill someone had dropped in the grass. Fifty dollars! A fortune for the ol' boy. He looked at it and muttered, "Hmmm. I'll pick you up tomorrow. I ain't 'bout work on my first day in Chicago."

I saw a man selling roasted chestnuts from a cart on the sidewalk and thought, there it is, just like in the song. New York is where Christmas lives. I felt as if I had found the home I had always dreamed of. I looked at all the theater marquis. *Long Day's Journey Into Night*, the revival with Gabriel Byrne and Jessica Lang; *She Loves Me*; the crazy, crazy, sardine-packed *Noises Off; Falsettos; Hamilton*, oh my god; *Hello Dolly* with the incomparable Bette Midler;

Tennessee William's masterpiece, *The Glass Menagerie* with Sally Fields. I was in heaven, even though buying a ticket to even one of those shows might necessitate a battle between sleeping on the street or paying rent for a week in whatever cheap abode I could find.

The abode I found for that first night in the city was better than cheap. It was free. It was the Catholic Worker's St Joseph House on East First Street, way down in the lower end of the East Village. I'd never heard of the Catholic Worker. I found out about it from a guy I met in Central Park. I wandered from the park down through Chelsea, where I browsed a couple of art galleries, and then across fourteenth Street to First Avenue and then farther downtown. The house itself was modest and not too unlike the house where we had lived in New Orleans.

The guy I talked to there wanted to know everything about me: where I came from, why was I there, how long did I plan to stay. He was an energetic little man about my age who was constantly in motion. He seemed leery of me, like he thought I was going to rob them or something. After what I thought was unnecessary grilling for a few minutes, he said, "All right. You can stay until Thursday, but we expect you to earn your keep by working in the kitchen." And his previously stoical expression gave way to a warm smile, and he extended his hand and said, "I'm Darren Pressman. Welcome to St. Joseph House."

The people were welcoming, down-to-earth, friendly. The house was operated by a religious organization and financed by donations, but they weren't pushy about their religion. I ended up staying a bit longer than planned. I can't remember exactly how long. Even after I found an affordable apartment in the Village (almost impossible anywhere in the city, but I lucked out) that I shared with two other aspiring actors, I continued to go back to the Worker's house and volunteer. I helped in the kitchen preparing meals that were served to the street people, and I helped put together the organization's newspaper that sold for—get this—one penny.

Darren Pressman from St. Joseph's House was one of the actors I shared the apartment with. The other one, who stayed with us a very short time, was Roy something or other. I never could remember his last name. Darren had been volunteering at the Catholic Worker for quite some time. He didn't live there, but he had stayed there a night or two when he couldn't afford anything else, and after that he volunteered as often as possible. Like me, he had aspirations of being a Broadway star. "I can show you the ropes," he said. Unlike me, he was a devout Catholic but of the revolutionary sort. His heroes were the notorious priest and anti-war activist Daniel Berrigan and Dorothy Day, the founder along with Peter Maurin of the Catholic Worker movement. I knew about Berrigan, but I'd never heard of Dorothy Day. So I read up on her. I learned there was a movement afoot to make her a saint. I know nothing about how those things work, but it sounded cool to me.

I liked Darren's style. He was a no-nonsense, gutsy kind of guy. Practically a midget at barely over five feet tall and no more than, by my guess, a hundred and ten pounds. I thought of him as a bantam rooster ready to rule the entire hen house and fight off the biggest and baddest of roosters to do it. Darren showed me where to go to get day jobs. It was an employment agency called Jobs First in the basement of a kind of flop house on Bleeker Street near Washington Square Park. It was a short walk from where we lived. "You gotta have a job, but you gotta control your work hours," he said. "You gotta be available for auditions and rehearsals."

Jobs First hired people by the day or the week, mostly at minimum wage. A lot of the jobs were brute labor, lifting and hauling, dirt and sweat. I marveled at Darren's ability to lift and haul as much as I could despite his diminutive size. Proof of the old saying about dynamite. A lot of the jobs we were sent on were simply weird. Like for instance, Darren and I got hired to stuff rolling papers in little cardboard packages, the kind of papers that were ostensibly used for roll-your-own cigarettes; everybody knew what they were really used for. Our fellow workers were mostly old hippies. We sat around a conference table and stuffed the papers for three hours, and then the supervisor announced, "Smoke break," and I started to stand up to go outside to smoke a cigarette, but Darren grabbed my arm and laughingly said, "Hold up. It ain't that kind of smoke break." And a couple of joints were lit up and passed around and everybody got stoned. Then we went back to work.

We were both hired as models for a figure drawing group. There were about ten people in the group. I had never before taken my clothes off in front of a group of men and women, and I was so nervous at first. I was horrified of maybe getting an erection. I could barely sit still, but the artists seemed to take our nakedness in stride, and so did Darren, who had done it before. I soon got comfortable with it—mentally, emotionally, that is; physically it was more torturous than any of the heavy-lifting jobs we worked. You can't imagine how hard holding still can be until you try it.

One day four of us were picked to distribute flyers in a residential neighborhood on Long Island. We all crammed into a little Datsun coupe and drove out, and then walked for miles around a neighborhood where every house looked the same and were jammed together the way we were in the Datsun. The trip out and back took longer than the work, but we got paid for travel time.

My best job—and it turned into a gig that lasted for quite some time—was working as a Shabbos Goy at a synagogue on the Upper Westside. A Shabbos Goy is a non-Jew who turns the lights on and off on the Sabbath. Certain things are not allowed by Orthodox Jews on the Sabbath, the rabbi explained. That's where Shabbos Goys come in. I flipped the switches on and sat on a chair outside the door during the service and flipped the switches back off when they were done. On the first day of the job, the rabbi handed me a *Playboy* magazine and said, "Here's something to read during the service." I never would have expected anything like that from a rabbi with one of those black hats they wear and the side braids. After that, I took to carrying a paperback novel.

After the service he asked me if I could kosher a kitchen. I said I didn't know what that was, but I was willing to learn. Koshering meant cleaning the kitchen and putting away the pots and pans. I guess he was pleased with the way I did it, because he kept offering me different jobs. In other words, I was basically a janitor. I was usually there all by myself, and I sang out loud while I worked. My favorite song to sing, especially while sweeping the roof, was "Hey Jude" by the Beatles. Also, while up there, I once sang songs from *Fiddler on the Roof* because it seemed appropriate.

Me, Debbi

Back to that Easter dinner with Moms and Pops. It was a rousing big family gathering with Bryce's brother Harrison in from Orange County in Southern California with his wife, Cindy, and their three kids; his cousin Belle, a shrill, mousey blonde-from-a-bottle who lived in Shreveport and was married to a fat man named George. Come time to hide Easter eggs in the grass for the kids, George's butt crack showed every time he bent over. One of Harrison's kids hollered, "Your crack is showing!" and George straightened up and tried with little success to pull his shirttail down to cover himself, and Harrison's children started calling him Uncle Crack to his great chagrin and to their great delight.

The children were all younger than ten, the adults, except for Moms and Pops, were mostly in their thirties. While the kids played in the yard, Bryce fired up the barbeque grill and the adults, all but Bryce, drank martinis and beer. Two or three times before dinnertime Moms made belittling remarks about me, nonchalantly as if I were not within her hearing. I think she knew I could hear and wanted me to. Some kind of malicious thrill she must have got from putting me down. She said things like "The poor thing, the first time we asked her to say grace, she didn't know what we were talking about. Bless her heart. I guess she never went to church or ate dinner with a Christian family. I think her mama believed in some kind of voodoo. What was it, dear?" This last aside was aimed at Pops, but I spoke up before he could.

With the sweetest voice I could muster, I came out with, "Oh no, it was nothing like that. Her voodoo hoodoo was kind of an act Mama put on. She was never serious about it. She did it to frighten the tourists, especially the hypocritical, self-righteous so-called Christians who looked down on her and smothered her with attitude."

I don't think Moms even got that I was referring to her. My sarcasm was too subtle for her apparently pea-sized or pickled brain.

George served the burgers and hot dogs hot off the grill and everyone took their plates to the oversized dinner table from the dining room that Bryce and Harrison had carried outside earlier, along with two smaller tables for the kids. Pops came to dinner with a lit cigarette, which was usual for him. He took his place at the head of the table and everyone else waited until he was seated. He flicked ashes on the grass. Harrison said, "Do you have to smoke at the table, Pops?"

"Why? You got something against smoking?"

"Naw. But well . . ." I could see on his face that standing up to the old man was a struggle for him. "Yes, I do," he finally said. "You know I don't react well to cigarette smoke. It affects my asthma. You know that."

Pops said, "Buck up, son. Be a man. I been smoking since I was nine years old, and it ain't never hurt me none."

Moms said, "Why not be nice for a change, honey, and put the cigarette out? It is pretty nasty."

"Oh what a bunch of pansies ya'll are," Pops said, but he did squash his cigarette out underfoot, and he coughed, a dry, hacking cough that lasted almost a full minute. His eyes watered, and his face reddened, but then he shot Harrison a look that said he'd better not make any smart-alecky remark about his coughing.

Moms asked me to say grace. Of course she couldn't not ask after making such a to-do about it earlier. "Why sure, Moms. I would be more than happy to," I said, still with that sugary little-girl voice.

Saying grace had never been a thing we did at home, nor did Bryce and I ever say grace before a meal. Mama always prayed before meals. She left it up to me whether to close my eyes and say the words, which were always the same. "Hail Mary full of grace. Thank you, Mother Mary and our sweet Lord Jesus for our many blessings." She was Catholic of a sort. Bryce's parents went to a Baptist Church in Grapevine. Bryce had attended the same church when he was growing up, but never again attended after he left his parents' home.

Somehow, I plowed through what I hoped was a satisfactory blessing of the meal, ending with "Amen, pass the taters," and Moms said, "Thank you, dear. That was lovely."

While platters of potato salad and bags of chips and condiments were being passed around, Moms called for a toast. "We need to toast our newest family member." Raising a glass in my direction, she said, "We're all just tickled pink to welcome Debbi Mason to our Easter dinner, and I guess to our little family. Debbi and Bryce are living together now. Oh my goodness, living in sin, as we used to say, but in this day and age it seems to be acceptable, and I for one am broad minded enough to welcome her just as much as if she was my own blood daughter, even if she is a quarter colored." And looking directly at me and cooing as to a baby, she added, "That's all right, honey pie. We all love you just like one of our own. Ain't that right, everybody?"

There was a chorus of welcoming grunts and cheers, and Harrison leaned over to whisper to me, "Don't you mind Moms. In her world it's still 1850. But she means well." I wanted so much to say meaning well was a sorry excuse for bad manners and downright viciousness, but I held my tongue.

Remember what I said in the beginning about being a loudmouthed rabble rouser? I was certainly not acting like that woman at that Easter dinner, and I hated myself for it. I couldn't believe I had become such a lily-livered suck-up, but I knew it was only a matter of time before the real me burst out, and I figured Moms and Pops and Bryce and Harrison and George and the whole lot of them would be knocked clean off their feet when it happened.

Moms went on to announce, while Pops surreptitiously lit another cigarette, "Debbi is the cutest thing you've ever seen, and . . . and (getting all fluttery) she has the cutest way of talking. Tell them where you come from, honey."

Slowly, haltingly, not knowing whether to be mad or flattered or tickled, and not knowing what could possibly be so cute about where I came from, I said, "New Orleans."

"No, not like that. The way you say it."

"Oh, you mean like Nawlins?"

"Yes. That's it. Isn't that so sweet. I swan, if she don't sound as dumb as a hound dog."

That was the trigger it took to set off the explosion that had been building force all day. No more sweet affectation, my voice was a spear of ice aimed right at Moms' heart. "You're the one that's howling like a brain damaged hound dog, you pompous b b b . . . (I caught myself before I said it). And by the way, do you recall how I said my mother's voodoo was an act. Well I lied. I was trying to avoid shocking you. But oh yeah, Mama was a voodoo priestess all right, you can bet your sweet bippy. And a conjurer, too, and I'm proud to be her daughter. She cast spells and told fortunes and from time to time she was known to bite off a chicken's head and smear the blood all over her naked body and dance in the moonlight. And if I take a mind to call her and ask her to, she'll cast a spell on you that will make you wish you'd never been born."

Harrison laughed at that. So did his wife and kids. I was really warming up to them. I imagined that Moms had probably treated Harrison's wife with similar disdain and it thrilled him to see someone giving her what-for. Clearly to Moms, not a woman in this world was good enough for her boys.

The rest of the table sat in stunned silence. Bryce looked mortified. Pops? Hmmm, I think I detected just the slightest hint of a satisfied grin about to pop out on his face.

I thought I had got the best of Moms and shut her up for the rest of the evening at least, but she wasn't done. Oh no. I had under estimated her. Sometime after we scoffed down colossal quantities of hamburgers and hotdogs and potato chips and potato salad, and after the mosquitoes came out in kamikaze droves and everybody retreated to the house, and after Moms had downed a few more drinks, she said to all and sundry, "Did you know Debbi was a dancer. She performs—or she did until Bryce whisked her away—in a Bourbon Street nightclub called . . . what was the name of it, dear?"

How did she know about that? Had Bryce told her? I couldn't believe he would do that. He was the one, not me, who was ashamed of it. Had she investigated me? Surely that's easy enough to do nowadays. You just type in a name. Debbi Mason, New Orleans. And as if by magic the Internet pulls up my stage name and the name of the club where I performed. Darlin' Debbi. Lipstix on Bourbon Street, with an address and a photo of the outside of the club showing one of the girls in the swing and a photo of me in costume.

Livid doesn't describe the half of what I felt. Enraged doesn't do it justice. Throwing a hissy fit is an understatement. I wanted to pull her hair out and choke her with it. "Lipstix!" I shouted. "Lipstix is the name of the club where I took all my clothes off and sat in the laps of fat drunks and rubbed my perfect little ass against their so-called manhood."

I never did any of those things. Complete nudity and lap dancing were not done at Lipstix. But I was going for all the shock I could squeeze out of my tirade.

"Now dear," Moms said, still honeysuckle sweet. She wasn't even phased by my outburst.

That was when Bryce finally spoke up, but not exactly coming to my defense. He said, "Honey . . . take it easy."

Take it easy—ha! I figured I'd show him. I'd show them all. I was fed up to my eyeballs with Bryce and his entire family. Getting to my feet, I announced, "Ya'll want to see what kind of dancing I do? Okay, sure. Let's have a little show, howzabout it? Have a look. See if you like it." And I jerked my top off over my head. It was a simple pullover with a scoop neckline, and I was wearing a bra, so nothing was exposed. But they didn't know how far I might go, and to tell the truth, neither did I. I waved my shirt by a sleeve like a lariat and started a bump-and-grind, the kind of thing I never did in my actual dance routines, while singing out loud the wordless tune everybody knows as "The Stripper." Ba bah boom, bah bah boom, bah bah boom boom boom.

"Yah ha!" Harrison shouted. "Go, go go!" His wife covered her mouth with her hands and giggled.

Bryce pushed himself out of his chair and grabbed me around my chest and shoulder, pinning my arms to my side, and hustled me toward the door. As he pushed me out the door, I shouted back over my shoulder, "Ya'll have fun now, ya hear."

I have no recollection of what was said on the drive home. A lot of cussing from Bryce, and just as much from me. So much for my long-ago vow to not cuss. And the argument continued at home while we changed clothes and got ready for bed. I remember some of it. I remember him saying, "Don't you ever talk to my mother like that. My mother, for God's sake."

I accused him of being a mama's boy and a weakling and said, "Are you still nursing on mama's tit or what?"

That was when he struck out with his fist. A single blow to my face. I didn't see it coming. It knocked me to the floor. On the way to the floor I banged against a chair and knocked it over. It felt like my jaw was broken. His fist was like a wooden bat against the side of my face. I was dizzy and nauseous. I tried to crawl out of his reach. He took a step toward me. I didn't know if he was coming to help me up or to hit me again. Halfway between lying down and pushing myself up off the floor, I reached and grabbed a leg of the chair I had knocked over and swung it blindly. I felt it hit something. I think it was his arm. The shock of it ran up my arm to my shoulder. He shouted "Goddamn you!" And that was when he hit me again.

I rolled away from him just as he fell on top of me, and I thought he was going to try and suffocate me or hit me again, but instead of that he started crying and begging me to forgive him. He flopped over on his back and then he was on his knees and cradling me in his arms and saying, "Oh baby, I'm so, so sorry. I don't know what came over me. I'll never do that again, I swear to God. Please, please forgive me."

I thought my jaw was broken. It wasn't, thank God, but it was bruised and swollen for days after.

Me, David

"Being an actor ain't easy," Darren said. "You got to want it more than anything. You got to be willing to suffer, work your butt off, work an eight-hour shift at some shit job while sneaking in a reading of impossible-to-memorize lines every spare moment you get and then rush straight from work to rehearsals that usually run till midnight or later. If you're lucky, you'll get good directors and good stage managers, but you might just get the stage manager from hell. And all that's only after you get the part. First you have to audition for about a million plays including some of the worst ever written, and you have to withstand humiliation and insult and the feeling that nobody even sees you, that you're a ghost, that you never even existed. When they never call you by name and you don't get a call-back or even a thanks-no thanks, Man, that's rough. But when you do get a good part in a play worth its salt, you'll find that the theater community can be the most encouraging and supportive family there is. Really. You'll find that most actors are great people. And then when the play finally opens and if it's successful and you get a standing ovation no matter how big or how small the audience, it's like you won the Nobel Prize or scored the winning run in the World Series."

I found myself gulping air in sympathy because he was talking so fast without stopping to take a breath. I couldn't resist a sarcastic comeback. "Uh huh, and this is all coming from the guy who in the past year has had a small role in precisely one play—one measly play that ran three performances, and a walk-on part in a student film project you didn't even get paid for. Ha! This is the voice of experience talking? I don't think so." In the brief time Darren and I had been best buddies, we had fallen into an easy routine of lovingly bullying each other.

At that point in my New York adventure, I had not yet dared start my search for an acting gig. A regular old job-job had to come first. But I was beginning to see some light, enough that I felt ready to start pursuing my "real" work as an actor.

Darren said the first step was to get a good headshot. "You need to hire a professional. I know you can't afford it, but you have to do it. I know a good photographer who is quite reasonable."

The guy he recommended charged $150, which Darren swore was by far the cheapest I could find in the city. And that wasn't the end of the expense. Next, he insisted I had to get a cell phone with access to the Internet so I could check the audition announcements. "You probably ought to get a laptop too. Get on Facebook and Linked-in. Put yourself out there."

My god, I was barely making enough money to pay my part of the rent and groceries, even though we were getting by on mostly rice and beans and ramen noodles, vegetables from the day-old bargain bin, and hardly any meat.

"Here's how it works," Darren said. We were sitting outside one of the few remaining packing houses in the old West Village meat packing district, right in the shadow of the High Line, smoking. He said, "You find out about auditions from *Backstage* or *Broadway World*. They're both online. So you find a play that looks like something you could do, right age, right size. I mean, like, they break it down for you. Sometimes they'll say something like two male and three female, one African, or Hispanic, whatever. Thirty to fifty years old. Pretty specific like that. And they'll give a bit of a description of what the play is about. So if it looks like something you can do, you send them your headshot and a resume, except you don't have any acting credits so just the headshot. And then you wait. There's going to be a hundred people, two hundred trying to just get an audition. If you're lucky enough to get called in, the call will most likely come from the SM by phone or email, so you got to have both."

"SM?" I queried. Feeling inadequate already because I didn't even know the language.

"Seriously? Stage manager. My god, you are a novice."

"Yeah? Well we all are at some point. Must I point out once again your stellar achievements so far?"

I didn't want to dip into my somewhat pathetic savings account—money I had set aside to use only in an emergency—but Darren convinced me that not having a cell phone and email was an emergency. It was, I guess, sometime in February when I got my phone and started looking for acting jobs. Over the next few months, I auditioned for a dozen or more plays. Some of the audition notices called for actors to do a monologue of their own choice. Darren helped me pick them. He kept a file of monologues on his computer, arranged by category: comedy, drama and Shakespeare. And some were cold readings, meaning, Darren explained, that they would hand us scripts when we got there. The thought of that scared the hell out of me, but at least with a cold reading I wouldn't have to memorize lines, which scared me even more.

Most of them didn't call back at all. Left me hanging in the wind like forgotten underwear hung out to dry. They could have at least thanked me for reading and wished me luck, but I guess they couldn't bother with that. A few sent formal-sounding emails. One even said, "We enjoyed your reading and hope you will try again when we audition for other shows." A little hope at last.

One of the first shows I tried out for was Paula Vogel's Pulitzer Prize-winning play *How I Learned to Drive*. I had seen it in New Orleans and loved it. It was an intense play about incest and pedophilia, with, basically parts for one man and one woman and a small ensemble cast.

Darren said, "Wow, man! You really go for the top, don't you?"

"What do you mean?"

"I mean like this is a tough, tough play to do, and it's practically all just you and the woman, with a hell of a lot of lines to learn. I mean this is like a huge challenge even for an experienced actor."

"You mean like you?" I put in.

"Yeah, like me, A-hole. It's a killer. But what the hell. Give it a shot."

I did. That was one of the one's I never heard back from.

Another one was some little theater in SoHo that was doing a version of *The Tempest* set on the moon. I did one of Darren's Shakespeare monologs, Ariel's speech about three men of sin belched up on the island. I only barely understood it, but I liked the sound of it. I got a form rejection from that one. Then there was another strange one that was a lot of fun. It was an update of Moliere's *Tartuffe* set in 1930s Hollywood. (Who does these crazy updates on classic plays?) I had heard of that one. I mean people we knew were gabbing about it. But I'd never seen it or read the script. The fun thing about that one was they gave us about fifteen minutes to read over our lines backstage and then brought everyone out so we could be audiences for each other. The scenes we read were hilarious, and the audience of fellow actors laughed wildly. It made me feel for the first time that I was a member of the acting community. But, of course, I didn't get a part in that one either.

One that was hilarious was an uproarious take-off on 1950s sci-fi called *The Head That Wouldn't Die*. I wish we had all been allowed to sit in the audience for that reading as well. I didn't get cast, but Darren did, and I saw him in it. It ran for three weeks in a theater that seated less than a hundred.

One of the best was a play by an unknown playwright from Seattle or someplace like that, *Seven Ways to Get There* by Bryan Willis. It was about a woman therapist who runs a therapy group for a bunch of men. There were six or seven parts for men and one for the lone woman. I thought for sure I nailed a part in that one, but no such luck.

I could go on and on about every play I tried out for. Another good one I didn't get cast in was *Boy Gets Girl*, a contemporary drama by Rebecca Gilman, and one I would have loved to be in was Edward Albee's strange comedy about a guy who falls in love with a goat, *The Goat, or Who Is Sylvia?* There were only two parts for men, and I was not the right age for either. I probably shouldn't have bothered auditioning for that one. I don't have a clue why they called me in.

By the end of summer I was so dejected I was ready to pack it in and go back to New Orleans. Or at least admit I was never going to be an actor. How audacious and dumb I must have been to have set a goal for myself of getting an acting job in a year or pack it in. By September the odds against me meeting that goal were astronomical. I had given it my all for nine months. If I were a woman, I could have had a baby by then. A star is born by Christmas—bah, humbug.

But giving up didn't necessarily mean going back to New Orleans. I could be a failed actor in New York as well as in New Orleans. I could be a bartender or work in a bookstore just as well in one place as another. Or even a flocker. That was my job that fall, and it was full time, and the pay wasn't bad. I worked for Haruto's Warm Lamps. My job was flocking lamps. Strange sounding, I know, but their product was wildly successful. I'd been on the job since the last week in July. Haruto was an enterprising immigrant and entrepreneur from Japan, and his business was going great. His name meant something like first warmth, which gave him, if not the idea for the business, at least the idea for the name. He manufactured flocked lamps—flocking, like the fuzzy stuff that goes on artificial Christmas trees. Those of us who put the flocking on were called flockers. The lamp bases were ceramic dolls, teddy bears, ballerinas and whatnot. They were cute, and the business really boomed starting in September as we headed into the holiday season. I joked to my friends that I was the best flocking flocker in the whole flocking factory. My job started out part time but soon became full time with the promise of a lot of overtime in November and December, so there was no way I could do any acting before Christmas, even if my one-year, self-imposed deadline were not a pipe dream.

Darren gave me hell for giving up. "You'll regret it, my friend. You'll regret it the rest of your life."

"Maybe," I said, "and maybe not. Maybe I'm just not cut out to be an actor. Maybe it's time I faced the truth."

He said giving up on a dream is never a good idea, and he tried his damnedest to convince me I really did have what it takes. "I've seen you in auditions. I've seen you rehearsing monologs. You're a better actor than a good half the people I've seen auditioning. Better than a lot I've seen on stage."

Trying to encourage me was nice of him, but I felt so dejected by that point I was convinced that whatever talent I might have, if any, and my college education were all for naught. The only thing I was capable of was flocking ballerinas. Darren kept saying I would regret giving up, but every time he used the word regret, the only thing I could think of was how badly I regretted losing Debbi. I was still in love with her and thought that would never change.

Me, Debbi

My jaw was aching like crazy when I got up the next morning. My first thought was to look in the mirror to see how much damage he had done. My eyes were red-rimmed, not from the hit I took but from crying. The right side of my jaw from ear to chin and up to my cheekbone was swollen and colored the purple of a rotting prune. I wanted to say something into the mirror, to say anything, just to see if I could talk. I slowly opened my mouth, moved my jaw side-to-side. It was painful. Tears came to my eyes at the first movement. I said to myself in the mirror, "Good morning. You look like Russian dancers have been dancing on your face." I laughed at myself. That hurt too. The old joke: it only hurts when I laugh. Then don't laugh.

Bryce was already gone. Skedaddled, apparently before daylight. In our bedroom were two overstuffed easy chairs set on either side of a round, glass-top coffee table. There he had left a note, a corner of it edged under the heavy ashtray that always stood on that table, saying again what he had said the night before, how dreadfully sorry he was, and begging my forgiveness. He had left a pack of cigarettes on the table. I took one out and lit it and drew smoke deep into my lungs, even though I was not a smoker. (Once in a blue moon I might smoke a cigarette at a party, but seldom inhaled.) The cough that naturally ensued was painful, and again tears came to my eyes, and then I not only had a sore jaw, but my throat burned.

Shivering from the cold, I pulled on a heavy cotton robe, one Bryce had given me. It was white with pictures of red roses on the vine. I tried applying a little foundation and powder to my face, but it didn't cover my bruises sufficiently, and I figured putting it on heavy enough to hide the damage would make me look like a mime. I didn't want to leave the room because I was a horrible mess, and I didn't want anyone to see me in the condition I was in, not Martina or anyone else, even though Martina had surely heard the ruckus the night before.

I knew I would eventually have to eat, and I was craving coffee. I had to bite the bullet and call Martina in. I couldn't avoid her forever.

"Good morning, Miss Deh . . . ," she chirruped like a cheerful cricket, shutting up halfway through my name when she caught a glimpse of my face. "Oh my goodness. That must hurt like the devil. Did he do that?"

He. Of course. She knew it had to have been him. I figured— actually the thought dawned on me for the first time—that she had probably been on the receiving end of his fury at some point. I asked her to bring me some coffee, "and maybe something I can eat without having to chew."

She said she could bring me some oatmeal.

"No, don't go," I said after she brought the oatmeal and coffee on a lap tray and turned to leave. "Stay and talk to me a bit."

I couldn't think of any way to soften it, so I blurted out what was thinking. "He's done this to you, too. Hasn't he?"

She didn't answer out loud, but there was an almost imperceptible nod of her head, and she looked down at the floor as if ashamed to let me look into her eyes.

Before noon that day, UPS delivered a bundle of yellow roses. From Bryce, of course.

Me, David

Crunching peanut shells underfoot was the thing I loved about Tally's. That was the bar on East Tenth where Darren and I liked to go when we had an evening with nothing to do. It was small and dark with what must have been fifteen or twenty tables, four seats to a table, so I guess the seating capacity was around eighty when the tables were jammed together so tightly knees bumped. I don't think there were any two tables alike, but they all had one thing in common. On each sat a bowl of salted peanuts the servers constantly refilled, plus there were five or six bowls of nuts on the bar. The thing to do was crack the shell and toss the empties on the floor, thus the crunching underneath.

Most nights Tally's was not crowded, meaning we could hear each other talk. Saturday nights, however, they had live music on their little stage. We never went on Saturday nights, not we discovered crowded and noisy Saturday nights were. Wednesday night was also busy. Wednesday was story night, and we went as often as we could. We loved story night. Darren even told stories sometimes. It was open-mic. Anybody could tell a story. The rules were first, they had to be true stories (but everybody fudged on that), and second, keep them under six minutes. A warning light flashed at five minutes and flashed repeatedly at six. After that, if the story tellers didn't wind it up, the audience shouted them down. It was all in good fun, but some people—wow! You couldn't shut them up. I remember there was one lady who seemed to think she was the first woman in America to break the glass ceiling. She was an insurance adjuster and the only female adjuster in the company where she worked. She went on grandly aggrandizing herself for almost fifteen minutes. When she wouldn't shut up, somebody started singing "Stuck in the Middle with You," and everybody joined in until the woman finally got the message and exited the stage. And there was a guy who was upset because he couldn't get laid, and he bored everyone with tales of his failed attempts with women. Blaming, of course, the women.

One night when we were there for story night—it was early and it was quiet—a woman approached our table and said, "You guys are actors, aren't you? Sancho Panza and Don Quixote."

I thought she meant she had seen us playing those parts. I wish. But before I could say, "You must have us mixed up with some other guys," Darren said, "That's us, my dear, and who might you be?"

"Rain."

Reflexively I looked toward the door to see if it had started raining outside, and Darren started singing "Don't Rain on my Parade." It took me a second, but I got it.

Darren asked if Rain was a stage name.

"Nope. That's the name my mama gave me, God bless her hippie-dippie soul."

"Just Rain? No last name?" Darren was doing the talking for us. I sat back and listened.

"My last name is Weiner."

"Like a hot dog?" I asked.

"No, like a whiner."

Darren asked if she was Jewish.

She said, "Yeah, but not religious. My grandparents were in a concentration camp. They never made it out, but my mother did. She grew up to be a hippie. Obviously. Only a hippie would name a daughter Rain. I know ya'll from auditions for *Tartuffe*. Wasn't that a hoot?" She spoke softly and slowly with the remnants of a Southern accent.

I had barely glanced at her, and she was rubbing her forehead so I couldn't see much of her face. When I finally got a good luck at her, I was flummoxed. She looked just like Debbi. Well, maybe not *just* like her, but enough so that in the dimly lit bar the resemblance gave me a shock. How many times had I fantasized bumping into Debbi in some unexpected way. For what must have been no more than ten seconds, I truly thought it was her. I said, "Deb . . . uh, Rain." Recovering, I went on. "Yes, I think I do recall seeing you there. Why don't you join us?" I thought I was being quite gallant.

"Thanks. I'll be happy to join you." She took her seat between us, and Darren offered to go up to the bar and get her a drink. She had asked for a club soda. In rapid-fire succession, she cracked open peanuts and popped them in her mouth and washed them down with her drink. Not much talking after that, because of the story tellers, but when the last one finished his story, a fish tale about the big one that got away—literally—a whacked-out version of that cliched fish tale, and it was hilarious.

The place soon cleared out and got quiet, and the three of us had a long conversation about theater and how tough it was to break in, and about our own personal stories.

Rain was most recently from Tacoma, Washington, but for most of her life before that she had lived in Nashville. She had been, as she put it, a big deal actor in community theater, and she thought she could find similar success New York. She had a deep and resonate voice, and to me she was stunningly beautiful. Rain was wearing a scoop-neck shirt that exposed part of a tattoo on her chest. It was not like Debbi's but close enough. I thought I had succeeded in putting Debbi out of my mind, mostly. But Rain brought it all back. I longed to hear Debbi's incredible humor. She could be a winner at story time. I remembered how her wild streak often left me overjoyed but dumbfounded, such as when we came across a jazz trio playing on a street corner on Canal Street and she did an impromptu dance on the sidewalk and doubled the crowd that had stopped to listen to the music.

I think Rain and Darren were both silent while I was spacing out. And then Rain brought me back to the moment. She said, "You're staring at my boobs, Dude." Not accusatory, but she put me on the defensive.

I said, "No, I . . . I didn't mean to, it's just . . ."

"You're embarrassed," she laughed. "Hey, it's no biggie. They're just . . ."

"It's the tattoo," I stammered.

"Uh huh. I get that a lot. I guess that's as good excuse for ogling as any. Next thing you're going to ask if you can see the rest of it. Forget it. We're not that friendly yet."

At that point, I guess she got it that I was shamed to my core and didn't know how to react, so she placed her hand on top of mine and said, "It's all right, dude."

Making sure to look her smack dab in the eye and not let my gaze wander south again, I said, "This is embarrassing. It's just that you look a lot like someone special, someone I lost, and the thing is, she had a tattoo a lot like that one. I mean not the same picture, but, you know, splayed across her chest like that. I know I shouldn't have."

"It's okay, dude."

Darren jumped in. "Time out. Looka here. I'm here too. Me, right here. I'm a pretty interesting guy, too, if you care to hear about me."

"All righty. I see you. You want to take a gander at my boobs too?" I expected her to call him Dude, but I guess one dude per table was enough.

Darren told us an abbreviated version of his life story. He was a Southerner too. That made three of us. He grew up in South Mississippi and spent his days lounging on the beach in Biloxi, worked on offshore oil rigs, and was married and divorced twice before he was thirty. Like Rain, he had been a big-deal actor back home, with leading roles in nearly all his high school and college plays. "I was even in a show in David's home town once. Maybe you saw it. I was Bob Cratchit in *A Christmas Carol* done by Whatchacallit Theatre. Maybe you've heard of it."

"Nope. Never heard of it."

"I'm not surprised. It's kind of a fringy-type theater in a tiny space on Rampart. They're probably not even there anymore."

He went on to regale us with funny stories about some of the characters that worked with him offshore. I had heard him tell some of those stories at the open mic. From there he worked up to a synopsis of his three years in New York. I already knew most of that part of his story, and I let my mind wander again back to Debbi. I wondered how she was doing. I told myself I hoped she was happy, but I really hoped she was miserable, so unhappy she would leave the guy in Texas and go back to New Orleans and search for me. But that narrative came to a halt when faced with the reality that none of our old friends in New Orleans knew where I was. Until just recently, I didn't even have a phone. Nobody knew how to contact me—nobody, that is, except for a bunch of directors and stage managers who were not calling. I was not on any social media, and even if I could work up the courage to try and contact Debbi, I wouldn't know how. In an age of instant communication between everyone, Debbi and I might have well been on different planets.

Me, Debbi

Y ou couldn't be more in the dark about Martina's life than I was before the morning after the night I did a strip tease at Moms and Pops' and Bryce clobbered the side of my face. Tentative talk at first as she tried to draw me out about what had happened, meaning how and why and what was said, as if there were any question about what happened. He beat me, period. That was it. Nothing else need be said, except of course much more needed saying, and that brought us to the note again, the one slipped into my bag that said "Run, girl, run."

It had to have been her note. She knew it, I knew it, and she knew I knew it. "But why?" I asked. "Was it because you knew something like this would happen?"

But she said, "I wasn't lying to you. I am not the one who wrote that note." She still wouldn't admit it, and she would not look at me. She kept moving her hands in jerky circular patterns on the table top. And suddenly she burst into tears, and she who had been trying to console me was being consoled by me.

As a young child, she and Bryce had been playmates. They played hide-and-seek on the vast Fisher property, outside in the spring and summer and even on balmy winter days, and in the big house when it was cold and rainy outside. Before she even entered first grade at Grapevine Elementary, she declared her undying love for Bryce, to his mortification and his parents' delight. I might add here that they were delighted only because they saw her love for Bryce as childish and cute, and because they were sure it wouldn't last. If they had entertained the least suspicion her crush for Bryce might last until adulthood, they would have been horrified. Especially Moms. On the other hand, Martina's mama discouraged them from the start. She knew it could never be, and she was afraid Martina would end up broken hearted.

Martina chased Bryce around the house shouting in her little girl voice, "I'm gonna kiss you," and he fled her pursuit in mock terror, letting her catch him only when they were out of the grownup's sight. He didn't fool her one bit; he liked the kissing as much as she did, and she knew it. I'm talking maybe seven or eight years old. Understand, of course, kissing at that point meant on the cheek, and it was always a one-way street, she being the kisser and him the kissee. Until about the third or fourth grade, when he started kissing her back. For a few years after that, Bryce and Martina declared themselves boyfriend and girlfriend, and there was a lot of hand holding and kissing, and not always just on the cheek.

One of them, and she said she couldn't remember which one came to it first, heard about and told the other about French kissing. Oh boy, that lifted it to a higher level. Stuff getting serious, you know. They didn't hide it from the other kids at school. We've moved up to the fifth or sixth grade now, when they started going steady, and proudly announced it to everyone. At school anyway. At home, they continued to hide it. They had to because it was as clear as a flashing neon sign that neither his parents nor hers would approve. The class divide between them was as wide as the great Mississippi River. He was the son of the lord of the manor, and she was the kid of a lowly servant.

That Bryce was comfortable with those roles and expected her to be also was shattering to her. Not only classism but sexism was beginning to screw with their lives.

As is common with kid romances, they broke up and later got back together and then broke up again. During the times when they were broken-up, he was cold and aloof. He found other girlfriends.

Starting when he was in the eighth or ninth grade and she in the seventh and just beginning to come into puberty, he began to treat her more as a servant and less as a playmate. For at least part of a school term they were girlfriend and boyfriend at school but worker and boss at home. To Martina, it was confusing at best. From moment to moment there was kissing and hugging and sweet words of endearment, and then he was Mister Bryce the master she was not supposed to be familiar with, while she remained Martina the Mexican girl. Add a helping of xenophobia to the stew of class and sex.

When her breasts began to develop, he begged her to let him see them, touch them. And finally she gave in, saying, "Promise you won't let anyone know."

Naturally he swore up and down it would be their secret, and just as naturally (why didn't she see it coming?) within a day or two it was all over school. "Martina Lopez showed Bryce Fisher her tits."

And that wasn't the half of it. What really stuck in her craw was the kids saying "What do you expect? She's Mexican." She was heartbroken and mad, and she swore she would never speak to him again, but he begged her forgiveness so sweetly and with such believable abject sorrow that she finally gave in and welcomed him back into her affection.

And then there came the time when she finally gave in and let him take her to bed. He was a junior in high school then, almost as tall as his father and handsome as could be, albeit with an unfortunate spray of pimples to mess with his beauty. The sex was clumsy but enjoyable for both, and then it became horrifying to her once it was all over, because they did not use protection that first time. They waited in trembling until she got her period. There was no thought or talk of STDs but there should have been.

The second time they were more careful. After that she said, "We can't do this anymore" and was shocked when he said, "You will or you'll live to regret it."

After that he molested her routinely and she didn't dare refuse him.

"Why did you let him get away with it?" I asked. "Why not just say no? What could be have done? You had the right to refuse him your body."

For the longest time she didn't say anything, but at last she said, "Because my mother is here without papers."

She said, "I'll never forget what he said after that or the way he said it, like a guard in a prison or—dare I say it—like a master to

136

his slave. He said, 'You're going to let me do it whenever I want, and you're never going to tell a living soul. Or you're going to get to watch the immigration cops come pick your mother up and send her back to Mexico.'"

We held each other, and we blubbered like babies in each other's arms. I asked her again about the note she had slipped in my bag. "That was you, wasn't it? I knew it was. It had to be."

"Yes, it was. I had to warn you." She apologized for not coming clean right off the bat. "I just never know what to do. I never have, not since Mister Bryce started messing with me."

But here's the thing: she was not the person who wrote the note. She had fessed up to it only to get me to quit asking about it, because it really didn't matter if I thought it was her. It took me a while to figure that out.

If I had not hated him enough and feared him enough after he hit me, finding out how he had treated Martina made me despise him even more. But the weird thing was, and God alone knows why, there was still a self-loathing or desperate part of me that wanted to forgive him. And there was something else I thought about that Martina couldn't let herself believe or say out loud to me, and that was that maybe so long as I was there, she was safe from further advances from Bryce.

Me, David

I think Rain must have sent signals I didn't catch. I never was good at catching those kinds of signals. It happened with Debbi when she was dropping hints all over the bookstore. Same thing with a server at the Polish café down by Tompkins Square where we sometimes ate—best breakfast in the city. She was young and blonde and cute as a kitten. I didn't notice, but Darren told me she was trying to flirt with me. "Really?" I asked. "How can you tell?"

He seemed flabbergasted. "How can I tell? Christ, man, she might as well been wearing an I'm-available sign around her neck."

I couldn't believe it. I said, "Maybe it was you she was flirting with."

"Are you kidding? She never even looked at me."

I guess being that oblivious was typical, or so I was told. Not that women flirted with me that often. So anyway, Rain was flirting with me the night we met at Tally's, and Darren caught on when I didn't. He bowed out, and Rain and I wound up alone together when the crowd cleared out. And there we were, me and Rain in what I guess was a romantic setting, and it somehow ended up that she asked me to take her to see *Casablanca* at a movie house right around the corner from her place, a third-floor room in a brownstone that she rented from the old lady who lived there with a pair of Pomeranians. I walked her home, and she invited me up and introduced me to the old lady who chatted nicely for a few minutes and excused herself saying it was past her bedtime. "She always waits up for me," Rain said, "And then if I bring my date home, she gracefully bids us goodnight and leaves us to ourselves. But don't get me wrong, it's not like I bring dates home very often. Hardly ever, in fact."

It was a warm and muggy evening. She wore a light jacket over a sleeveless blouse. As soon as we stepped into her apartment, she whipped that jacket off and hung it on the back of a chair and opened a window. "Something to drink?"

"Sure."

"Rum and Coke okay?"

"Yeah, that would be great."

She mixed the drinks with plenty of ice cubes and put some cheese and crackers on a plastic tray and said, "Let's take it to my room."

Furnishings in her room consisted of a queen size bed, an office-type chair on rollers, and a computer desk. A single window opened wide to let in the night air. I sat down on the chair and she sat on the edge of her bed. Her walls were filled with movie posters, including one from the film we had just watched. "I never get tired of that film," I said.

"Me either. I've seen it about six times. Now tell me all about yourself."

"Well, I don't know where to start. I grew up in New Orleans, the youngest of six kids. My parents were hippies."

"You're lucky they didn't give you some far out hippie name."

"You mean like Rain?"

"Yeah, like Rain." She shrugged her shoulders.

"You could change it, you know."

"I know, but I actually kind of like it."

I said, "Maybe my folks were just half hippies. My dad was a school teacher, and my mom was an artist. She did pastel portraits of tourists on the sidewalk by Jackson Square."

She said, "I grew up on a communal farm outside of Nashville. It was called The Farm. Original name, huh?"

I noticed a pastel portrait on the wall of a young girl. "Is that you?" I asked.

"Yeah, one of my mother's, when I was fifteen."

"Not bad," I remarked. "You were cute."

"Still am."

She was, too, but did I take the bait. We finished off the cheese and crackers and our drinks, and she took our glasses and refilled them with rum and Coke.

I pulled out my pack of Marlboros. "Is it okay if I smoke?"

"Sure. It's fine. But let's go out on the fire escape to smoke 'em. Light me up one too."

Outside we sat with our feet dangling over the edge, and I lit our cigarettes. She asked me about how I came to New York, and I told her the whole story about Debbi leaving me and about hitchhiking, leaving nothing out, not even the whore in Georgia or the self-professed killer and kidnapper. She said, "That's the funniest story I ever heard. You should tell it a Tally's."

Even New York City sometimes gets quiet, and after a while that part of Chelsea became not quite so eerily silent as a three-o'clock Sunday morning, but quiet enough. Traffic at Seventh and Twenty-third, both vehicular and pedestrian, became slow and muffled after midnight, and we looked down on the tops of parked cars and rows of garbage cans and the halos of street lamps cast on the sidewalk, and everything was foreshortened, big on top and tapering down. We soaked in the quiet. And it became too chilly for us to remain on the fire escape, so we went inside and sat together on Rain's bed. We ran out of things to talk about and didn't want to refill our drinks but did not want to separate. I could have said "I should go," but I didn't. She should have said, "I guess it's time for you to leave," but it didn't seem she wanted to. Long, awkward silences. I wondered why she had invited me on the movie date and then asked me to come up for a drink. I felt as if there was an attraction between us that might go beyond casual enjoyment of one another's company, but I didn't know if that was true on her part or not. Nor did I know if it was true on my part. I still missed Debbi terribly and did not want to throw myself into what is commonly called romance on the bounce. I suspected she was not the kind of person who hops into bed on a first date, and neither was I.

Finally, we addressed the fact that it was time for me to go. We stood awkwardly at her door and wondered whether we should shake hands of give each other a hug or even a kiss. We settled on a somewhat uncomfortable hug.

Me, Debbi

I don't know how to explain it. Something happened to me after Bryce hit me that night. It was like I had been drained empty of whatever was inside me that made me what I was. No longer the brash, ballsy chick I had seen myself as or had at least acted as if I were, no longer the loudmouth, fun loving, rabble rousing woman I had been. I was a punctured helium balloon taking a nose dive to earth. The feeling didn't come all at once. When he hit me, my first emotion was shock, disbelief, followed quickly by a rush of anger such as I can't remember ever feeling. And then when he crumpled at my feet in a puddle of regret, I felt sorry for him. My impulse was to believe in his sincerity, to cradle him in my arms and say, "It's all right, baby." My thoughts and feelings vacillated between hate and forgiveness. When I was on the forgiveness end of the pendulum swing, I would think of how horribly he had treated Martina, and that would send me swinging back the other way, and I was ready to kill him. His cruelty to her angered me more than did his hitting me.

The one thing I did know was if he ever hit me again, fighting fair would not be on the agenda. Fighting fair was something that happened in the movies and in the boxing ring. Fighting was something that happened out of desperation, a last resort. I would kick, knee, hit, gouge, bite. I would go for the most vulnerable parts of his body, the eyes, the groin, and with any weapon I could get my hands on.

Or would I? That was the thinking of the person that was me before it happened, boldly imagining what I would do if it happened. But after the imagined thing happened I was no longer that me. I did not know what to think or feel or, most importantly, what to do. And it wasn't just that day or just that moment, but gradually over the following days when Bryce did not come home—thankfully, because I did not want to see him and did not know what I would say or do when he did come. I came to the realization that I had to get away from Bryce. I needed to go where he could not find me, because if I left him he would search for me, I knew he would. His stupid pride would not let him let me get away. Or would it? I couldn't even imagine that he would just move on and let me go.

I could not go home to the apartment with Lucy and Randy and Hopper, because that would be the first place he would look for me. The next place would be Lipstix, so I could not go back to my old job. Mama. Yes, my mother. I could flee to mother's protection. He didn't know her name, I don't think, or where she lived. But even at Mama's I wouldn't be safe for long, because I had told Bryce enough about her that it wouldn't take him long to find her. And then I thought of Stormy. Stormy Days, my best-bud dancer at Lipstix. Stormy would be willing to put me up until I could get a job and a place of my own.

Maybe I wasn't so much planning as fantasizing. It was like a movie playing in my head, a sleazy made-for-television movie about a former stripper escaping an abusive relationship. I would go to Stormy's abode, wait for her on the stoop late at night, waiting for her to get off work and walk home. It was a secluded, ground-floor place off a garden patio reached through a brick archway between a grocery store and a bookstore. Ironically and romantically resonating with the real story, the bookstore was Crawdads, the very same store where David had worked and where we had met. Stormy would not get home until sometime in the quiet hours of early morning shortly before dawn. Her eight-year-old daughter would be peacefully sleeping inside, and the babysitter would be asleep on the couch with the television still on but the sound turned down low. I would not dare ring the bell and wake them. As soon as Stormy got home I would jump up to greet her and fall into her arms and pour out my story of grief. Stormy was a big woman, almost six feet tall, with muscular arms and hands to hold me tightly and ebony skin that felt like fine leather to the touch. The men who watched the shows at Lipstix, almost exclusively white men, loved her. I guess she was exotic to them, representing a kind of dark and scary sensuality that existed only in myth and in their minds. Stormy would welcome me into her home. She would help me change my identity, dye my hair red, help me choose a new stage name. We would try out names like Cherry, Kitty, Star, Misty, Jezebel and Stella (a New Orleans favorite because of *A Streetcar Named Desire*) and combine them with various last names mostly taken from places, such as Canyon, River, Miami and Phoenix. Stormy's daughter would help, tickled to death to be a part of the intrigue. I'd have to get a job as a stripper in some other club.

Stop it! I told myself. I was being ridiculous. I didn't want to be a stripper again. Burlesque, sure. I mean that was something I could be proud of. There was humor to it, fun, surprises. Yeah, so what if some of the men in the audience got turned on? There's nothing wrong with a little titillation if it's done in fun. But most of the other clubs in the Quarter were about nothing but the titillation. I'd seen the girls in those clubs listlessly pole dancing, walking around on stage with about as much energy and style as a butcher chopping meat, lackadaisically bumping and grinding, drunks stuffing dollar bills in their G-strings, lap dancing for god sake. I wasn't about to do any of that. I wanted to be a legitimate dancer. I wanted to be appreciated for my art. I wanted to go to Hollywood and become a movie star or to New York and dance on Broadway.

As soon as I thought of Broadway, I thought about David, because he had talked so much about wanting to go to Broadway and see all the shows. And the thought of David made me stupidly start bawling, and I had to blow my nose and wash my face. I didn't have any idea how in the world I could get to Broadway or Hollywood anyway. I couldn't even make my way out of Dallas on my own, much less Broadway or Hollywood. I didn't have a car, and I couldn't drive if I had one. Never learned. Never had any reason to learn. And I didn't have any money. I still had friends in New Orleans who could save me, but I didn't know how to contact them. Can you believe I left home without getting phone numbers or addresses of anyone I was leaving behind? Other people were all over social media—Facebook, Instagram, Snapchat, probably others I'd never even heard of—all but David, the one person I'd give anything to see pop up on my laptop if I had one, or the computer in Bryce's home office, which I wouldn't dare use. He would know how to search the files for any messages between me and Stormy or David or Hopper. It was useless. David was techno ignorant, and I was pretty much a luddite. Neither one of us had a laptop or I-pad or anything like that. I didn't even own a cell phone, and I didn't think David did either. We might as well have been time travelers from a time before any of that stuff existed.

And I have to admit that at the time I didn't know if I really wanted to get away. Oh my good God in heaven whom I wasn't even sure I believed in, there was so much about Bryce I hated, there were so many reasons I wanted to be shut of him forever. Yeah, sure, he was handsome, he could be unbelievably charming when he wanted to (although he had seldom wanted to since leaving New Orleans). He took good care of me, provided a comfortable home with amenities I had never before dreamed of—a giant television screen, a fully stocked kitchen with hired help to prepare all my meals and serve them to me and wash up after, a bed and couch and easy chair that were each more comfortable than any I'd ever had, my own in-home dance studio. He bought me beautiful clothes, and when he took me out to dinner it was always at the best restaurants. Perhaps I could never forgive him for hitting me, but he was so pathetic when he begged my forgiveness. Could I trust him? I didn't know. Did he love me? No, I don't think he did. I think I was a possession to him, precious only in the way his father's trophy fish were precious to him. I mean after all, didn't he practically keep me prisoner in his house? Didn't he go away for days at a time without even telling me where he was or what he was doing? And to be brutally honest, I didn't love him either. He was just a meal ticket to me, a trophy husband for a trophy wife. That was the deal we made. Why should I want or expect anything different?

Me, David

I spent Christmas day alone. Darren spent the day with a friend in New Jersey, and Rain went back home to spend Christmas week with her parents. No Christmas tree for me, no presents. I spent the day and most of the night alone watching old movies on television. There had been that silly vow I made to myself to get a job acting before Christmas or give up on acting and go back home to New Orleans. But there was nothing in N.O. to go back home to, and I had a good job. Flocking lamps might not have been glamorous, but it was easy work and the pay was not bad. Haruto had given me a raise.

What social life I had centered around Darren and Rain and storytime at Tally's. Time passed slowly, snow in January and rain in February, a surprising warm spell in early March. I told myself it was a good life. Every once in a while Rain and I went to a classic movie together, and always would end the night drinking on her fire escape, no matter the weather. I thought it would be nice if someday I could find a woman to love as I had loved Debbi, but until that happened, I at least had Rain's friendship. I even entertained the thought that maybe our friendship could grow into romance. I could see it happening because Rain was a practical kind of person, the kind of woman who, unlike Debbi, didn't want to be swept off her feet, did not seek excitement in a relationship but would be sensible enough to see that a best friend could be the best kind of lover, steady and dependable. Debbi was a hot Corvette convertible. Rain was a Volvo station wagon.

To feed my theater bug, I wondered if I should volunteer at one of the little non-profit theaters in town, although I hadn't stepped into that yet. Maybe be an usher or work the box office or brush up on my tech skills and work backstage. That way I'd get to see theater at least. And when Rain or Darren either one got a part, I would go see them. In the months I had known them—almost a year in Darren's case—neither of them had landed a part.

"Just give it one last try. Please, for me," Rain begged of me, wanting me to audition for a show with her.

"No way," I said. "I'm worn out and smart enough to know when to quit battling windmills. You and Darren, you just keep on tilting at 'em. I'll cheer you."

Bug by Tracy Letts was a play Rain said was made for the two of us. She wouldn't cease begging me.

The audition notice described it as a study in paranoia or a psycho-thriller about lovers staying in a seedy Oklahoma City motel room who think their room is being bugged by government spies. While caught up in paranoia, they are infested with real bugs; i.e., insects.

Rain said, "I saw it last year. It's great. The main characters are a female drug addict and a male army vet with PTSD. We could play them, dude. I know we could."

The woman was supposed to be forty-four and the man only twenty-four. I teased Rain about being perfect for the part because she was so old, and she came back with, "And you're such a baby. Also perfect for the part."

I said I couldn't do it, but she wouldn't let up. She said, "I want this one more than any part I've ever tried for. I gotta have it." She said she wouldn't feel right auditioning without me. "I just can't," she said. "If you don't do it I won't either."

"Yes you will. Nothing has stopped you from auditioning for other parts without me."

"Yeah, and I didn't get any of those, did I?"

They held the auditions in an artist's loft in SoHo. The producer, it turned out, was the artist whose loft was being used. A hand-lettered sign taped to the side of the building directed actors to a freight elevator that spilled out ten or more people at a time into the loft. In all, there must have been forty or more people auditioning. We all chatted in a friendly way as we found places to perch. "Any place you can find," said the young woman who introduced herself as the stage manager. "There are a few chairs, and you can sit on those crates over there. Otherwise, just sit on the floor or lean on any vertical surface that won't topple."

She introduced the director, Sam. He said, "Okay, boys and girls, here's what we're going to do. I'm going to pair you up and hand you copies of the scenes you're going to read. We'll give you fifteen minutes to read over the scripts, then I'll call you one couple at a time. The first couple will be number one, the second number two and so forth. Got it?"

Most said, "Yes." I didn't say anything, assuming his "Got it?" was rhetorical. Rain and I looked to each other and whispered, "I hope he pairs us." He didn't. He said, "You, striped shirt, and you, tall redhead" and "You and you, over there," and so forth, while the stage manager moved about helping clarify which couples he was pairing. He paired Rain with a guy who looked too short to be with her and paired me with a woman I thought was too young for the part. Rain and her partner read their parts before me and my partner, and I got to watch and listen. She seemed lost. I was afraid she had counted on being with me—she should have known better—and felt lost and helpless without me. Or maybe I was giving myself too much credit. Compared with me, Rain was a seasoned professional. I thought the lost and confused look, intentional or not, fit the character perfectly.

When it was my turn, I promptly missed a whole sentence. Nerves, I guess. My eyes skipped over a line, but my partner covered by skipping her next line too, and going straight to the one after, and I picked up where I was supposed to. Aside from that one little glitch, which I hoped the director would not notice, I thought we did well. When we were done, I whispered an apology, and she said, "Don't worry. It happens all the time. Believe me, if he doesn't pick us that won't be the reason. I think you did well. In fact, if I was the director I'd cast you."

"Thank you," I stammered. "I thought you did really well, too."

After everybody read their parts, there was a lot of shuffling around of bodies as they tried to see how couples looked together, and then they had us read different scenes with different partners. I was a nervous wreck by the time it was over. As soon as they let us go, Rain and I went to the nearest bar to wind down.

The place made me feel old. Wow! That I could be made to feel old by a watering hole jampacked with people who looked barely old enough to drink was a kind of revelation, though I couldn't tell you what exactly it revealed to me. Disdain for youth, I guess, a kind of in-my-day-we-didn't blah blah blah sort of attitude. Hell, I had only recently turned thirty myself. But the loud laughter, the jokes we overheard that were crude and juvenile to our ears, the clanging of plates and glasses, all made me feel like an old man who just wanted to go home and have a hot toddy and read a good book. There was music from multiple speakers and a basketball game was in progress on televisions at three different spots high on the walls. We drank our beers and practically shouted at each other.

"I think that went well."

"What?"

"The audition."

"What? I can't hear you."

"Let's get out of here."

We wandered through Washington Square and headed in the general direction of Rain's apartment. It was a cool night, sometime near midnight (neither of us bothered to check the time). She reached for my hand, and we held hands while strolling Christopher Street. We stood for a while in front of the Stonewall. "So this is where it happened," I pondered.

"Yep. This is the place."

We strolled over to a little park at Seventh Avenue, where we sat on a bench and I smoked a cigarette. She said, "You know, you really ought to think about telling that story about hitchhiking from New Orleans at Tally's. The bit about the whore giving you a freebee was funny and kind of sweet, as odd as that may seem, and then them chasing you. And then the part about those scary guys. What were they? A killer and a burglar?"

"A killer and a kidnapper."

"Yeah. That was one of the wildest things I've ever heard. I mean that actually happened to a real person I know. Did you just make up the part about saying your mother gave you the watch?"

I said, "No, I didn't make it up. I really did say that. I don't know why. It just popped into my head." I dropped my cigarette and ground it out underfoot and picked up the butt and sat it on the bench with the intention of carrying it to a garbage can before we left.

Just then the most delightfully weird thing happened. A tall man wearing a white wedding dress came gliding by on roller skates whirling about in and out of the halos of street lamps. "How lovely," Rain said. "Only in New York."

I responded with, "You've never been to New Orleans."

She said, "That bit about the watch seems like it was almost suicidal, like you were daring the guy to shoot you."

"I don't know," I said. "I don't think I had a death wish." And out of nowhere I thought about my mother, who never gave a me a watch or much of anything else. I could not remember my mother ever being affectionate. She took care of me well, made sure I was fed and clothed and all of that, but if she ever hugged me or kissed me, I don't remember it. I can't remember her ever laughing or being playful.

When I was five or six years old she walked me to the kindergarten and left me there as usual and never came back for me. I remember it well. The teacher called our house but never got an answer, and then called my father at work, and he said she was probably just a little late and would be there soon. But she didn't show up and didn't show up, and the teacher finally called my father again and he came and picked me up.

The woman who was my mother never came back. Did they eventually get divorced? I really don't know. I just know my dad raised me by himself from then on, until I was in the eighth grade when he brought home another woman who became like a mom to me even though they never got married. I called her by her first name, never Mom, because . . . because even though she never said it, I don't think she wanted me to call her Mom. But I liked her. She was kind to me. It had never before dawned on me that when Debbi left me it brought up abandonment issues I had been suppressing pretty much all my life. Maybe that was why I made the risky decision, so unlike me, to hitchhike, and why I made up tales, inventing whole new personalities to present to the people who gave me rides.

Me, Debbi

Something totally unexpected happened. It started with the persistent noise of the front door buzzer. I didn't want to answer, but whoever was insisting on being answered would not give up and go away. I tried holding my hands over my ears. I tried burying my head in my pillow. It was mid-morning, I guess, not long after Bryce and I had the big argument and he hit me. He still hadn't come home. I was still in bed, having insisted I wasn't hungry when Martina tried to get me to get up and eat some breakfast. "I can make some waffles," she said. "I know you love them."

I said, "Go away." She was standing outside my door. She would never come into the bedroom without permission.

I heard her steps receding, and then blessed quiet for a little while, and then the buzzing. Martina came back to my door and said, "Somebody's buzzing."

I was like, "I know somebody's buzzing. Answer them. Tell them nobody's home."

The constant buzzing ceased, but there was a pounding in my temples that matched its rhythm like and echo that wouldn't go away. I could barely hear the mumble of Martina talking to whomever it was, but I couldn't make out the words. Then the click of her shoes on the hardwood floor again, and then she knocked on my door once more and said, "It's Mister Fisher, Bryce's father."

"I know who Mister Fisher is."

"He says he really needs to talk to you."

"Really, really, really. Well I really need some quiet. And a pain killer." I can't remember if I said that out loud or just thought it. I pulled myself out of bed and shuffled into the bathroom and found a bottle of Tylenol in the medicine cabinet. Downed two of them with a sip of water, then thought about it and shook two more out. From inside the bathroom I could hear Martina's voice but not her words. I wondered what Mister Fisher could possibly want with me. He hardly knew me. The few times we had visited with them, he had very little to say. The strong, silent type. His only interests seemed to be hunting and fishing and football, and I didn't think he even liked his son. So what in the world could he want to talk to me about? But then I thought something might have happened to Bryce. He could have been in an accident. He could be dead for all I knew.

I pushed and held the button on the intercom. "Are you still there?"

"Yes, I'm still here. This is Ron Fisher. Can I come up and talk to you please?"

I asked, "About what?"

"About Bryce. About Bryce and you."

Since he said "and you," I knew he was not coming with the news that Bryce had been in some terrible accident. I was like, "What about us?"

"Could I just come up, please?"

I hate it when they do that. Just answer my question, please, and not with another question. I said, "I'm not decent. Can't you just tell me over the intercom"

He said, "I'd rather not. Look, I talked to Martina. I know what happened. I know he hit you, and I know you want to hide your bruises. I understand. You're probably embarrassed. But believe me, I know my son. I know it's not your fault."

Somehow, he looked diminished when he stepped off the elevator, slump shouldered and inward looking. Not that his eyes had ever sparkled, perhaps when he was a younger man and before business and fatherhood and marriage to Moms had worn him down, but whatever light there might have been had been turned off. "Come in," I said. "You want me to ask Martina to get you anything?"

"A cup of coffee would be nice. And do you mind if I smoke?"

"No, not at all." I called Martina in and asked her to fetch him a cup of coffee and an ashtray.

Settled in with his coffee and cigarette, he said, "I don't know, I don't really care to know about, you know, whatever's going on between you and my son. It's none of my business." He was right about that. "But I know it ain't your fault. My son can be a mean S.O.B. sometimes. I reckon it's my fault, mine and Charlotte's. We let him get away with way too much when he was growing up. So far as Charlotte was concerned, he could do no wrong. He could'a driven that Mercedes of his eighty miles an hour right through the middle of downtown and she'd a said well the boy's just working off steam. I reckon we taught him that whatever he took it in his mind he wanted was his for the asking."

I noticed he never referred to Bryce by name but always as "my son" or "the boy." I figured that had to be significant, but signifying what, is something I couldn't figure out.

He told me they knew, even as far back as when Bryce was in high school, that he was having sex with Martina, but so long as it was just sex, they could nod and wink and pretend it wasn't happening. Boys will be boys, the code of the West or some such. Screwing 'em is fine, but loving 'em ain't. Not if they're below you, not if they're servants, especially not if they're not real Americans. I guess that was the sum of their feelings about their teenage son diddling the hired help.

Pops said, "She told me he hit her. Not just once neither, but a regular thing. That was not right. I can't abide with that. That was when I put a stop to it. I told him no son of mine had better ever hit a woman. I told him if he ever hit her again I would cut him off. No more working for the family business and no more money from me. Not a dime. Can you believe it, he said, 'That's all right. I'll get it all when you're dead,'" and I told him I'd take him out of my will too. That made him sit up and take notice. And now I'm gonna to tell him he ain't allowed to hit you either. One warning, and that's all."

I figured even giving him a warning was being too easy on him. Hadn't he already told him not to ever hit a woman, and am I not a woman? He ought to cut him off right now. But then I thought (how self-serving of me) if he cut him off while I was still living with him, that would be cutting me off too. Where would that leave me—so long as I was living with Bryce and with no way to make it on my own? And I thought I must be a bad person for thinking that.

He said he would help me in any way he could. "What do you need? What can I do for you?" he asked.

I said, "I don't know. Maybe nothing yet. Maybe let's wait and see what happens." I was being pulled in two directions at once. Part of me wanted to leave, to go back to New Orleans and rebuild the life I had abandoned. But there was still a pull from the part of me that fell for Bryce in the first place.

Before he left, Mister Fisher said, "You call me anytime, you hear? Day or night. I'll be there for you."

He was halfway through the door when an unexpected thought occurred to me and I called after him. "Pops, the first time we came to your house for supper something strange happened. When we got home I reached into my purse for something, and I pulled out a note that said 'Run, girl, run.' By any chance could that note have been written by you?"

"Why girl, I can't imagine me ever writing a note and slipping it into your purse. Whaddaya think? I'm in junior high?" He said it with a big smile, and there was a noticeable sparkle in his eyes. But maybe that was just the glint from the light over the door.

Me, David

We both got the part. Rain was cast as Agnes the drug-addicted waitress, and I got the part of the war vet, Peter. I got the call from Brenda, the stage manager, and I called Rain the moment I hung up. "I know," she blurted before even saying hello.

I had been at work when the call came. My boss at the flocking factory was a friendly and easy-going fellow. He said, "Okay, what's so important you have to stop working in the middle of the day to make a phone call?" He wasn't angry. It was one of those things you can just tell once you get to know someone.

"I got the part," I practically shouted. "And my girlfriend, she got the part too. I mean we both got parts in the same play." I had never before spoken of Rain as my girlfriend. "We're going to be doing a play together. Just like Susan Sarandon and Tim Robbins (my favorite actor couple), or like Brad and Angelina."

"You do know they got divorced, don't you?" was his smart-alecky rejoinder.

And I said, "Don't be a spoil sport."

Haruto said getting the part was great and I should take the rest of the day off to celebrate, which I did, gratefully. But there was nobody to celebrate with. Darren and Rain were both at work, Darren doing some job through the temp agency, and Rain at the new job she had started with the Post Office. So I went home, practically skipping as I walked the streets and stopping at a grocery store to buy a yellow marker. I Grabbed a Sam Adams from the fridge and slipped on a sweatshirt and stepped out on the fire escape with my script to start highlighting my parts. I read and re-read dialogue until Darren got home, loving in particular the parts in the end when my character starts going off the deep end explaining his paranoid fantasies. He was a real nut job.

"Whatcha doing, man?" Darren asked as soon as he got home and saw me out on the fire escape marking up pages."

"Highlighting my lines. I got cast. Me and Rain both. Can you believe it?"

"No I can't. Damn, that is great. We have to celebrate. Hey, tomorrow is story night at Tally's. We should go, me and you and Rain."

We drank too much and laughed too hard at the stories told at Tally's, and Rain, in her playful and innocent way, took turns sitting on my lap and on Darren's. And she even put her name in the pot and got up and told an impromptu story about how we met and often went to auditions together and finally got cast in the same play. "It's coming up, folks, in two months at the Back Alley Theater."

Rehearsals were held in the same artists' loft where we had auditioned. We were still on book, it was in the middle of (I think) our third run-through when the director stopped us and said, "You should kiss now, and then we fade." End of the first act.

"There's no kiss in the stage directions," Rain said, and my immediate reaction was to feel rejected, like she didn't want to kiss me.

The director said, "It doesn't have to be. She's asking you to go to bed with you. It would be pretty freaking natural. Now let's see it. Drop the books. Surely you can be off book for one freaking line."

I didn't like his attitude, but I did like that he wanted us to kiss. I wanted us to kiss too. But if it wasn't in the play it probably never would happen. So here's the thing, a make believe kiss in a play is still a kiss. Rain flashed a reassuring smile my way and then to the director, she said, "Okay. One kiss coming up."

She said the line where Agnes asks Peter to go to bed with her, which was highly appropriate because if it ever happened with us not on stage, it would be her doing the asking, not me. We tossed our scripts to the floor, and we kissed. Simple as that. Perfunctorily, passionlessly.

"No! Not like that," the director grumbled. "Do it like you mean it."

So we kissed again, and again he complained. "Come on, guys. Have you never been in love? I want it to be like you just discovered your feelings for each other and you want to devour each other. Rain mock-growled at me and laughed, and then she said the line and we kissed like we meant it, and—that time we did it right.

A few weeks later I tried to tell the same story at Tally's Rain had told about how we met at an audition, fudging the truth to claim the audition for *Bug* was the one where we met, and telling about our first stage kiss. I rehearsed for the storytelling as diligently as we rehearsed for the play. The big difference was for the storytelling at Tally's I was the writer and the director, and I kept changing the story to try and create the feeling for what that kiss was like without making it sound like something out of some sugary love poem.

The easy way would have been to say it was electric, that there were sparks, that I was dizzy. But it wasn't like that at all. That's what I had felt with Debbi, not with Rain, and as beautiful and all-encompassing as it was with each in their separate ways, let's face it: that is passion but it isn't love. It isn't real. It never has been. (What horribly misleading role models Romeo and Juliet were!) What I felt with Rain in the staged kiss and what I still feel for her was (is) something different.

I guess I don't know what love is. Who does? There's agape, Biblical love, the love Jesus preached, the love of Gandhi, Nehru, Mohammed, yeah, that I get. That's not a feeling; that's a doing. That's what someone at the Catholic Worker described as doing for others without hope or expectation of personal reward—a goal we all should strive for, that I strive for and always fall short of. And it is or should also be a part of romantic love. I say that because I think it is important, because I suspect that any love entered into as if diving into a Hallmark card is doomed to failure. That's what Debbi and I did. The feelings we shared were like and unlike that sucker punch that slapped me when Rain and I kissed on the floor of that artist's loft.

We should not have been surprised when Darren told our story on stage at Tally's, but we were. The third time the story had been

156

told, each from a different point of view. He got up on that little stage and in less that the allotted five minutes he told about meeting a shy would-be actor while staying at the Catholic Worker and about how he taught me the ropes and how I was scared out of my wits the first time I auditioned, and the second and the third, and how we met an actress named Rain and how he (his unnamed friend; i.e., me) fell in love with Rain and she with him, but neither one of them (us) was willing to admit it, which made me and Rain give each other confusing signals and clink our glasses together, and finally how the two of us got cast in Tracy Letts' play *Bug*. And then he said, "Hey Johnny, can you point this spot at that table right there, the second one to the right? Right there, my friends, are the actors in this little story, my friends . . ." and he named us and told us to stand up and take a bow.

Me, Debbi

I made my escape in style. It was after Christmas. I had been living with Bryce more than a year, and in that time we had maybe ten reasonably happy days together. There was nothing dramatic about our parting of the ways. After that one time when he walloped me, we both knew it was just a matter of time. We tried to salvage whatever it was we had, and we got along okay, but we both knew there was nothing there. Yeah, he had once told me he'd track me down and come get me and bring me home if I ever left him. Like I was a cow that strayed off the ranch. "I'll spare no expense and no effort to find you," he said.

"Why? Why would you do that?"

"Because I love you."

And I was like, "That's not love. That's stalking. If you think that's like all romantic and stuff, you've got another think coming."

And he said, "Well all right then. I won't come after you. You're not worth it." If that was meant to hurt me, it didn't work.

So when it finally came to the time we both knew it was never going to work, he said goodbye and watched me walk away. Neither of us said anything about where I was going to go or how I was going to get there. The assumption was I would get Anders to take me to the bus station, or if he wasn't available I would walk. It wasn't too awfully far. And I'd catch a Greyhound. I had enough money for a ticket and probably enough to live on for a month if I was frugal. I got all that from Bryce's petty cash stash. figured I could stay with Stormy until I got a job. Unlike in my previous fantasy about it, I wasn't going to have to go incognito, and I was sure Jazzy would give me back my old job dancing at Lipstix. I was Jazzy's favorite. Thinking I wouldn't have to go begging for work at any of the other clubs—let's face it, the other sleazier clubs—was quite a relief.

I had two hours to kill at the bus station, and while I was waiting I thought about Pops. I had been so afraid of him at first, and I had entertained such a messed-up picture of him in my head before I met him. Never would I have expected a guy with trophy animals all over his house to be so kind and gentle as he turned out to be. I decided to call him and tell him goodbye, thank him for treating me so nicely. I thought it would be a two-minute call—Hi, it's me, Debbi. Bryce and I have decided to go our separate ways. I just wanted to call to say goodbye and thanks for being nice to me. But he showered me with questions. "Where are you? Where are you going? How are you going to get there? Is this separation for good? He didn't hit you again, did he? How long before the bus gets there?" Somewhere in there he wedged in the statement that he was really sorry it hadn't worked out between me and Bryce, although it didn't surprise him that it hadn't, and he hoped I would be okay, and then he said, "You wait right there. My driver will be there to take you where you're going."

"I'm going to New Orleans," I said. "He can't take me all the way down there."

"Sure he can," Pops said.

It couldn't have been more than fifteen or twenty minutes before his driver showed up. I was somewhat surprised I had never seen him before, but then I hadn't seen Pops very often either. The driver was a big man. Looked like he might have been a former football player, and it turned out he really was—a defensive tackle for the Cowboys. He was gentle and kind, and he even wore a kind of chauffeur uniform in navy blue with a matching cap. He had no trouble picking me out of the crowd of people waiting in the station. I saw him open the door and knew immediately he had to be the driver. He looked around quickly and marched directly to me and said, "Miss Debbi, I am Tuma, Mister Fisher's driver. My friends call me T-Man?"

I liked that. I said, "Can I call you T-Man?"

"You betcha," he said, all grins.

T-Man escorted me to a white Cadillac Escalade with white leather seats. He opened the back door for me, but I said, "Can't I sit up front with you?" I'd never been chauffeured and felt funny about it.

He said, "Yes ma'am, if you insist. But the TV's in the back."

"I'd rather talk to you if you don't mind." No way was I going to watch TV in the back seat of a car moving so smoothly and quietly down the freeway that it felt like we were floating in air.

We talked and talked. Well, I talked; he listened. And what did I talk about? Ha! I talked about David Parker and what a great guy he was, how smart and how sensitive. T-Man asked if David was waiting for me in New Orleans. Those might have been the only words he muttered the whole way other than "Uh huh" and "Yes ma'am." I had to tell him I really didn't know, that I hadn't heard from David since I left. I said, "I hope he'll be waiting for me. Oh my god, I do hope so."

I got excited when we skirted Lake Ponchartrain and felt the thrill of homecoming when I saw the old brick and wrought iron of the Quarter. I gave T-Man the address on North Galvez.

"This is it, right here. That one."

He offered to carry my bags in. I had a big suitcase on rollers and a smaller carry bag, both stuffed with clothes and shoes Bryce had bought for me. I said, "No, I've got 'em. Thanks a heap."

Nobody answered my bell ringing. I sat on the stoop and waited. I started getting hungry and finally felt so hungry I couldn't wait any longer. I lugged my suitcases six blocks to Steamboat Suzie's and ordered a shrimp salad. I tried calling Crawdads. They said David didn't work there anymore. "He's been gone a year or more." They said he moved to New York. I asked if he maybe left an address or phone number. Whomever I was talking to (he made it clear he knew me, but I didn't remember him, whatever name it was he gave me) said, "You know David. He never owned a cell phone. He's just gone, man, gone like yesterday's gumbo."

I trudged back to North Galvez and rang the bell again. This time somebody answered, but it wasn't Lucy or Randy or Hopper. It was an old man who made me think of Uncle Remus. He said, "Them young'uns don't live here no more. It's just me and my Lilly and our little granddaughter Katie. But looka here, honey, you look like you been abandoned. You wanna come on in her and maybe call somebody?"

"Yes sir. Thank you. That's mighty nice of you."

It turned out that granddaughter Katie was a grown woman probably not much younger than me. She asked if I would take some coffee or tea, and I thanked her and took her up on a cup of tea.

I called Lipstix and got a hold of Stormy. She said of course I could stay with her. Katie said she could take me. I felt like Blanche in *A Streetcar Named Desire*. I didn't tell her that Stormy didn't get off until three o'clock in the morning. I was afraid she would insist on waiting with me in the courtyard if I did.

Anyway, that's pretty much my story, for what it's worth. I went back to dancing at Lipstix, and I found myself a new boyfriend. His name was Hopper. Yes, that Hopper, our old roommate from when I was with David. I didn't love him the way I loved David, and he wasn't rich like Bryce, but he was kind to me. He was fun to be with. He was well read, which has always been an important thing for a friend or partner. We had similar taste in literature and movies, and he didn't mind me stripping. After all, it ain't really stripping. I've explained that already. It's a sophisticated art form, and I'm damn good at it, if I do say so myself. We never take it all off anyway, just down to pasties and a g-string. Oh, and I'm back to cussing again. No sense in imposing such arbitrary restrictions on my natural inclinations. Besides which, I could not have survived the end with Bryce without a slew of juicy cuss words.

Me, David

*B*ug was not as successful as we had hoped. It ran for six weeks, and we managed to get a good many butts in seats most nights in the first week, six nights a week and twice on Sunday. We even got reviewed in some of the smaller papers and blogs. One reviewer called me an exciting newcomer. After the first week, however, audiences started thinning out, and we ended up playing to audiences of fewer than a dozen and once to one old woman in a red hat.

It's been almost eight years since I landed in New York. It's Christmas week. I don't recall the exact date of my arrival in the city, but I celebrate the week leading up to Christmas as my New York anniversary, and I always mark the week as a time to take stock, see how I'm doing. Not bad, if I do say so myself. Haruto offered me a partnership in the business, and I took him up on it. I'm doing more supervising now than hands-on work, and I'm making a lot more money. Haruto thinks of me as a son. He's single, always has been, and never had children of his own. As a partner in the business (and pseudo son), I can usually take time off whenever I need to, so that makes it possible to keep acting. I've done four shows now, all as far off Broadway as you can get and still be in New York. Two of them with Rain. We're starting to call ourselves Bogart and Hepburn, playfully of course. And Darren is doing great. He's now playing Chelsea's boyfriend, Billy Ray, in a revival of *On Golden Pond*. Still not on Broadway, but a pretty big theater. Rain and I kid that we're honored he still deigns to speak to us.

Storytime at Tally's has become something of a big deal. It's three nights a week now, and they have "headliners." That's what they call them (us)—up-and-coming actors or comedians who serve as hosts and tell stories or jokes. Tally's always posts the headliner's head shot in a glass-fronted display board on the outside of the building. "Storytelling with your host Darren Pressman" That kind of thing. The headliners get a stipend, twenty-five bucks. For everybody else it's still open mic and no pay. Darren is a frequent headliner, and I've been the headliner twice. I tell stories about Debbi and our crazy housemates in New Orleans, and I've told tales about the time I hitchhiked to New York. I'm always nervous as all get-out before I start, but once I start talking the nerves settle down. I might as well be talking to a handful of friends.

So let's back up a year. It was Christmas Eve-eve, and I was the headliner. The place was packed. Rain and Darren were in the audience, seated at a table close to the stage. "The better to heckle you," Darren kidded.

I told a story with hardly an iota of truth to it about when I first met Debbi. I started out with, "You know what New Orleans is famous for? I mean other than Mardi Gras and jambalaya and Dixieland jazz. Strippers. That's what. Badda boom, badda boom. Twirling titty tassles. Every place on Bourbon Street is either Dixieland jazz or twirling titty tassles. So it was on a night like tonight, cold and rainy with Christmas lights up and down the street and strippers taking off their clothes to the beat of "Jingle Bell Rock."

My housemates, Lucy and Randy and Hopper had forced me to go with them to this raunchy strip club called Lipstix. The announcer, a very fat and painfully unfunny comedian, introduced the next performer, a lady called Darlin' Debbi, a little woman barely more than five feet tall with huge ringlets of coal black hair and gorgeous tattoos all over her body. And believe-you-me, it didn't take me long to see the proof that her tattoos were indeed all over her body, because she went into a slow and sensuous dance with her slim body like an undulating snake and started taking stuff off until there was nothing on her body but ink."

"That's a bloody lie!' a woman's voice cried out from the darkness out front. I was floored. Because it was Debbi's voice. I'd recognize it anywhere. She stood up and started making her way toward the stage, squeezing herself between tables and talking as she walked; and Johnny, the guy running the lights, spotted her. It was her. In the flesh. Shorter hair and that perfect body hidden under a bulky sweater, but unmistakably the Debbi I remembered. I felt like somebody had hit me in the stomach. I lost my breath, and I think I might have started crying. She brazenly walked up to the stage and said, 'I was never a stripper. I was a high-class burlesque performer. I was the queen of Bourbon Street. I was entertainment royalty. And I never took it all off. Never. You know that. If I had, there would have been men passing out on the spot from sheer ecstasy. And women, too.'"

When she stepped up on the stage, we clasped each other in a big hug and held each other long and hard, and when we finally broke apart—not really breaking apart but turning to face the audience with our arms still around each other, I said to the audience, "Oh my god, oh my god, ladies and gentlemen, this is Darlin' Debbi, Debbi Mason. Debbi is the dancer I was talking about. Debbi was the love of my life. I haven't seen her in eight or ten years."

I don't know if the audience thought it was an act or if they got it that I was totally surprised when Debbi shouted from her table in the audience, but they broke into applause. I said, "Let's take a little break, folks," and we stepped off the stage and joined Darren and Rain at their table, and I introduced Debbi to them.

Me, Debbi

F inding David was easy, since he had finally joined the twenty-first century and got on social media. He had a Facebook page and a Linked-in account. I sent him a friend request, and we exchanged emails. When Hopper and I went to New York, we let him know we were coming, but I didn't tell him we were going to Tally's the night he was headlining story night. I wanted that to be a surprise. I didn't tell him Hopper and I were a couple, either. I thought that needed to be in person. He hadn't told me he was with another woman either, but I should have expected it.

It must have been three or four months after I returned to New Orleans that Pops contacted me again. Despite me and Bryce breaking up and despite Moms' unreasonable dislike of me, Pops had taken a real liking to me. I was like a daughter to him. Some of that, I guess, was because he was so ashamed and angered that he had not protected me from Bryce. Part of it was because his son had turned out to be such a sorry excuse for a human being, and Pops felt a lot of responsibility for that. I guess he wanted to be a good father to someone, and I was perforce that someone.

Pops fronted the money for the Debbi Mason School of Dance. I told David about it that night after meeting him at Tally's. After his part of the show was over but long before the club closed down for the night, the four of us wandered down to Washington Square Park with a bottle of wine in a brown paper sack, and huddled close together in our winter coats, we talked long into the early hours about all the things we had done together and separately since the time I stupidly abandoned David in New Orleans. That night was one of the most special nights in my life. From the moment I stood up and shouted, "That's a bloody lie!" my heart was in my throat, and I was shakier than I had ever been in my life. But I did not dare let David or

165

anyone else know how scared I was, determined to put on for him the bold and brash face I had always worn.

We all knew that David and Rain together and Hopper and I together would live out the rest of our lives as we should, with few regrets.

Nine Stories

Hot on the Tracks

Janet and Brad could not have picked a better time for a train trip to San Francisco. Record heat was predicted for the usually balmy Pacific Northwest, while down in the Bay Area early August temps were predicted in the high seventies and lower eighties—ideal for lounging around Janet's sister's pool.

On the night before departure their neighbors Ralph and Margie stopped by to have a beer with Brad, as they often did, India Pale Ale for Ralph and Janet and for Brad a Dick Danger Ale, a rich dark beer brewed by a local craft brewery in the nearby town of Centralia. Margie drank tap water, no ice. They watched Rachel Maddow, and Ralph and Margie talked through most of the show as they usually did. Their chatter irritated the hell out of Brad, but he didn't complain.

Janet, the constant organizer, waited until a commercial break to ask, "What time are we leaving in the morning?"

"Leaving for where?" Margie asked.

"The train station. Remember? You're taking us to the train station."

"Shit. Is that tomorrow?"

"Yes. We've been talking about it for a week."

Margie said, "Oh gosh, I forgot all about it."

"Me too," from Ralph. "What time does your train leave?"

"Eleven."

"Ah heck. All right, I'm gonna have to get you there a little early. I'm playing golf with Paul, and we gotta get there and get in nine holes before the heat hits. It's supposed to be up in the nineties. I'll have to drop you off no later than nine."

Way to go, asshole, Brad thought.

Continuing to bitch about the neighbors after they went home, Brad said, "Now we'll have to wait two freaking hours in the train station."

"Oh well, we'll have books to read on the train, and we can get some coffee. It won't be so bad."

Brad grumbled, "We should be given distinguished service metals for putting up with them. Why do we do it?"

"Because they're our neighbors and we're nice people?"

"Yeah. Geez. I hate that. And the way they chatter away while we're trying to watch TV makes me bananas."

"So why don't you ask them to be quiet while you're trying to watch the show?"

"I know I should."

"You don't have to be so damn polite to them. After all, it's our house and your beer."

Brad had been re-reading Hemingway's *The Sun Also Rises*, but he decided to bring something lighter, something mindless and escapist. He didn't want to have to think on his vacation. He picked from his bookshelf a copy of Twilight, the vampire story set not far from where they lived. It had been Margie's Christmas present to him six years ago when it first came out. He had never read it, of course. Had never seen any of the dumb movies either.

Up at seven the next morning, they were coffeed, breakfasted, packed and ready to go when Ralph banged on their door at eight-thirty. They tossed their suitcases in the back of Ralph's Rav 4 next to his golf bags. "Hurry up," Ralph said. He was anxious to get to the golf course.

Not a hundred feet from their house, they almost had a collision when Ralph turned right onto Twenty-sixth without looking both ways. An oncoming vehicle almost hit them. Ralph never even noticed. He blithely accelerated while the car behind them braked.

Not a good start, Brad thought.

Two miles farther on, Ralph slammed on his brakes at a four-way intersection, shouting, "Damn! There's a stop sign. I almost didn't see it."

This does not bode well for this trip, Brad thought. It crossed his mind that they might not even get to the train station in one piece. But they did.

Ralph wheeled his Rav into the sparsely filled parking lot at the Centennial Amtrak station in Lacey at precisely 9 a.m. It was already getting hot. A few people were waiting outside by the tracks and a few more were standing by the door waiting to get in. Brad and Janet lugged their baggage up to the door where they saw a sign stating that the station opens at 8 a.m. "Damn," Brad said. The station attendant was an hour late, and Brad's blood was boiling.

Half an hour later someone showed up to open the doors. He was a bustling little man with a handlebar mustache who profusely apologized. "This is only the second time in the twenty-four years this stationhouse has been open that an attendant has failed to show up to open on time. Luckily, a city bus driver called me. Sorry, folks"

For the waiting passengers who were now finding seats inside, he gave a brief history of the station, which was built by local volunteers and had been staffed by volunteers for all those years. The bantam rooster of a station master was right proud. "I was on the team that built this station. I installed these lights my own self."

Brad wanted to hear the porter shout "All aboard!" But the porter, a tall, handsome Black man with gleaming white teeth, did not shout out the time-honored phrase. He took their bags and helped them into the car. He introduced himself as Stanley, and—what with his uniform and solicitous manner—made Brad think they had stepped back in time to the heyday of Pullman trains. All that was missing was a big gold watch on a long watch fob. "Welcome to the Coast Starlight," he said, and took Janet's hand to help her in.

Stanley led them forward as far as the car went, opened the door to their sleeping compartment and set their luggage down. "You have a twelve-fifteen lunch reservation. You'll be called when it's time. Take the stairs to the upper cars and go back three cars. If you want drinks before lunch, you can stop off in the lounge. Call me when you're ready for bed tonight and I'll let down the beds."

They settled in and watched an elderly couple across the way get situated in their seats and then close the curtain. The old man's hands shook as he lowered himself to his seat. His wife wrapped a shawl around her shoulders. In Brad and Janet's sleeping compartment, two cushioned seats faced each other with a pull-down bunk above. "Comfortable seats," Brad said.

"Uh huh. This is nice."

They watched out the window as the train pulled out of the station and gathered speed. Soon they heard an announcement: "Eleven-thirty lunch reservations may now come to the dining car." A door opened to an adjacent room in front of their car and a family stepped out. Mother, father and teenaged son. All three were tall and thin, elegantly dressed in mostly black clothing. The father had a shock of blond hair. The mother's hair was long and black with a silver streak—natural or dyed, Brad could not tell. She looked too young to be going gray. The son was wearing an Oakland Raiders cap. All three carried themselves stiffly erect and looked straight ahead. Brad said, "Hey there, neighbors," but they ignored him.

Snooty, he thought. He felt a chill. And something dawned on him that he had not thought about at first. He parsed it out bit by bit. First, the neighboring families room had to be bigger than theirs in order for three people to sleep in it. Second, their room had to be in the very front of the train because the passageway ran right to their door and stopped, but that was impossible because he clearly remembered they had walked toward the rear of the train to get to their car, and he had seen many cars in front. So how could you get in front of them? Would you have to go to the upper level and walk past them and back down? That seemed very, very odd.

Soon the train slowed down as it pulled into the station in Centralia, home of Dick's Brewery, the town's one claim to fame other than labor wars sixty years ago. He wondered if they served Dick's beer in the dining car. The station was on the opposite side of their compartment, so all Brad and Janet could see through their window was what looked to be the back of a warehouse and a raggedy yard inside a chain-link fence with two antique cars parked in the grass, neither of which looked like they could be driven. It didn't even look like they were being restored but had been parked there and left to rust as grass grew all around.

"I kind of forgot that trains always go through the most rundown parts of town," Brad said. "I guess we can forget about a scenic route."

But they soon did see some beautiful scenery from the lounge car where Brad was able to order a beer almost as good as Dick's. Janet had a lemonade. They sped past mountainous terrain on the left and rivers and streams on the right, past the towns of Longview and Kelso. They hoped to catch sight of Mount Rainier and Mount St. Helens, but were not able to see either. What they did catch sight of was the vampire family, which was what Brad had started thinking of them as. They were in the dining car ahead. From where Brad and Janet were seated, they appeared to be not speaking to one another and not particularly enjoying their meal. When they finished eating and passed by going back to their room, Brad once again tried to greet them, and once again they walked by without so much as a nod.

The twelve-fifteen reservations were called, and they were escorted to their table. The waiter explained to them that it was Coast Starlight tradition to seat diners with different table mates at each meal to encourage them to get to know each other—where are you from, where are you going—it made the trip more enjoyable for everyone. Brad and Janet were introduced to their table mates, June and Rod Barefoot, a Muckleshoot Indian couple on their way to Las Vegas for a bookseller's convention. The Barefoots owned a small, independent bookstore in Seattle.

"I imagine you sell a lot of Sherman Alexie's books," Brad said.

"Yeah, we do," Rod Barefoot said. "But don't jump to conclusions. It's not like we cater to Native American readers."

"Oh no, I wasn't thinking that."

"Actually," June put in, "that book you got in your hand is one of our best sellers. The whole series."

June said, "You know that's based on an actual event, don't you? A series of events, in fact."

"No, I didn't know that." Of course it wasn't, but he decided it wasn't worth arguing. He listened politely as she told how there had been a series of disappearances in and around the town of Forks on the Olympia Peninsula. "It was kids who came up with the fantasy that there were vampires in the woods. It became a fun thing to spread the rumors, and I guess people believed some of the missing people had been turned into vampires. It was pretty brilliant of the writer, if you ask me, to turn the legends into a whole series of novels."

"Damn crazy Indians," Brad said to Janet after they were back in their compartment.

"They were putting us on."

"Yeah. Damn crazy fun Indians."

After a stop in Portland there was an announcement that the train had to limit its speed to fifty miles per hour due to excessive heat. It was over a hundred degrees outside. "I wonder what the heat's got to do with the speed," Brad said.

"I don't know," Janet said. "Maybe when it's hot and dry they're afraid sparks from the rails will start a fire."

Brad was reading the vampire novel. Periodically he stopped reading and spent long minutes looking out the window. It was amazing to see how fast things zipped past even though the train had slowed down, much faster, it seemed, than when the landscape rushed past when driving a car on the highway at even higher speeds. He figured that was because they were much closer to cliffs and trees than when on the highway. Sometimes the sheer faces of hills or mountains were so close that if he could open the window he could reach out and touch them. He couldn't imagine what that would be like. It would probably rip his hand to shreds. When another train passed by on another track it seemed the trains were going a hundred miles an hour or faster. When they crossed a bridge, the dizzying empty drop-off was right at the edge of the tracks. A rock on the tracks could sling them off into the abyss. It was as thrilling and terrifying as a roller coaster ride.

At dinner that evening that were seated at a table with Ronnie and Jimbo, a gay couple from Portland heading to Los Angeles. Brad and Janet ordered the grilled Norwegian salmon with wild rice and green beans, Ronnie had the roasted chicken breast and Jimbo—a bear of a man if there ever was one—ordered the vegetarian pasta.

"We're going to Hollywood," Ronnie said. "We're going to break into the movie business or die trying."

"The latter is the most likely," Brad said.

Janet said, "Now, Brad."

Jimbo said, "We've both done some acting, and Ronnie has written a screen play. We know it might be a pipe dream, but we're willing to do whatever it takes to get a foot in the door. Fetching coffee for the crew. Whatever."

Brad said, "You want a . . . what do they call it . . . a project that's surefire. Vampires and trains. Vampires are hot. And look around you. There's such a rich cast of characters right here on this train. We had lunch we a couple of Indians. American Indians, not from India. There's rich and poor, a potpourri of fascinating characters. Look at that family over there, tall, proud, aloof. Who do you imagine they are? They could be your vampires. And that fat dude all by himself in the lounge wearing a Seahawks jersey? He could be your first victim. The pitch could be Dracula meets The Orient Express in modern day California."

Ronnie laughed. "Hell, you oughta go to Hollywood. You could have those studio execs eating right out of your hand."

Janet rolled her eyes and said nothing.

Brad said, "Speaking of vampires, those Indians we had lunch with told us the most fascinating story. You know the Twilight series? Did you know it was inspired by a series of real-life events?" and he proceeded to elaborate on the tale to make it sound convincingly true.

Both couples retired to the lounge after dinner but there were not available seats for them to sit together. "God, I think they believed me about the Twilight series," Brad said. "Crazy gay dudes. Going to make it big in Hollywood. Shee-ish."

Janet said, "You ought to be ashamed of yourself."

"Oh, I am, honey. Really I am."

They watched the sun set in the west, and then retired to their compartment, and Brad sought out Stanley the porter and asked him to turn their beds down. The facing seats pulled together to make the lower bed, Janet's, and Stanley pulled down a shelf with a thin mattress for the top bunk, Brad's. Brad tipped him five-dollars. He noticed an odd glint to Stanley's eyes from the way the light struck him.

Brad turned out the light. There was plenty enough light oozing in from the passageway. Uncomfortably lying down on the bunk, he could see only the top few feet of the passageway on one side and out the slice of window only a few lights that flickered by like fireflies as the train sped through the night. Suddenly it became pitch black as the train went into a tunnel. Goddamn long tunnel, Brad thought. They rode through the blackness for minutes and minutes and minutes, and when they finally came out he saw movement through the top part of the door. The old man from across the aisle opened his door and stepped out. Brad could see him only from his shoulders upwards. He stood a moment, and then turned, then turned again as if disoriented. Maybe he was sleepwalking. Then the man from the front room stepped out, his blond hair like a puffy white cloud. The two men circled each other as if each were saying to the other, "You go first." And then the tall, elegant, blond man pounced on the frail elderly man and sunk his teeth into his neck and slung his arm around his shoulder and quickly dragged him into his room.

Brad must have been dreaming. Ten minutes later the old woman stepped out, searching perhaps for her missing husband. And swift as the lights flashing past the train, the vampire stepped out and whisked her into their room as well.

The next morning Brad said to Janet, "I had the strangest damn dream last night. It was really disturbing and seemed so real."

"Probably that salmon we ate. It was super rich."

Greeting the new day and in preparation for coming into a major destination, San Francisco, people were in and out of their compartments, a constant shuffling in the aisle, Stanley was busy converting passenger's beds back into seats. The family that had been so formal and aloof the day before stepped out into the aisle with bright smiles. "Good morning," the father said. "It's going to be a great day."

In the aisle and up the stairs and in the dining car, Brad and Janet saw what must have been every person on their end of the train, but they never saw the old couple from the compartment across from theirs. "There might have been some stops during the night that we slept through," Janet said. "They probably got off."

"Yeah, you're probably right."

Later, stopped at the station and while dragging their luggage out into the passageway, Brad noticed what looked like a spot of blood on the floor. "Let's go," he said, and they stepped off onto the platform.

He left his book on the seat in their compartment.

Ruination

Liz and Mandy were putting hands all over the items in the Shop-N-Go, picking stuff up, holding knick-knacks and toys to look at them from various angles, trying on hats and sunglasses, and generally driving the store clerk nuts trying to keep an eye on them. Liz and Mandy were sisters, thirteen and fifteen years old. Liz, with a mound of orange hair piled on top of her head and wearing a yellow shirt and green shorts, was the younger of the two. Mandy, the older sister, was more sedate in style, with a tan raincoat over a white shirt and tan pants.

It had been raining earlier but had stopped, and bright sunlight streaked through the shop windows.

Glancing to see if the shopkeeper was looking—he wasn't, he was checking out a customer buying a six-pack of beer and a bag of potato chips—Mandy picked up a disposable cigarette lighter and dropped it into the deep pocket of her raincoat. Mandy didn't smoke and had no use for a cigarette lighter. She knew it would end up in the junk drawer with all the other useless items she had shoplifted.

The girls left the shop without buying anything, and walked three blocks to Grayson's, a drugstore with a lunch counter, a coin shop in one corner, and a back room where the town's movers and shakers met to talk politics and make deals. Their grandfather, Clyde Grayson, owned the store and was one of those movers and shakers, a longtime member of the city council and a major donor to the state Democrats. Billy Brown, movie-star handsome in his white shirt and jeans, was the only customer in the store at the time. He was drinking coffee at the lunch counter. "Hi there, Mister Brown," Mandy chirped. "How are you today?"

"Just fine, Miss Grayson. What are you girls up to?" She loved being called Miss Grayson like she was a grownup.

"We're fixing to go down to the Ritz to see Butch Cassidy and the Sundance Kid."

"Is that thing still playing? Ya'll must'a seen it a bunch a times."

"Just about a gazillion," Liz said. "I could watch it a gazillion more."

"And just what is it you're coming in here for, as if I didn't know?" their grandfather asked.

"Money for tickets and popcorn," Mandy said.

"I ought'ta make you girls work for your money," their grandfather said with a chortle, pulling out his wallet and fishing out a twenty and handing it to Mandy. "Tell the mayor to come by later." The town mayor was also the owner and operator of the Ritz, a movie theater greatly in need of repair that showed nothing but old films. The mayor and Clyde and a few other old timers decided what shows to show—almost exclusively hit movies from their younger days.

After the girls left, Clyde said, "I really oughta put those girls to work. They need to learn to appreciate where their money comes from."

Billy Brown said, "Youngsters nowadays don't appreciate anything."

"Ain't that the truth? I don't hold out much hope for the younger generation. But Liz and Mandy, they're okay. They been raised right."

Billy said, "I don't hold out much hope for this town, neither. Looks like just about everything's going to hell."

"Ain't that the truth," Clyde said.

"I see that Greg Johnson's place is closed and boarded up, and Town Hardware."

"Uh huh. You gotta drive all the way to the Walmart in Smithville if you want to buy a chainsaw or a decent drill. Everything's drying up. There ain't no money no more ever since they re-routed the railroad."

Billy Brown had been back in town only a week, having been living out on the coast for close on to a dozen years. He said he wanted to check the town out and see if it looked like a place he could set up business. Billy had made a fortune as a developer out there in

California, and Clyde and some of the other good old boys in town hoped he would settle in and bring some of his magic back to the town of Burr. He reached in his shirt pocket and extracted a pack of Lucky Strike filter tips. "Can I hit you up for one of them cigs?" Clyde asked, and then noticing the pack was squashed flat said, "Lessen that's your last one. I wouldn't want to take your last cigarette."

"Nah, I got one more. I'm saving it for after dinner. Then it's going to be my last one forever. I swear. I promised Honey I'd quit and I'm gonna do it. I'm gonna save this one for just the right time and really savor it. My last smoke for a lifetime." Clyde took a cigarette and handed the pack back to Billy. Billy pulled the last one out and stuck it behind his ear and crumpled up the empty pack and tossed it in the garbage can.

"I reckon I'm gonna head on out, Clyde, walk around a bit, try to get my bearings, see what I can remember of the old town. Thanks for the coffee. It's good seeing ya."

Clyde said a silent prayer: Please, Lord, don't let him go south of Front and Market.

Billy Brown left a fiver on the counter and walked out to Main Street and headed east to Front and south on Front to Market. He spotted a cigarette lighter someone had dropped on the sidewalk and picked it up, tested it to see that it worked, and shoved it in his pants pocket.

He saw the Grayson girls in the clothing store next door to the Ritz.

Mandy took two skirts off the rack and headed into the changing booth, coming out a few minutes later wearing one of the skirts and twirling around for Liz's approval. "That one looks all right," Liz said, "But I think I like the other one better. Try it on and lemme see."

Before they managed to get out of the store, they ended up purchasing both skirts and a shirt for Liz. They paid with their mother's credit card, knowing that when the bill came their mother would pay it without noticing what was on it. Mother was unconscious that way.

They were already late for the start of the movie. A few minutes more wouldn't matter, and Mandy wanted to smoke the cigarette she had stashed in her raincoat pocket. Reaching for it, she felt the cigarette but not the lighter. Fingering the lining of the pocket she discovered a good-size hole. "Crapola. I lost the lighter."

There would be any number of their friends in the movie, and she could hit one of them up for a match or a lighter after the film.

Still headed south on Market, Billy Brown reached behind his ear for the cigarette. He put it between his lips but didn't light it.

That part of town was nothing but blight. Store fronts with smashed windows or plywood sheets covering the windows, most of the buildings empty, and the ones that were occupied run-down and dirty. Hardly anybody on the streets, neither cars nor pedestrians. Where two streets came together down by the railroad track, his old favorite sandwich shop still stood. What a strange shop it had been back when he was in school, three barstools at the counter and two old fashioned school desks serving as a makeshift booth by the window. The baldheaded Greek who used to own the place no longer stood behind the counter. Instead, a woman Billy recognized as the Greek's daughter was dishing up the same goopy roast beef sandwiches he had loved in his youth.

"What'll you have, buddy?"

"Roast beef of course," he said while squeezing into one of the old desks. And then, "You don't recognize me, do you?"

"I'm afraid not."

"Billy Brown. We went to school together. I haven't been back in town for nearly thirty years."

"Oh my God, yes, I do remember you. How are you?"

"Fine. And you?"

"Could be better, but it don't do no good to complain."

"Tell me 'bout it."

They reminisced about old times, who had died, who had moved on, who was still in town. Do you remember that time when . . . blah, blah, blah, while Billy played with the found lighter, flicking it, watching the flame, and then shutting it off, waiting for his roast beef sandwich, watching the way she turned the meat on the grill just the way her father used to. The daughter, now owner—he finally remembered her name, Cathy Demitrio—said, "I'm afraid this end of town is dead. I don't know how much longer I can hold out down here."

"Well I'm glad you're here. It's good to see you again." He took the cigarette out from behind his ear and tapped it on the desk. Across the street there was a bar in what used to be the kitchen entrance to the old Burr Hotel. The sign hanging over the door read Clancy's Saloon. Windows from the second floor and up were boarded over. A yellow light shone weakly from a window on the ground floor. There were two such lighted windows next door to the saloon. Billy Brown didn't know it, but this was the apartment of the bartender at Clancey's, Red Reid, and his girlfriend, Charlene, and their baby boy. The baby was five months old. Charlene was a drug addict trying her level best to kick the habit—for the sake of their baby. Red's older brother, Steve, owned the saloon. He let them stay in the dingy little apartment rent-free. Billy Brown saw that the glass was missing from three of the eight window panes.

Billy glanced out the window and spotted the Grayson girls walked past with a couple of boys. Mandy had ditched the trench coat somewhere. She and the boy she was with had arms around one another's shoulders. Liz's boyfriend had his hand in the back pocket of those gaudy, tight-fitting green shorts. Billy Brown noticed that the girls were acting a lot more grown-up than he had at first thought, and than they had seemed when in the drugstore with their grandfather. It also dawned on him that he must have spent a lot more time wandering around town than he thought. Either that or the Grayson sisters didn't go to the movie after all. Could they have already seen Butch and Sundance and were now wandering around with the boys? That didn't seem possible.

He left the sandwich shop and slowly walked in the direction the teenagers had taken, following a block behind them. He passed what was once the Sports Center, now a pile of rubble. He remembered hearing that the old sporting goods store had burned to the ground. Apparently no one had bothered to clear up the broken-down and charred shelves and display cases that were left behind in the ash. The kids ahead circled a block and headed back past the sandwich shop and Clancy's Saloon. Stepping into an alleyway next to the saloon entrance, they lit up what looked to Billy like joints and tossed the spent matches to the ground.

Near the door to Clancy's there was a concrete pillar that had once been the base of a statue of a man with a big beard and a derby hat. Billy had always assumed the man was some local hero from back when the town was first established as a railway hub. He had no idea who the man might have been, but whoever he was, he was long gone now. Billy decided it was time to smoke that cigarette he had been carrying. He sat on the pillar and smoked his cigarette. From where he sat, he could see Mandy and Liz and their weed-smoking boyfriends, but they could not see him. He watched them smoke their joint, and he saw the one boy slide his hand under the waistband of Liz's tight green shorts and down to grip the cheek of her ass, and he saw her grab his wrist and pull his hand away. Perhaps there was hope for decency in her after all.

Dark clouds began to gather. He finished his cigarette and flicked it toward the side of the building, and pushed himself up and walked away, heading back toward the west side of town where he was staying in a Best Western Plus.

He did not see the cigarette sail through the opening where one of the missing windowpanes should have been in the room where Red and Charlene's baby was sleeping. The cigarette landed on a stack of paper. A thin wisp of smoke rose from the edge of the papers, and glowed red before it burst into flame. The flame caught on a curtain next to the baby's crib and climbed up. The baby woke and started crying. Charlene, asleep in the next room, had no idea that her baby's room was on fire. Wiping the bar with a damp cloth and listening to The Doors on the jukebox next door, Red had no idea either. The only person who saw the smoke and then the glow of fire was the teenage boy who was kissing Mandy Grayson. "Fire!" he shouted, and the two boys ran toward the building that was on fire, followed closely by the girls.

Billy Brown, by then, was far enough away that he didn't hear the commotion. All he knew was that there were dark clouds overhead now, and wind was beginning to blow, and he had better get back to his motel before the storm hit.

The teenagers heard the baby cry. They tried to open a door to get in, but the door was locked. They could feel the heat of the fire on their hands and faces. Smoke was now pouring out the window. The oldest Grayson girl, Mandy, saw that the window pane was missing. Her boyfriend lifted her up to where she could crawl through the window. The other boy lifted Liz up in the same way. Mandy grabbed the baby out of his crib and rushed with him to the door and out onto the street. Liz found the mother asleep in her bed, could not wake her, so she lifted her by reaching under her arm pits and dragged her outside. By then, Red Reid had heard the commotion and rushed outside along with the few drinkers in the bar. He took the baby from Mandy. He hugged the girls and thanked them for saving his wife and baby. Cathy Demitrio came running out of the sandwich shop, and everyone celebrated the Grayson girls as heroes.

Time travels at a different rate of speed in the world of Clyde Grayson's eleven-and thirteen-year-old granddaughters, Amanda and Elizabeth, than it does in the world of the slightly older Liz and Mandy Grayson. Amanda and Elizabeth are playing with a Lego city and little plastic men and women. They have built a plastic town and populated it with plastic people, including little doll people representing their grandpa and other people they know plus people they have made up, about whom they fabricate elaborate stories featuring their daring self-avatars. Now they're tired of their game and decide to put away all the pieces. But first, Liz, as she always does, scatters the pieces all over the floor shouting, "It's a tornado!" Or a hurricane or an earthquake. That part of the story varies from time to time, but it always ends with them tossing the pieces one-by-one into a cardboard box. When they finish putting all the pieces away, Liz says, "Billy Brown is missing. Where is Billy Brown? He is her favorite little toy man and always plays a major role in their stories.

In Billy Brown's world, it is now hours past when he unknowingly tossed that cigarette through the window. He stopped at a store on his way back to his motel, and now he is seated under an awning by the pool in defiance of the wind and rain, smoking. It hadn't taken him long to give up on quitting once again. He is going to wait one more day and start over.

The twister roars down the street like Yosemite Sam throwing a hissy fit, and Billy jumps up to run for cover. But not fast enough. It's a small but powerful tornado that picks him up and hurls him through the air where he lands on grassy knoll thirty feet away. He hits the ground rolling, and he slides underneath a truck and stays there until the storm passes by, bruised and with a cut on his arm but otherwise unhurt.

"Here he is! I got him," Elizabeth says as she sweeps her Billy Brown doll out from underneath the couch.

The Littlest Football Player

(And earlier version of this story was published in Creative Colloquy)

From the time he was knee high to a grasshopper, Kevin Lumpkin's greatest ambition was to be a football hero. His twin brother Evan. Loved the game as well. The twins looked so much alike that half the time even their parents couldn't tell them apart. In high school they were the smallest kids in the whole school. Smaller than lot of the girls. But did that keep them from going out for football? From butting heads with guys big as the two of them put together? No way.

Kevin wanted to see his picture on the first page of the sports section in the Journal. Better yet, a picture of the two of them leaping for the ball. They'd seen that movie about Crazylegs Hirsh running like a dervish for the L.A. Rams. Their daddy had taken them to see Burt Lancaster in *Jim Thorpe—All-American*. Kevin wanted to be Crazylegs Hirsh; he wanted to be Jim Thorpe, All-American. Evan didn't share his brother's dreams of glory. He just liked to play the game but couldn't care less about getting his picture in the paper.

Over six seasons of junior high and high school football, the twins warmed the bench while waiting for a chance to play. On the practice squads they were used sparingly as running backs and tried their churning legs as kick returners, and finally were switched to defensive backs, which seemed absurd because they were too short to guard pass receivers, even though they certainly had the speed and could leap like crazy. They thought they were pretty damn good in practice, but Coach never seemed to notice. Kevin was convinced that coach was afraid to put them in a game for fear they'd get hurt and he'd get blamed for letting such little boys play. "Just 'cause we're

185

little don't mean we're more likely to get hurt than other guys," Kevin complained."

"Yeah, he thinks it's all right for us to get hurt in practice, but not in a real game. Oh yeah, that makes a lot of sense," was Evan's comeback.

Another reason they didn't get to play was that they did what the coaches told them. The supreme irony of that drove Kevin wild and made Evan mad as a crazed bumblebee. That was a big difference between them. When Kevin was overlooked or slighted in the least little way, he felt hurt; when Evan was overlooked, he got mad. But here's an example of what I mean when I say doing what the coach told them was one of the reasons he wouldn't put them in a game. On the grassy side of Hawkins Junior High the kids played a wild and dangerous brand of football at which the twins excelled. No uniforms, no pads, no teams, no scoring and no rules. They called it killer ball. On any given day there would be anywhere from fifteen to twenty kids playing. Someone would throw the ball up in the air and all the players would scramble for it. Whoever caught the ball or picked it up then ran in no particular direction, not going for a score but just running pell-mell around the field until he was either tackled or passed off to someone else. The twins were almost impossible to bring down. They were slippery as greased pigs. They could change directions in a flash, stop on a dime and spin out of tacklers' grasp, and each always had an eye on the other to be ready for a quick pass-off when trapped. Kevin often thought that if only the coach could see him running in those games he would realize what a talented runner he had on his team.

But running the ball from their backfield position in team practice was a wholly different kind of game. They were instructed to follow their blockers, who may or may not do their jobs. There were pre-planned patterns, and they had to keep moving forward. Never, never, never go back toward your own goal, coach said. The wild scrambles allowed on the school yard were not allowed on the practice field, and that took away the twins' greatest offensive weapon, their scrambling ability.

One day a new guy tried out for punt returner. He was short, almost as short as the twins, but fifteen to twenty pounds heavier. They watched the new guy catch a high punt and take off running toward the opposing goal. They watched him spin and change directions and circle back a good thirty yards toward his own goal—coach should have raised hell about that—and run toward the far sideline before heading up field again. He did all the things the coach had told them never to do. It was as if he was playing killer ball. That guy, that upstart, that where-the-hell-did-that-showboat-come-from-anyway, on his first day on the team, on his first punt return, scored a touchdown, and the whole team and the coach were screaming and jumping up and down on the sidelines like they thought he'd just scored the winning TD in the Rose Bowl. He was an instant hero and was the team's kick returner from then on.

It wasn't fair.

Finally, in their last season, in the last game for Tupelo High School, the coach put Kevin and Evan in as left and right cornerbacks. It was well into the fourth quarter and Tupelo was ahead by three touchdowns. The other team had the ball at midfield.

At five-foot-four and a hundred and twelve pounds (Evan was larger at a hundred and fourteen) Kevin was assigned to guard a six-foot-three, hundred and eighty-pound wide receiver. It had rained earlier in the day and the field was still soggy. The other players on the field were mud-splattered from kneepads to helmets. Evan and Kevin lined up ten yards deep in the secondary in their spotless purple and white uniforms. When the opposing receiver headed downfield, Kevin backpedaled a few yards and then turned and ran with him stride for stride, taking two churning steps to the other guy's every loping stride. The receiver made a sharp cut to his left, and Kevin tried to go with him. His cleats dug into the wet field and his foot refused to swivel along with his leg. He felt something move sideways with sudden and searing pain, and his right leg collapsed. It was his knee. As he lay on the ground in agony, the receiver angled to the other side of the field completely unguarded. Kevin tried to push himself up and take after him, but the moment he put weight on the injured leg his knee gave out and he crashed back down to the turf. From the ground he looked downfield and saw his brother Evan suddenly turn and rush to guard the open receiver just as the quarterback released a long lob of a pass that went wide of his target. Gaining ground with amazing speed, Evan leapt for the ball and easily picked off the pass. He hit the ground running, and with a couple of neat spin moves to avoid tacklers ran into the end zone.

The crowd went wild. Teammates mobbed him, slapped him on the back and on the side of his helmet, and ran with him off the field. Evan's touchdown on his first ever play in an actual game knocked the wind out of the other team. For the remaining five minutes or so they didn't even try. Both teams sluggishly went through the motions of letting the clock run down, while on the sidelines the Tupelo players comforted Kevin, saying, "Too bad" and "Hang in there, man" as a couple of second-string defensive linemen helped him hobble into the dressing room, helped him get dressed with coach hovering by, and carried him to the waiting ambulance.

An alert Journal photographer caught the interception on camera, but a copy editor made a mistake and credited the wrong twin. Both boys laughed at the mistake when reading the write-up from Kevin's hospital bed the next morning. The caption read: David and Goliath. Five-foot-four Kevin Lumpkin out leaps six-foot-three opponent in thrilling Tupelo victory.

Aikiko's Last Fight

Akiko Durant didn't much like boxing, but she was good at it and it provided her with a handsome living. She sometimes didn't much like her live-in boyfriend, who was also her manager, either. More precisely, she didn't like herself for liking him, but she was a sucker for his slick charm.

Akiko held the women's welterweight championship for ten years with a record of 86-2-0 until she was finally defeated by Dana Mitchell, a tall, blonde brawler who started her career in the ring as a wrestler popularly known as Dominatrix. The championship bout was a split-decision that boxing fans argued about for months while Dana the Dominatrix strutted her stuff in all the places where the in people were seen, while Akiko retreated from the public eye. Her only public appearances were when she was pictured in a suburban newspaper, once escorting her six-year-old son, Hiro, to his first day of school, and a second time when she worked with a local church's efforts to raise money for victims of a tsunami in the Philippians (pictured in the same suburban newspaper holding one end of a banner while the church's popular pastor held the other end). She did not appear to be particularly athletic in either photo. At a slim 140 pounds, the lowest weight in her division, Akiko looked more like a dancer than a boxer, especially in the sleek black dress she wore for the charity event.

A gorgeous woman with luscious lips, high cheekbones, and copper toned skin as unblemished as a baby's cheek despite having absorbed thousands of punches, Akiko was the most celebrated female boxer ever. She and her longtime manager and lover, Jimmy Joe Cranston, the proud father of her son, were worldwide celebrities far beyond sports circles, not so much for anything they had done (other than winning a boxing championship), but because of their glamour. Jimmy Joe dressed like a showboat gambler and wore his golden hair swept back in a tall pompadour, and she looked like a porcelain doll by his side. They were often pictured in celebrity magazines.

Twenty-five-year-old Dana Mitchell was twelve years Akiko's junior. Fans hated Dana Mitchell as much as they loved Akiko. Naturally larger than her ideal fighting weight, Dana had to starve herself before every bout to get down to welterweight size. Her style was lumbering, a brawler more than a boxer, and she was often accused of dirty tactics. In her wrestling career she had been the wrestler fans loved to hate. But her nastiness was an act, something Akiko understood since the two were friends when not in public settings.

The fans really hated Dana after she took the title away from Akiko, because not long after Dana became welterweight champion Jimmy Joe dropped Akiko and teamed up with Dana as both manager and lover. And then, to everyone's surprise, he left Dana and went back to Akiko, begging her to forgive him and take him back. Her fans howled, "No, never take him back!" Imagine if you can, and if you're old enough to remember, how Americans would have felt if Eddie Fisher had dumped Elizabeth Taylor and gone back to Debbie. Should she or shouldn't she take him back became a hot topic on social media and in the popular press for a few short months. But take him back she did. For the sake of the child, she told herself. So, it was not long before all was forgiven and Jimmy Joe and Akiko were America's favorite couple again. And once again she did not like herself for liking him.

And then Akiko announced she was going to come out of retirement. At the age of forty-one, when few of her fans believed she could do it but fervently hoped she could, Akiko Durant met Dana Mitchell again in a championship bout.

It is now six o'clock in the evening of the bout. Madison Square Garden is quiet, only a few maintenance workers near the ring, the big lights not yet turned on, someone doing a sound check. Akiko shows up two hours before the bout to work out in the ring with Jimmy Joe as was her custom. She climbs into the ring and drapes her robe across the ropes. Moving with grace, punching Jimmy Joe's oversized punching mitts with sharp jabs, working more on movement than on hitting, getting accustomed to the feel of the ring, she moves like Muhammad Ali in his prime. She even repeats his mantra as she boxes: "Float like a butterfly, sting like a bee."

Perhaps a dozen people drift in to watch her workout. Trainers, a couple of sports writers, more Garden workers; and Dana Mitchell sitting three rows back with her new manager, Hulk Montague of professional wrestling fame. "I gotta admit, she's got the moves," she whispers. "I can't out box her."

"Sure you can. You just gotta set your mind to it."

"I'm gonna have to overpower her and hope she can't last ten rounds."

"She's fucking old," Hulk Montague says. "There ain't no way she can last."

"That's what I'm counting on."

"No mercy. Go for the kill from the first bell."

"Look at that move. She's fucking smooth."

"She won't be so fucking smooth after she takes a few of your rights."

For the first time in her career, Dana feels a momentary shudder at the thought of hurting an opponent, but she knows she can shake that once she climbs through the ropes.

It is now eight o'clock at night. Dana and Akiko are seated on stools in their respective corners, towels draped over their heads, rolling their necks and shoulders to work out the kinks, slapping their gloves together, their managers squatted down in front of them giving last minute instructions, pep talks. Jimmy Joe is on one knee. Akiko says, "I'm going to kill her. I'm coming out with everything I've got. I've got to win it in the early rounds, knock her out."

"That's the worst thing you can do," Jimmy Joe tells her. "You've never won by knockout. You're not that kind of fighter."

She knows he's right. Furthermore—and Jimmy Joe has always criticized her for this—she never wants to hurt her opponent. She doesn't have the killer instinct.

Jimmy Joe says, "Fight angry and you lose. Don't forget what took you to the top before. Finesse and skill. Keep moving, counter punching."

"You're right, you're right. I'll do it your way."

Both women are on their feet now, dancing in place, shadow boxing. The bell rings, and Akiko shuffles softly toward the middle of the ring. Dana blasts off from her corner like a rocket from a launch pad. She attacks like a mad dog. She meets Akiko with a flurry of punches before she has gotten five feet from her corner. Akiko never sees it coming. A quick left and a right to her cheeks, an undercut like a sledge hammer to her gut. For a second she can't see. She tries to cover up. She backs up, tries to circle. Dana has her against the ropes. She's landing body blows that take her breath away, hurtful hooks to the face and shoulders. Akiko clinches, holds on for dear life. The referee breaks them apart. Dana is on her again. She clinches again. Akiko is unconscious on her feet, backpedaling. She wraps her arms around Dana in a desperate attempt to hold her arms to her sides. Dana brings her knee up to hit her between her legs. Akiko gasps. She's woozy. Dana whispers, "Sorry." She means it. It was an accident.

The referee breaks them up again, stops the fight to ask Akiko if she's able to go on, warns Dana no more knees. Akiko says she is all right. There's a cut over her right eye. Blood is streaming into her eye and down her cheek. The crowd is booing. The bell rings and Akiko staggers to her corner, sits on her stool. Jimmy Joe applies astringent to her cut. "I'm afraid there's going to be a scar," he says. He asks her if she wants him to throw in the towel. She shakes her head no.

"To hell with boxing," she says. "I'm going for the kill. Gotta get it over with."

Jimmy Joe now knows better than to try to talk her out of a desperation strategy. It's all they've got. She comes out for round two as recklessly as Dana had for round one. She doesn't have the strength Dana has. She's two inches shorter with a shorter reach, and she's five pounds lighter. In terms of the power of her punches that five pounds could be twenty. But she has gained the advantage, if only momentarily. She catches Dana with an unexpected flurry of blows that has her back on her heels, and she keeps pummeling her until the bell rings.

Akiko wins the second round as decisively as Dana won the first. After that, the brawl settles into a boxing match, and for that

Akiko has the edge. Dana had counted on Akiko being out of shape after years out of the ring, but what she had not counted on was that Akiko had never stopped training while she, Dana, had spent most of her time since winning the championship partying.

By the eighth round both women are rubber-legged. They can barely hold up their gloves. They both begin to wonder what in the hell made them think boxing was a good way to make a living. They clinch so much you might think they're making love, not fighting, and in a way they are. Over the course of ten, three-minute rounds they have come to admire the hell out of each other.

Akiko is declared the winner by a split decision. Not long afterwards they both retire from boxing. Jimmy Joe finds himself a hot new up-and-coming boxer to manage and drops Akiko. Leaves her for the younger woman. Akiko and Dana start hanging out together. They're seen in all the in clubs, and they're pictured on the cover of People magazine looking more like lovers than rivals. Their closest friends know they are, and it won't be long before they make it public.

The Soldier

The soldier was hunched in the shadow of an abandoned automobile of an unrecognizable make and model, dull gray, a layer of fine dust on the hood and the door panels, the windshield shattered, shards of glass and rock and hunks of concrete all around. Holding his gun at an angle across his chest, he dared to lift his head above the shield of the hood. He looked to his left, to his right, gazed far ahead and scanned every doorway and window. Everywhere he looked it was gray, gray, gray. The city had been bombed to shreds. Sides of buildings stood like jagged rows of broken teeth. Only one intact building stood. It was three stories high with picture windows on the ground floor. It must have been a retail store before the war came to town, with apartments on the upper floors. Its walls stood undamaged, but all its windows were gone as if a hurricane had blown them out from the inside. There was no movement anywhere.

Vigilant. He must remain vigilant. The enemy could be anywhere. Behind that vehicle across the street, just inside that open doorway to his left, around any corner, most assuredly behind any upper floor window with a clear view of the street. There could be explosive devises planted anywhere. The sun was high and hot, white in a bleached-out sky. No traffic moving on the streets; neither walkers nor trucks nor cars. What looked like a small pond in the middle of the street he knew to be a mirage created by the wavering heat. The silence was eerie; the only sound he could hear was the far-off echoing bark of dogs. The soldier was lost from his patrol, had not seen any of them in more than two hours.

One more furtive look around and then he ran as quickly as his legs would carry him across the street, bending low and running in a zig-zag path to the shelter of the empty building. Quietly he inched up the stairs to the second floor, expecting at any moment to be

194

confronted by the enemy. Would he be quick enough to react? Would he have the nerve to shoot? What if he didn't? Or what if he did shoot and his target turned out to be a civilian? A woman? A child? If he reacted too quickly he might kill an innocent person, if too slowly . . . He wiped sweat from his eyes with his shirtsleeve.

He was in an abandoned clothing store as evidenced by the overturned shelves and debris underfoot—shoes, pants and shirts now painted the ubiquitous gray of dried mud. Everyone needs clothing, but would any of these clothes ever be worn again?

He slowly opened a door to a darkened stairwell leading up to the second floor. A door on the landing opened onto a large room, a continuation of the store below. There were racks of men's and women's clothing, some of them tipped over onto the floor, a children's section to the back. He picked up what looked to be a red and white soccer uniform shirt with a team name in letters he could not decipher. He banged it against a wall to knock off some of the dirt. He stuffed it inside the blouse of his own uniform. He knew not why.

A small door at the back of the room opened to another set of stairs leading to a short, dark hallway with three doorways on either side. Carefully, as quietly and slowly as possible, he opened the doors one after another, fearful of death waiting behind. Each room was the same, an apartment with a single bed, a desk and a chair. There were clothes hanging in closets with no doors and draped across chair backs and tossed haphazardly on beds, books strewn on the floors, paintings and photographs ripped from the walls. Each apartment had a small kitchen with a stove and sink, a two-shelf cabinet, a bathroom with a toilet and shower. Unlike the rest of the city, the building had not been bombed, but it had been ransacked.

A door at the end of the hall opened onto another stairway, this one to the roof, where he hoped to be able to observe the city in relative safety. If the enemy were not already there. Slowly he ascended one step then pause. Another step. He pushed open the door to the roof and stepped out. All appeared to be clear. He let go and the door slammed behind him. Instinctively he reached to pull it open again, to make sure it would open. And it didn't. The door had locked itself when it closed. He tugged, he rattled, but to no avail. He could not open the door. He would have to find some other way to get down when he was ready. He foresaw enemy troops coming down the street lead by a tank, armed soldiers with guns trained at any place their enemy—he—might be hiding. From his vantage point he could pick them off one-by-one. He wondered how many he could kill before they killed him. Did he have sufficient ammo? He prayed for his own troops to arrive. He prayed that the enemy had long since abandoned the town and would not come back.

He crawled to the edge of the building and peeked over the parapet. No troops were in sight, neither friendly nor enemy. There was a ledge below that looked to be about six inches wide. He calculated that if he hung from the parapet his feet would come close to the ledge. It would be a drop of no more than three feet. This could be his escape route when the enemy soldiers stormed the building and came up the stairs. There was a pipe that ran from the roof to the street below. With luck, if he could reach out and quickly grab it at the moment his feet landed on the ledge. If the pipe was strong enough. But from there could he drop to a second ledge? It was too far to drop all the way to the street, and from his vantage point he could not see a ledge farther down. To get to the ground that way would take a circus performer.

There were three other sides to the building. He crawled to each edge, but could find no way to escape.

He waited, hoping his own troops would arrive, sure that their arrival, if it ever happened, would be his only chance for survival. He waited and waited. After what seemed like an hour, he heard a voice.

"Johnny. Where are you, Johnny? Dinner's ready, Johnny. It's time to come home."

Johnny threw down his toy gun and stood up and ran to the far-side parapet and shouted, "Mama! I'm up here, Mama. I'm stuck. I can't get down."

After trudging up the stairs in the empty building on the corner half a block from their house and opening the door for her brave little soldier and hugging him, she said, "How many times have we told you to stay away from this building?" She vowed to call the city again and demand they board it up or put a fence around it or tear the damn thing down. Why hadn't they done it already?

The Face on Facebook

I stared at her profile photo for a good ten minutes, wondering if it could possibly be her. I scrolled through her photos. Susan climbing a tree, in the stands at a football game, camping beside a river, and mostly her with a handsome man I assumed to be her husband. Susan Brown Jansen Roebuck. She looked a lot like the girl I remembered, but it had been more than thirty years, and I didn't have a photo from that time to remember her by. She was sixteen then, and would be close to fifty now. Same thin body and long, dark brown hair, same megawatt smile with an almost too wide mouth. She had been so pretty at sixteen. But my god, I've got friends I haven't seen in a year or two and I'm not sure I could recognize them if I saw them today, much less a woman I barely knew when she was a girl. On the other hand, you'd think no matter how long it had been a guy would recognize his own daughter.

My mind struggled to dredge up a vision of that sixteen-year-old girl and compare her features to the woman on the Facebook page. They did, by god, look a lot alike. As well as I could remember, at any rate, and to be truthful, what I could remember was little indeed. The only truly distinguishing feature was a small mole on her left jaw. In none of the photos on her Facebook wall was that side of her jaw in view. The woman on Facebook looked forty-five-ish. The little girls with her in some of the pictures looked too young to have a mother that old. They could have been cousins or nieces. But yes, they could be her daughters. Hell, they could even be her grandchildren.

Staring at a photo on Facebook and wondering if it could possibly be her, afraid to send her a message. What would I say? I think I might be your father? What if she says yes you are, I'm so glad to see you; and what if she says yes you are, and don't ever try to contact me again? What if she wants to be my friend? What could we possibly say to each other after apologies and recriminations and catching up on our separate lives? Would it be better to not know?

Two years after the divorce, her mother asked if I would sign papers allowing her new husband to adopt our child. I didn't want to agree. Her mother sent me a letter threatening to have me arrested for non-payment of child support, which was true. I wasn't making much money and had missed a lot of payments. I felt boxed in and guilty as charged so I agreed, hoping it would be the best thing for her.

More than thirty years ago her mother called me. I had not heard from her in a dozen years, not a word, not since Susan was about four years old. She said, "We're having problems with Susan. She's so rebellious. She won't do anything we ask her to. She says she wants to go live with her real father. So, we were wondering if you'd mind if she moved in with you."

The nerve of that woman! After so many years of not letting me visit my daughter, after not even letting me know where they were living or even giving me their phone number—she sure as hell knew how to get in touch with me if she needed something. And now she wants me to let our daughter move in with us, to be her father again. But I was overjoyed at the thought of getting to be a dad to Susan at long last. I asked my wife and my children what they thought about it. My wife said, "Of course," and the kids said they'd love to have a big sister. Well, the youngest did; the older—thirteen years old and beginning to show the same signs of rebelliousness I assumed Susan was displaying in her home—was indifferent but she didn't object.

I guess her mother had driven her from wherever they were living, but it was her grandmother who dropped her off in front of our house, who sat at the curb with the motor in her old Ford running and then drove off when she saw me coming down the sidewalk to meet her and help carry in her one little suitcase inside.

Oh my god, she was so pretty, so shy. The evening of the first night after she came to live with us, we sat on the couch with my arm around her shoulder and her chin snuggled against my shoulder. She was all bones and harsh angles but felt frail and soft as a pillow in my arms. We told each other stories about our lives, and I was careful not to say anything bad about her mother. I didn't want to be that kind of dad.

After a few days she asked if she could visit her grandmother, her mother's mother. "Sure," I said. We drove her to her grandmother's house and said we'd be back to get her after dinner. When we returned almost eight hours later, she was gone. Her grandmother said her mother had come and picked her up. The only thing the grandmother had to say about that was, "Well, she's a teenager. You know how teenagers are. The only reason she wanted to live with you in the first place was that her real parents made her do chores around the house, and she thought she could get away with not doing them at your house. When you made her help with the dishes, she figured what the hell, might as well go home. Besides, she missed her friends back home in Texas."

Texas. Ah, at last a bit of the puzzle. That was the closest I came to finding out where they lived. Her grandmother would not give me their address or phone number. In those days we didn't have smart phones that could tell you who called and give out their numbers.

I had met Jennifer in a honkey-tonk where I played drums in a country swing band. I was a senior in college, playing in the band on weekends. The band and its followers were a hard-drinking bunch. Every Saturday night after the club closed we would go to the piano man's house and jam until the early morning hours, often crashing on a couch or a spare bedroom with whatever woman we were dating at the time or might have picked up in the club. One Saturday night the singer in the band showed up with another woman saying, "This is Jennifer. She's my best friend." Jennifer glommed onto me like a dog with a bone and wouldn't let go, clingy from the start.

Throughout that summer we were together constantly. She said she loved me. I thought she was too needy, and I wanted to break it off, but when I tried to—not once but many times—she threatened to kill herself. She tried it twice, once with pills and once by cutting her wrist. I bandaged her wrist. When she took the pills, I rushed her to the hospital and they induced vomiting.

And then she told me she was pregnant. And then her mother called me and told me that Jennifer was only sixteen years old. How could that be? I had met her in a bar where you had to be over eighteen to get in. She had told me she was nineteen.

We were married by a justice of the peace with only our parents in attendance. We moved into a garage apartment near the college, and we were not unhappy there.

I walked to class every day while she stayed home. I thought she should look for a job, at least part-time, something to keep her occupied, and the money wouldn't have hurt, but she said she wouldn't be able to work for long because of the pregnancy. She wasn't showing yet, she didn't have morning sickness, and she never talked about the baby. One day I came home from class to find her hugging a pillow on the couch and bawling. She told me she had a miscarriage. It seemed too convenient, and I suspected she had made up the pregnancy to get me to marry her, but then I scolded myself for judging her so harshly.

The thing was, I had grown to like Jennifer. I didn't love her, but she could be fun to be around even though we had little in common. Her honkey-tonk country friends and my college friends inhabited different worlds. Her countryfied speech embarrassed me when we were with my college friends.

If I had been less happy, I could have asked for a divorce, but I didn't. I decided to stick it out because that was what I thought you were supposed to do. I thought I could come to love her by pretending to. We stayed together while I was in graduate school and through my first year teaching in a dismal little town in Missouri. We stayed together through her pregnancy and Susan's birth and first birthday. And then, just when I thought we were going to make it as a family, out of the blue Jennifer asked me for a divorce. She said she didn't love me anymore. No matter how hard I tried to persuade her to stay—"we can make it work"—she would not be swayed.

We rented a U-Haul and I drove her and Susan to her mother's house, and then I drove back alone to the duplex we had rented in Missouri. The landlord, a single woman who lived in the other half of the duplex and a fellow teacher where I taught, asked me to move out because in such a small town it would not look proper for us to be sharing a duplex. So I rented a room in the Sycamore Hotel to finish out teaching the school year. I tried writing Jennifer, but she didn't reply. I tried phoning, but she refused to talk to me. I did not renew my teaching contract for another year, but went back home to

Mississippi. I visited with Jennifer and Susan when I could manage to make the trip, but she made it clear there was no chance of us ever getting back together. And that was that—until she remarried and moved away without telling me where they were going.

I kept skimming Susan's Facebook page. There were a lot of photos of her, all of them looking more and more like they could be the daughter I remembered. There was a picture of her in front of an American flag and another one standing in front of a silhouette of the Statue of Liberty with fireworks exploding in the background. And there were some sappy religious memes. If there's anything I can't stand, it's people who wear their patriotism on their left shoulder and their religion on their right. The face on Facebook belonged to a woman I might not like if I got to know her, and who might not like me either. What chance could it be if it were really her that that we could build a loving father-and-daughter relationship?

Still I hoped. I went back to her page every day and looked at the photographs and read the posts. I thought of sending her a private message telling her who I was, but at the thought of doing that I would begin to hyperventilate. I wrote and re-wrote messages to her, terrified of her possible reaction, and I trashed them all without sending.

Finally, I did what was irretrievable. I moved my cursor to the top of her Facebook page and clicked on the button that said, "add friend."

Picnic in the Grass

"Next time we get together, let's have a picnic on the grass," she said.

"But what if there is no next time?" he asked.

"What do you mean?"

"Well, if we never separate we can never get back together."

She asked if he was suggesting that they stay together.

"Day after day, you mean?"

"Maybe. I'm not sure. That just popped into my head."

He was twenty-six years old, but still looked like a kid. Tall and lanky, he was called Beanpole by his friends. He grew up on a farm an hour's drive from Warsaw and moved to the city right out of school. She was a year younger, grew up in a different small village not far from him, and, like her, moved to the city immediately after finishing school. They had gotten jobs in the same office building, he as a file clerk and she as a cleaning lady.

He stayed over in her apartment that night. Shyly, they undressed and quickly slipped under the sheets. When he awkwardly wrapped her small body in his slender arms and tried to snuggle closely against her, she said, "Can we just hold each other and not do anything more tonight? Maybe more tomorrow night after we've grown used to our bodies touching."

He had never imagined such a thing: sleeping together naked but not making love. What kind of thing was that? But he found that much to his surprise, it was a relief.

The sun rose early, and there were birds chirping outside her window. After coffee and sweet rolls and a morning lounging together, she made ham sandwiches on dark bread with lettuce, tomatoes and onion. She dished sauerkraut into a container and packed plates and napkins and two forks and a butter knife from the silverware handed down from her grandmother. There were two bottles of beer in the refrigerator, and she put them in a basket with the food.

But before they left for their picnic in the grass, the German soldiers came banging on their door with their guns, their dogs barking angrily, and herded them like cattle, along with crowds of their neighbors to the railroad station where women and children were forced into one boxcar and men into another.

One of the soldiers grabbed the sandwiches and beer and sauerkraut from their picnic basket and stuffed them in his backpack.

Lyla Goes to the Mall

Lyla goes to the mall, not to buy anything but to hang out, people watch, window shop, to dream of wearing the dress in The Bon window, of seeing her name on the marquee at the cinema. There are a million malls in Los Angeles, but this one is her favorite because there is an old-timey soda fountain and a movie theater that shows classic films—meaning films from her recent youth. She'd give up anything, even the love of her life, to be in a movie.

She's done her hair up like Wynona Ryder in Bettlejuice, and she's wearing a bright red dress. She walks slowly past shop windows, The Bon, Victoria's Secret, the Apple store, and watches her reflection, pleased with her dark eye shadow. She decides that yes, she does have a nice shape. She stands for a long time in front of the cinema reading all the words and looking at the pictures on the movie posters. They're showing the first *Star Wars* again. Coming next is a real oldie, *Rebel Without a Cause*. She wonders what it would be like to play Natalie Wood's part. Poor Natalie. Drowned, probably pushed overboard by what's-his-name. She wonders what it would be like to kiss James Dean. She catches herself mimicking a passionate kiss, and quickly looks around to see if anybody is watching.

There is. There's a man no more than twenty yards away is unabashedly watching her. He smiles as if in delighted recognition when her eyes momentarily meet his. She turns away, pleased that he seemed to like her looks. He's a handsome man who looks a bit like Richard Gere in Pretty Woman.

She wanders into the food court, orders a root beer float at the soda fountain and takes a seat at one of the high tables, turning sideways to get a better view of passersby, carefully crossing her legs. She sees the man again, watches him order a cup from Starbucks and take a seat across the food court where he looks directly at her. She thinks she should feel creeped out, but for reasons she can't fathom she doesn't. She watches him watching her. She sips on her root beer and re-crosses her legs, giggling to herself as she thinks about Sharon Stone in *Basic Instinct*. Of course, she is not nearly so exposed. Would she have the nerve to shoot a scene like that? Maybe. She thinks maybe she would. Hey, if someone as classy as Sharon Stone could do it, why not?

The man finishes his coffee. He tosses the paper cup in the trash and walks away, appraising her as he passes close by. Now she does feel a bit creeped out.

Half an hour later he appears again when she has stopped in front of Victoria's Secret to look at the window display. This time he approaches her without hesitation and with a serious look on his face. He reaches out to hand her a business card, and she takes it in reflex action. He smiles warmly, turns and walks away. She stares at the card in her palm as if wondering how it got there. It is cream-colored with embossed, midnight-blue lettering. T. Parker, Producer.

She almost throws it away, but places it on the bottom edge of her dressing mirror at home. She picks it up many times to stare at it. Three weeks go by before she calls him.

"Mister Parker, this is Lyla Evans. You gave me your card at the mall. You probably don't remember me. It was 'bout a month ago. I . . . I was wearing a red dress. Black hair all piled up on top of my head."

"Yes, Lyla. I remember you. Are you an actress?"

"Well no, I . . ."

"But you'd like to be."

"Of course. I mean, who wouldn't."

"Are you over eighteen?"

"Yes sir. Twenty-one next month."

"Can you meet me at my place for a screen test next Wednesday, say 1:30 p.m.?"

"Yes, yes. I'd love to. Where do I go?"

"It's in Laurel Canyon. Do you have a way to get there?"

"Yes. I have a car."

"Give me your number and I'll text you the address."

It's a three-story white, Spanish-style house with a red roof, three double-car garages and a cascading waterfall into a reflecting pool in front. She thinks the guy must be a gazillionaire. She wonders why she's never heard of him. The house is surrounded by tall palms; none of the neighboring houses are visible from where she stands pushing the doorbell. Mister Parker ("Call me Trip") opens the door himself. She was expecting a doorman or butler. He leads her into the studio, a room with a few chairs and a couch, b-movie posters on two walls. One entire wall is a green screen, two cameras set on tripods. A third camera sits on a small table and is attached to a shoulder mount.

Not one to beat around the bush, Parker says, "What we make is trash. But if you're willing to do nudity, it's a real door into the movie business."

Her eyes dart around the room as if searching for an escape route. She looks at the posters again, and at Mister T-for-Trip Parker. There's nothing threatening in his expression. It's not like she hasn't thought about it. She knows the kinds of things that are supposed to be expected of women who want to be stars. She always thought she would know what to do when the time came, and now the time has come. The casting couch. Will I or won't I? She's been in L.A. three years and has yet to get so much as a callback.

"Yes," she says. "All right. I can do that."

Trip shouts, "O.K., Billy. We're on. Come on in."

Billy is middle aged and bulky like a former football player. He's wearing a gray suit and his dull gray hair is slicked back.

"It's a kidnap scene. You're naked. You just got out of the shower. You walk out drying yourself with a towel. Mostly drying your hair. Billy is hiding. He jumps out and grabs you, forces you out the door and locks you in the trunk of a car. You think you can play that scene?"

Yikes. Hesitantly, she says yes, she thinks she can. She feels scared and her hands tremble. But she's going to be in film at last. Will he notice her hands shaking? No matter. It fits the scene. It's acting.

"All right. Down that hall to the right there's a bathroom. Go in there and take your clothes off and get in the shower. Get yourself thoroughly wet. Make sure your hair is wet. When you get out of the shower, wait just behind the door for me to call 'action.'"

Billy gets into place, and Trip mounts the shoulder camera. Lyla walks out on cue, swaying her hips and looking seductively at the camera.

"Cut!" Trip shouts. "Don't look at the goddamn camera. You're not trying to seduce the audience. You're an innocent girl coming out of the shower. This ain't a striptease. And don't look at Billy. You don't know he's here. Now let's try it again."

This time she does it right. Billy grabs her suddenly and so strongly that it hurts. She's truly terrified now. She fights to get out of his grasp. She's not acting. She kicks and squirms, but his hold on her is unbreakable. Her towel falls to the hardwood floor as he carries her to the door and kicks it open. The car is a black sedan with a foot pedal to open the trunk. Billy does that tosses her in and slams it shut.

Again, Trip calls "Cut." He opens the trunk and helps her out and places a large beach towel around her shoulders. She pulls it together cover her nakedness.

"Good work. Now get in," Trip says. "We're going to start filming right away. You're going to be a star."

"But, but I need to get dressed," she stammers.

"Don't worry about it. We got a great wardrobe for you. Besides, the whole cast runs around naked practically day and night. You'll see. You'll fit right in."

"What? It's some kind of nudist camp?"

"Yeah, I guess you can say that. A kind of nudie movie lot."

"But I need my purse."

"Right." Billy retrieves it and hands it to her.

It's an hour-long drive, much of it on country roads. Billy drives, and Trip sits up front puffing on a cigar and blowing the smoke out the window. They finally arrive at a house that's even bigger than Trip's house, with five or six smaller houses on the property, all surrounded by a dense forest. "This is where we're going to film," Trip says. "Here. I'll take that." He snatches the towel away from her and casually walks ahead to the big house with Billy, leaving her to stand alone and naked by the car. A man approaches. She tries to cover herself, one hand in front of her legs with her bag and the other slung across her chest. He doesn't even look at her. He gets into the driver's seat and drives the car out of sight.

Something is terribly, terribly wrong. Panicked, she takes off running back down the road, thinking, I'll flag down a car, naked or not. Hopefully I won't get raped. Maybe they'll have something I can cover myself with.

A mile down the road, winded, the muscles in her legs burning and pounding with her heartbeat, she comes to a gated wooden fence that looms twelve feet high with no purchase for climbing. There is no way out. She tries following the fence line, and after an hour or longer fruitlessly searching for a way to escape, she wanders into the woods. She comes to a clearing wherein there are people. Three men and five women. They are all naked like her. They have unnaturally ecstatic expressions on their faces. "Oh my god, who are you people? Where are we? Is there any way out of here?" Lyla begs.

"Out of here?" an unusually beautiful woman asks. "Why would we ever want to leave? This is heaven"

"Do you mean we're dead? Am I hallucinating."

"Oh no, it's very much real, and we're very much alive," a handsome man says. Lyla notices that they are all incredibly beautiful and unblushing in their nakedness.

Another one of the women says, "It's not literally heaven, but it might as well be. We're all movie stars. Our fans adore us, and we have everything we could ever hope for. And now you do too."

Lyla asks, "Why are you all naked? Did they take away your clothes? How did you get here?"

"I don't understand the question," one of the men says. "We've always been here."

"Of course we have clothes," a woman says. "There are tailors who can make us anything we want. We go naked because we like it. It's liberating."

"And because the producer likes it," one who identifies herself as Rita says. "He's a dirty old man." She says that as if she thinks the producer being a dirty old man is terribly cute. She introduces Jeremy and Lance and Rex, Barbara, Lana, Shala and Anita. They all gush about happy they are she's come to join them.

"Come on, it's lunch time. You must be starving," Jeremy says.

Lyla is hungry. Extremely hungry. She had not noticed it until it was suggested.

The inside of the sprawling house is a movie lot with sound stages and dressing rooms and a commissary. Outside there are paths through the woods and a lovely little lake, and dormitories built in the style that mimics the look of stars' homes in the Hollywood hills. Lyla soon learns they call the property Hollywood, and she gets the eerie sense they've forgotten there's a real Hollywood outside and they are prisoners in this vast, sprawling wonderland.

In the commissary they sit four to a table in groups. Men who appear to be executives, cameramen, directors, sit in one section; writers and sound and light people in another, and the beautiful naked actors together at all the other tables. Looming like the photo of Charles Foster Kane is a larger-than-life portrait of Trip Parker projected onto a wall with the words The Producer. She learns that on the rare occasions when the producer makes an appearance he is fawned over as if he's a god.

"Who are those people over there?" Lyla asks. They are mostly middle aged and older men and women in casual dress. "Those are the character actors," Rita explains. "We love them to death."

The others chime in to babble about how much they love the character actors. They sound like people going on about a dearly beloved pet or like Lyla's aristocratic parents back home in Arkansas talking about their house servants whom they "love to death, just like members of the family."

A white-haired server wearing a tuxedo brings them bowls of soup.

"Don't we get to choose what we want?" Lyla asks.

"Well, surely we do. For the main course. But we always start with the soup. It is delicious. Try it. You'll love it."

She scoops up one spoonful and gingerly sips it. It is delicious. It is not a taste she can recognize. Everyone falls to, quickly slurping spoonful after spoonful. Lyla begins to relax. The tension she had felt lifts like the morning fog.

That night everyone goes to the theater to watch a remake of *Gone With the Wind* starring Jeremy and Rita as Rhett and Scarlet. Every seat is filled with still-naked actors and casually dressed character actors. She wonders why the character actors aren't naked. Possibly because they're older, and maybe their bodies are not so beautiful anymore. There's a standing ovation at the end, and the character actors shower Rita and Jeremy with flowers. Lyla is beginning to see why they are so beloved.

Day after day she walks naked in the woods and eats in the commissary with the actors, and every night they watch films starring her friends, who tell her that her time for glory is coming. Somewhere along the way she forgets where she left her purse.

Lyla gets cast as Maria in West Side Story, her dream role. She's not a singer, but she manages to get through the songs more easily than she ever imagined she could, and when she hears herself in the rushes, she is astounded at how clear her voice sounds. She is overwhelmed at the love showered upon her when the film premieres in the theater.

Lyla barely remembers life before Hollywood, but despite feeling uncannily happy day and night, there is an underlying feeling of dread or disconnectedness she cannot shake. She senses some of the same in Jeremy and Rita, who often separate themselves from the others. They, for instance, don't always eat the soup, which everyone else devours greedily.

One day Jeremy says, "I think I want to wear clothes."

"Why in the world would you want to do that?" Rita asks, and he confesses that he doesn't know. It's just a feeling. And they do get dressed, Jeremy and Rita both.

Shala asks, "Why are you dressing like character actors? You're going to be character actors soon enough anyway." Lyla assumes what they mean is that at some point all the romantic leads become character actors. At a certain age. She wonders what happens when they get too old to act. It seems there are no retired people in Hollywood.

Jeremy and Rita take their walks in the woods alone. Sometimes they let Lyla join them. And Lyla feels improperly dressed for the ball, because she is not dressed, so she starts wearing character actor clothes too.

One day when they are far off in the woods, Rita says, "I suspect the soup is drugged with something that makes everyone unrealistically euphoric and compliant."

Jeremy says, "I think they put something addictive in it. It's not natural that everyone loves the same soup."

Rita says she wonders if some of the other food is drugged.

Lyla has suspected that all along. She says, "I don't understand anything, if you must know. I mean, what is this place? Why was it created?"

Jeremy says, "I think the producer made it all so everyone will worship him."

"Maybe none of it is real," Lyla says. "Maybe we don't really exist. We are the producer's imagination."

They all get a big laugh out of that.

Jeremy and Rita co-star in Bonnie and Clyde. At the premiere, Jeremy says, "This will be our last starring role. We'll be character actors soon. Next thing you know, we'll be playing Clyde's brother Buck and his ridiculous wife."

The three of them, Jeremy and Rita and Lyla, begin to plot ways to get out. They start skipping meals or eating only parts of meals on the assumption that something they're eating is drugged. They explore the woods and along the fence for possible escape routes. They hide clothes in the woods and put them on only when they're safely away from the others.

One day they stumble upon what must be a gate and a road that are no longer in use. The pavement is broken, and the road is overgrown with leaves and grass. Saplings poke through cracks in the road. Best of all, the road extends to—probably—civilization. On the other side of the gate. And there is a hole in the fence. It is not a huge hole, but it is large enough for Jeremy to squeeze through, even though he is beginning to put on weight like a character actor. He scrapes some skin off, but he makes it.

But they're not yet ready. Jeremy squeezed back in. They wait until the night everyone is watching Grease, and then they sneak out of the theater and dash through the woods to where their clothes are hidden, make their way to the hole in the fence and escape. Once outside, they follow the road until they come to a house. It is a huge house, a rambling house surrounded by woods. The realization smacks them like a two-by-four upside the head. The house they have found is the house they have just escaped from, approached this time from the back where the cars are parked. The escape route they thought they had found circles back to where they started. They are in a world that loops back upon itself.

There is little sense of time in their Hollywood. At some point Rita and Jeremy no longer exist, and Lyla plays what she suspects will be her last movie. She's the 100-year-old Rose in Titanic, recalling the Heart of the Ocean and her romance with Jack Dawson.

Smoke, Smoke, Smoke that Cigarette

The first thing I did when I woke up was reach to the bedside table for my cigarettes, unfiltered Pall Malls. I thought of Kurt Vonnegut who, when asked what he'd been doing lately, said he'd been committing suicide by Pall Mall.

I lit one and took a deep and satisfying drag. It felt wonderful going down. And then I coughed like a son of a bitch, waking up Mary, my wife. She reached for her own smokes and lit up and joined me in a cacophony of coughing. We got up and made a cup of coffee and smoked some more. It was a lovely Sunday morning. Neither one of us had to go anywhere. We took our coffee out on the patio and occasionally coughed some more as we enjoyed a peaceful morning.

"Why are you rubbing your arm like that?" my wife asked.

"I don't know. It just feels funny."

"Funny how? You're not having a heart attack are you?"

"Lord no. It's nothing. It goes away after a while."

"A while? So, this has been going on for a while?"

I had to admit that yes it had. Months, in fact. Many months. But it was just a bit of discomfort and never seemed severe enough to worry about. Mary insisted that I see the doctor about it, and much harassing from her I agreed to. The doctor asked me a lot of questions, listened to my heart with a stethoscope, told me to breathe deeply and cough (which came quite naturally), and made me get on a treadmill. He said, "You might have some blockage or something else going on. You need to see a cardiologist."

The cardiologist did more tests and told me that ninety percent of the main artery going to my heart was blocked. He said I needed open heart surgery immediately. "No, it can't wait until next week. No, you can't go home to pack a bag. I shouldn't even let you drive to the hospital." His office was across the street from the hospital.

He also told me I had to quit smoking, and I knew it was serious enough that I really had to do it. I had known for years that eventually I was going to have to give it up. And now I knew I couldn't put it off any longer. I would just have one more Pall Mall—in the car while driving out of the parking lot and across the street to the hospital. My car reeked, but so far I hadn't noticed.

They gave me aspirin and nitro glycerin and hooked me up to an IV that was dripping I-don't-know-what into my veins. Early the next morning they wheeled me to the operating room. A couple of hours into surgery, a nurse came down from to the waiting room and almost casually told Mary, "He's got what we call a widow maker." That did not calm her anxiety. It made her so nervous, in fact, that she had to go outside for a smoke.

Recovering from a triple bypass is a slow process. It was about a month before I was able to resume normal activities, and I knew then, finally and unequivocally, that I had to quit smoking once and for all. I had a head start, first in the hospital and then while mostly bedridden at home under the constant and watchful eye of Mary, who would never in a million years let me touch another cigarette—or eat anything on the list of bad-for-me foods. Under her eagle eye I could not do anything that might increase my risk of a heart attack. I was already past the first stages of withdrawal. If I was still addicted to nicotine, it was psychological, not physical. I knew I could do it.

And then I made what I thought at the time was a wonderful discovery. At the corner store six blocks away from our house, you could buy single cigarettes. Hey, that was all I wanted, just one. I drove to a park and got out and smoked it outside of the car so there would be no telling odor of smoke in the car for Mary to smell. She still smoked, but in deference to me, not in the car and not in the house. I never before realized how much she smoked (and how much I had smoked) until she made the commitment to smoke only outside. We could never do anything or go anywhere without her taking a smoke break before we went and after we left and during breaks at whatever party or play or activity we were engaged in. I realized I was spending five, ten, fifteen minutes out of every hour waiting for her to go outside and have a smoke. Most of our friends had either quit, were trying unsuccessfully to quit, or smoked only outside. We had parties at which I never saw half the people who came except through the glass doors to the patio and through a haze of smoke.

And I was still having periodic chest pain and almost constant tightness and shallow breathing. The craving for cigarettes never went away. I had always heard that you can't just cut back; you must quit all the way or not at all. But I figured I could have one or two a day and sometimes go as long as three or four days without a single cigarette, but as soon as I put out my one smoke I started thinking about when and where I could have my next one. If I really was honest it was always on my mind.

Now I can't even remember when or where or how I finally managed to quit for good. I'm pretty sure it was at least five years after my open-heart surgery. During those years I ended up back in the hospital many times. I had three angioplasties and there are now five stints in my heart. Doc calls that the full metal jacket. But my heart is still pumping and I'm no longer puffing. It's been ten years since I lit up the last one.

Afterword

In 1973 I hitchhiked from Hattiesburg, Mississippi to New York, New York. It took me about four days to get there. People who gave me rides fed me and put me up overnight. I had left Hattiesburg with $100 in traveler's checks in my backpack. When I was let off from my last ride at the Newark Airport, I discovered that the traveler's checks were missing. I had ten cents in my pocket, which I deposited in a pay phone to call my only New York friend, who told me my brother back home had called her and told her the funds had fallen out of my backpack back in his car when he gave me a ride to the highway in Hattiesburg, and he sent them to her. She caught a bus to Newark to and took me to her East Village apartment where I stayed until I got a job and a place of my own.

In the basement entertainment room at Everything for Everybody, a service organization in Manhattan, I told the tale of my trip—turning it into a comic routine. The tale I told was mostly true. Forty years later I told a different version of the same story at a Story Oly story slam in Olympia, Washington, and then I turned it into a short story that was published by Creative Colloquy in Tacoma, Washington. With each retelling of the story, it veered further from the remembered truth of what happened. Some of the true story was even more outlandish than the fiction I made of it. Some of it, dear reader, you'll never know.

Unlike David's side of the story, Debbi's part of the story is a complete fiction. I hope that somewhere in the real world a Debbi exists, but so far as I know she exists only in my imagination.

About the Author

Alec Clayton was born in Tupelo, Mississippi and grew up there and in Hattiesburg, Mississippi.

His writing career began in New York City, where he edited a weekly newspaper from 1974 to 1977. In the summer of 1977 (the summer when fellow Tupelo native Elvis Presley died), Alec and his wife, Gabi, moved back to Hattiesburg where they published *Mississippi Arts & Letters*. They moved to Olympia, Washington in 1988. Alec has since been an editor and writer for periodicals including The News Tribune and the Weekly Volcano in Tacoma, Washington, and Oly Arts in Olympia. The Claytons continue to live in Olympia and are the founders of Mud Flat Press.

www.alecclayton.com
http://alecclayton.blogspot.com
http://www.mudflatpress.com